CREDENCE

MARTIN LINK

ISBN: **1539730468**
ISBN 13: **978-1539730460**

To Ann for her endless patience and support, Kathryn for her reread, and of course Carrie for her editing and proofreading.

And as with the first novel, there are many others, whom I will not list in case I miss someone, but you know who you are – a huge thank you!

And if you are enjoying these books, please look out for the forthcoming third in the series !

CONTENTS

ONE

It is 6am on April 24th, the fifth Sunday morning of spring, and I'm lying on my side in the spare bedroom, wide-eyed in total darkness, holding my breath.

Unmoving and silent, I strain for anything in earshot, but only hear my blood coursing and my heart racing. Thoughts bounce like pinball flippers as my mind struggles to latch onto some indication of reality.

I peel my left cheek from the sweat-soaked pillow and swing my legs round off the mattress of the Victorian bedstead, jumping slightly as my calves hit the cold cast-iron frame. I see a glint of eerie pink light through the small gap under the door to the landing: Daisy's old Hello Kitty plug-in nightlight. Since she was a toddler, she's insisted on a nightlight, and this latest one has been going since 2010; I think Hello Kitty is her guilty secret. To be fair, it's useful if we get up at night, as this private estate of ours doesn't have streetlights and is pitch dark.

Finally, after several minutes of motionless monitoring, my heart rate slackens and my mind throttles back.

I struggle to identify indisputable elements of corporeality. I need proof it is my conscious mind in control, and not again the lifelike imaginings of my nightmare.

Can I whistle? I can't in my dreams. Um, oh, I can, but why that piano solo?

Oh yes, I vaguely remember pulling onto the drive last night with it playing on BBC Sussex Radio – Joe Talbot's Drive Time. I smile fractionally, thinking my shrill noise is akin to the tune, although more Les Dawson than Elton John. These nightmares have been getting steadily worse over the last few nights as I near my return to work, and this is now the fourth time I've had this one.

Finally convinced I am awake, I get up, and, in pants and dressing gown, head out along the Hello-Kitty-lit corridor toward the bathroom.

I hang my dressing gown on the door hook, and tug the light's pull switch as I enter the white-tiled bathroom. The downlights burst into life, causing me to squint, and in the glare I knee the edge of the roll-top bath, which takes a small nick out of my leg. This only adds to my aching back from too much veg-patch digging yesterday afternoon.

"Bloody bollocks," I mutter whilst hobbling over to the sink, and grab the small tube of Fiery Jack from the cabinet. I squeeze a baked-bean-sized blob onto my right palm and rub it onto my lower back – hell, this stuff is hot – lovely!

Suddenly, I get an overwhelming desire to pee, and hop across the floor, just lifting the seat of the pan in time.

After the initial sense of relief, I feel an agonizing throb of pain.

I've inadvertently put Fiery Jack on to Jim and the twins, giving a very personal meaning to the phrase 'great balls of fire'.

With a stifled scream, I wrap a bath towel around my waist and rush out of the bathroom, down the stairs (only stepping on three of them) and across the kitchen to the pantry, where I grab a bottle of vegetable oil. Splashing a little on my hands, I rub it on Jim and the twins, which gives immediate relief from the pain.

I wipe off the excess with paper towels, drop them in the waste bin and rearrange the towel to cover myself, as, blushing, I run back upstairs.

"Sorry, sorry… Fiery Jack. Bloody agony!" I say over my shoulder to my wide-eyed wife and daughter.

This sets them off into hysterical laughter.

Back in the bathroom, I can still hear them chortling as I run the hot tap and stare at my red-faced reflection as it disappears behind the condensing steam on the cold mirror.

Still not fully awake, I rub some soap on my oily hands and plunge them into the water. "Bloody bollocks, that's hot!" I immediately run some water from the cold tap over my near-scalded digits.

Finally, I complete my ablutions, get fully dressed and limp, in more ways than one, downstairs for breakfast.

Can't help thinking of my mum, who always said, "Things come in threes." Gashed knee, Belisha-beacon bollocks – what the hell else is coming?

Let's hope it's one old wives' tale that's not true.

TWO

After bearing the brunt of twenty minutes of mocking, including *Great Balls of Fire* playing on Daisy's mobile – courtesy of a YouTube Jerry Lee Lewis video – and with breakfast complete, I ready our two retrievers for our customary Sunday morning hike. This takes place two hours later than their weekday 6.30am "walkies", and so the woolly beasts are more excitable than normal.

Their routine includes them hacking off through the kitchen and into the hallway, doing nose-to-tail circles until the doormat is rucked up. If there's more than a few minutes' delay in me getting the leads out of the under-stairs coat cupboard, they start whining.

The one thing I must not forget is Gracie's ball. Just like Dug in the film Up, she is mesmerised by a tennis ball, to the point of preferring one to a gravy-bone biscuit.

Today there's only Helen, Daisy and me, as my second daughter, Molly, isn't joining us. She's had a sleepover with her college friend Annabel, but both will be joining us for dinner this evening.

"So?" Helen asks, having finally run out of quips about my glowing nether region, "our usual route?"

"Yes." I look out of the kitchen window and smile at the clear blue spring sky. "Birling Gap and then on to Belle Tout."

We both had a fitful night's sleep, to say the least, and met in the kitchen getting decaffeinated coffees at 1.30am. I'm hoping the walk will clear the cobwebs.

As we approach the Greensward, a tree-bordered "village green" on our private estate, we see several of the resident gardeners out early with hover-mowers, trimming their front lawns. From yesterday's breeze, many of the premature blooms from the cherry trees are now on the ground, and there is a nasal potpourri of sweet blossom and freshly mown grass.

It's 8.30am on an already warm day, and definitely the start of the forecast Indian summer.

As we walk, I ponder the fact that, after dinner this evening, I have to drive to GCHQ in Cheltenham.

I worked there for several years until I moved to MI5 six

months ago, where I immediately took charge of my very first case.

Which is when I was on the sloppy end of a shit-storm of a successful international heist.

The gang got away with $48 million, destroyed two private jets, and nearly cost me my career and my marriage.

But I got away with a slap on the wrist: they gave me three months of gardening leave. "Lucky for you, Lucas," said my boss Jeff, Head of Section. It has certainly given time for the dust to settle, and for me to try to get my personal life in order.

Tomorrow is my first day back at work, attending a seminar on Memory and Associated Neurological Advances. Not the snappiest of titles, but it sounds interesting, and it's certainly a change from my daily hour-and-a-half commute to Thames House in London.

Anyway, it's still the weekend and I am at home, and can't imagine living anywhere else – Friston, East Sussex. The very first time I saw the neighbourhood I had a feeling of déjà-vu, as if every choice I've made in my life led to me ending up here.

But I am a fatalist and so maybe, as my dad used to say, "I always get what I never expect."

****

We've been walking for an hour, through East Dean Village, along Upper Street, and then Went Way.

Then it's down a track beside the cricket pavilion, past Birling Manor and the Sheep Centre, before pausing briefly at the 120-degree bend at Birling Gap.

Here, the view from the National Trust platform atop the steps down to the beach is fantastic. You can look west and see five of the Seven Sister cliffs, Cuckmere Haven beach, and on to Seaford Head.

Looking east, you can see the famous fishermen's cottages that are slowly being lost to the sea. Past those, the cliff rises majestically up to the Belle Tout lighthouse, which has been standing sentry to the rocks below since 1834.

Fifteen minutes later, we're all catching our breath, having clambered the 500-foot rise across downland grass. Now we stand only twenty feet from the sheer cliff face on the east side of this famous granite lighthouse. Below us are the white cliffs, and the dark blue ebbing tide splashing on the pebble beach. Up here there's only the whisper of the gentle breeze, and the occasional soaring, squawking seagull.

The 180-degree view south across the English Channel to France is truly spectacular, with Eastbourne to the east, and Seaford and then, on this crystal-clear day, to Brighton to the west.

As we stand here taking in this vista, I recall how, back in 1999, Belle Tout was moved 300 feet inland to avoid the ever-crumbling cliff. And before that, in 1986, it featured in the TV series The Life and Times of a She-Devil. But today it's a boutique B&B.

I look over my shoulder to Helen and say with a smile, "Do you remember what Dad called this place?"

"Yes," she sniggers, "Mange Tout."

Suddenly, there's a high-pitched whistle. "What the fuck!" I shout. A rhetorical question – I know that sound only too well, and once you've heard it, it's already too late: a bullet travelling at nearly twice the speed of sound will be long gone.

"Down!" I bellow, and as I drop to the floor, my right arm instinctively pushes Daisy to the ground, and then my left tries to grab Helen. But she is already lying beside me, her arm oozing crimson into the white chalk.

We three lie here face down, silent, still. Until Daisy gives a slight whimper through her hands as she struggles to hold back a scream, tears flooding down her teenage face.

"Stay down!" I demand, looking first at Daisy, and then at Helen. "Don't bloody move!"

Putting my hand in my pocket, I take out my iPhone and hold down the fingerprint-scanning button. After five seconds, the *Personal Alarm – Armed Assault* option comes on screen. It's activated!

I crawl the last twenty feet up to the crumbling cliff edge on my belly, and gingerly peer through the tall grass. Using my elbows as a tripod, I point my phone's camera out to sea. On maximum zoom I can see in the distance the glint of a sniper's scope at the rear of a speedboat.

After what seems like an age, he casually puts down his rifle, leaning it against the stern, and then turns away and sits on the side bench. As he drapes his arm over the side of the boat, his hand splashes the water and his wristwatch reflects the morning sun.

The boat's engines growl and power the craft south, across the English Channel toward France.

I jump up and dash back to my family.

THREE

I sit on the grass, cradling Daisy in my arms as she gently sobs, and I stroke Helen's arm as she comes back to consciousness, having cracked her head on a chalk boulder as she fell.

"Did I black out?" Helen asks me in a whisper.

"Yes… a sniper took a pot-shot at you, which grazed your arm, and in falling you banged your head on a rock."

"What?" she says in a daze. "Sniper?"

"Yes–"

"Where's Daisy?" She cuts me short, looking around. "Is she okay?"

"She's fine. She's here." And I stroke Helen's arm to reassure her.

"I'm fine, Mum," Daisy says, sitting forward to look past me at her mum, and bravely wiping away her tears.

"Just rest, Helen… cavalry's on their way."

I sense she's about to go off on one, but she winces and gently puts her head back on my leg. Within ten minutes, the armed response team is here, and after I give them a quick briefing, they whisk Helen, Daisy and me off around Beachy Head towards Eastbourne District General Hospital (DGH).

As the blacked-out Audi RS6 roars away, my phone rings. It's Suzi. "I've heard there's a sniper," she shouts anxiously. "You okay?"

"Yeah, I'm fine."

"Helen and the girls?"

"Yeah. We're all fine," I say, trying to sound convincing as I glance at Helen, who's barely conscious whilst I'm applying a pressure bandage to her wound, and Daisy, who's clinging on to my other arm, quietly sobbing.

"Come on," insists Suzi, "I can tell from your voice someone's hurt?"

"Helen has a nasty flesh wound, and Daisy is pretty traumatised… but we're fine."

"Look after them!" she says. "I'll get the gunman. I'm liaising with Coops – who sends her love. She's backtracking recent comms, and Tony's tracking the boat, with the French DGSE

(Direction Générale de Services Etrangères) monitoring their harbours. And Jeff's had a Typhoon redirected from its London patrol. Should come over your head any minute."

"Get the bastard, Suzi, before he gets to France."

"Don't worry, the Typhoon will deal with it!"

"Whatever it takes, Suzi," I say furiously. "They've attacked my family!"

"Go and get patched up. I'll get back to you soon as it's sorted."

"Okay." And the line goes dead.

Five minutes later and we've barely entered the car park of the hospital when my mobile rings – again it's Suzi.

"Hi, any news?"

"The target refused to stop, even after three warnings – so it's been neutralised," she says.

I close my eyes and look skyward. I don't speak for a second as pure rage ebbs from me.

"Thank you, Suzi." I whisper.

"Debrief later," she says firmly. "Get your family sorted."

At 10.20am, less than an hour after the shooting, and having been thoroughly checked over and patched up by the wonderful staff at the hospital, we're back in Friston.

As we drive into the estate, my driver advises: "Mr Norton. Armed response units are encamped on each of the estate entrances, one here" – he nods to our left – "and another by the pond on Windmill Lane."

I didn't see them, but then that's the idea of camouflage.

He continues, "Each team has four handheld Black Hornet drones flying an overlapping shift pattern to give a twenty mega-pixel infrared, colour view of the estate."

"Thanks… that helps puts my mind at rest," I say. "You staying local for the night?"

"I've got a B&B room at the Tiger Inn, on the village green."

"You'll like it there. Try the Long Man Blonde or the Harvey's – local brews."

"Will do, boss, cheers." He reverses on to our drive.

"Thanks for looking after us."

"No problem. You and the ladies try and have a restful night, there's loads of us out here looking after you."

We get out of the car, walk up to the front door, which triggers the porch light, and I let the girls in, waving goodnight to the driver.

Helen and Daisy go upstairs to freshen up, and, after letting the dogs out, I start looking for something as a quick snack for us all. I've no sooner opened the larder door than my phone buzzes again. This time it's an email from Coops:

Thinking of you, Helen and the girls. Just to let you know one of the new SRR (Special Reconnaissance Regiment) Solara drones, patrolling at 17,000 feet, has been re-tasked to cover your area. This has infrared and thermal, and the camera resolution is a massive 6,400mp, giving an image of five square miles which can be zoomed in to show the face of a wristwatch! And you can stream it to your iPad or iMac at home. Keep safe. xx"

I recall Coops showing me a paper about this a few months ago. Amazing tech with a grid of twenty by twenty (400) 16mp lenses, which feed into an on-board quad-octa-core computer that sews the images into a single, seamless video shot. Can't wait to see it on my twenty-seven-inch iMac!

Anyway, I need to focus on getting my family some hot food, and so I put some soup into two pans on the hob – cream of tomato and cream of chicken – and then put two part-baked baguettes in the oven. While the soup is simmering and the fan oven whirring, I can't help but wonder who ordered this hit, and why? Maybe revenge from my last case – Italian or Russian mafia?

For now, though, we just need to rest, and take a nap after we've had our soup. Then later I'll get some proper lunch.

FOUR

It's now two o'clock, and leaving the local farmer's veg in the steamer and the village butcher's chicken and ham pies in the oven, I walk out of the kitchen and into the living room.

Molly came home early, just after one o'clock, dropped back by her friend's mum, and now she, Helen, and Daisy are huddled together on the large sofa in the middle of the lounge, with Grace and Ellie curled up at their feet.

"Dinner will be another fifteen minutes. So, anyone for a glass of wine?" I say, upbeat.

"That would be nice," replies Helen with a slight smile. "A big glass."

Then, I look at the girls: "Would you two like some wine?"

Daisy and Molly glance at their mum, who grudgingly approves, and they whisper, "Yes please."

"Cool. Three glasses of wine then, and I'll bring in some nibbles."

I wander back out into the kitchen, and within seconds of my touching a bag of crisps, two retrievers rush to join me from the lounge. I put the sea-salt and crushed-pepper artisan chips in a bowl, then put that and the glasses on a tray, and return to the living room, shadowed by the dogs.

I put the glasses on the small tables at either end of the sofa and the bowl of crisps on Helen's lap. The dogs lie down, both mesmerised by the crisps.

We chink glasses and take a swig of wine, with Helen and I giving a small sigh. The girls smile at each other as they enjoy an indulgence normally reserved for Christmas.

"So… everyone okay?" I say, trying to keep things positive.

Daisy and Molly smile, but Helen glares at me.

"Oh yes, I'm bloody fantastic!" she jibes, lifting her T-shirt to show the stitched wound weeping slightly through the bandage.

"It's just a flesh wound, Hels." I try to lighten the mood.

"Just a flesh wound? Twelve stitches! From a sniper's rifle, for Christ's sake."

"Well, yes…" I say, knowing I've unintentionally lit the tinder paper again, "but we're all safe now."

"No thanks to your bloody job!"

Knowing it's pointless to argue, I shrug. "I'd better go and check on dinner. Back in ten minutes."

"Your job could have killed your family!" she shouts after me.

I bite my lip. Doesn't she think I don't know that? Doesn't she know I'm mortified I put my family in harm's way?

The doctor had warned us about the possibility of mood swings, not only from the head injury, but also from the trauma – both hers and our daughter's.

Right now, though, we need solidarity in front of our girls, not misdirected anger.

****

A few minutes later, I put our dinners on the dining table and then walk over and stick my head around the glass-panelled double doors to the lounge. "Dinner is served, ladies."

We all sit in silence eating, except Daisy, who grazes a little but mostly just pushes the food around her plate.

I put my knife and fork on my clean plate. "So… Anyone for some pudding? Only yogurts, I'm afraid."

Helen stares at me. "So now I've not got enough food in the house?"

I look at her, concerned. "I was just saying… No inference."

She continues to glare at me. "No bloody inference – oh, that's okay then."

Molly looks at me and quietly asks for a yogurt, and Daisy nods as well.

I get up and take the plates to the kitchen, leaving the girls and Helen at the table.

Returning with yogurts, I put one in front of each of us along with a teaspoon, and we sit quietly and eat. When we've finished, I put the pots one inside each other and collect the spoons, and as I get up I put my arm around Helen's shoulder, saying, "Look, I was only saying–"

She shrugs me off, and glowers at me again. "Just go to work and leave us alone, we'll cope without you… as usual."

"You won't be alone. The teams are outside, and they won't be leaving until we get these goons."

"Goons?" She looks at me incredulously. "Tim said

'professional sniper'!" She's almost stuttering with anger. "They… they knew our precise movements!"

"Look, you'll be–"

"No. You look. Just go to Cheltenham." Then she glances at Daisy and Molly, who are clearly getting upset, before staring back at me. She lowers her voice. "Come home when your family is more important than your job!"

With that she stands, strides out of the room and stomps upstairs, slamming the bedroom door behind her.

****

After clearing away the dining table, which I'm hoping has given Helen time to calm down a little, I go upstairs to check on her, and let her know I need to leave for Cheltenham.

Unmoving, she lies on the bed with her back to me, and grudgingly says goodbye.

I know there's no placating her in this mood and so I say farewell and then go to Daisy's room, where she's sitting with Molly, and kiss them goodbye.

Daisy, having glanced at Molly, gives me a tense smile. "We know things aren't good between you and Mum, and this sniper thing hasn't helped," she says. Then a tear runs down her cheek. "But don't give up; we'll look after Mum while you're away."

Cuddling both of them, and with my eyes welling up, I manage to say, "That would be great… thank you. I love you so much." It's all I can do to leave the room without blubbing. I give them a small wave as I gently pull the door closed.

As I've said many times, my girls can be so damned grown up, and it's so great having their support whilst their mum and I try and keep things together.

Feeling heartened by their words, I pick up my overnight case and go downstairs.

While loading my bag into the boot, I turn to see Tim come out of the shadows. "Don't worry Lucas," he says. "Helen and the girls are safe – I promise."

"Thanks mate," and I give him a back-slapping hug. "Anything happens, call me, and I'll–"

"Just go do your job – we've got things here."

It's now four o'clock, according to the digital readout on my car's dashboard; I should be at the hotel around six. As I drive out of the estate, I see a single green blink of light from a signal lamp in the shadows, confirming another team member's presence.

Once I get settled into my hotel room, I'll call Helen. Hopefully by then she'll have slept, and she'll see things in a clearer light.

FIVE

After just over two hours, I am on the final few hundred yards of my journey on the Old Southam Road, which, if I continued for another three miles, would take me to the main entrance for GCHQ. On past that and I would arrive at the majestic Cheltenham racecourse, and then if I continued further south a mile or so, I would be at the town centre.

But this evening I now turn right, through the grand gateway of the Ellenborough Park Hotel.

This yellow sandstone mansion, built in 1850, nestles into the rolling green hills of the Cotswolds, and only ten years ago was refurbished and reborn as a five-star luxury spa hotel.

The pillar-mounted CCTV pans to follow my progress, whilst the cattle grid gives a reverberating clang from the tyres that now scrunch noisily along the curved gravel drive, heralding my arrival.

As I admire the immaculate lawns, one dotted with six croquet hoops, and bounded by centuries-old dry-stone walling, several more cameras tilt in my direction. They monitor me as I reverse into my allocated space opposite the hotel's massive English oak double-door entrance.

After getting out, I open the boot and grab my overnight bag and laptop. Having scrunched across the last few feet of gravel, I wipe my dusty feet on the large "Ellenborough Park" coconut mat, and with a single *plip* of my key fob, the car is secure for the night.

At the main entrance, I turn the huge cast-iron latch and walk through the Norman archway to reception. I confirm my booking with the receptionist, and sign in to the guest register. "Up to the first floor," she directs, handing me my room key-card and emergency evacuation leaflet, "turn right along the corridor and room seven is at the end."

"Thank you. Is Nicky on tonight?"

"Yes. She noticed you were booked in, and said she'll see you before dinner. She's only just got over a chest infection that seems to be doing the rounds!"

"Oh, bless her." And with a nod and a smile, I walk toward the stairway.

Wandering across the deep pile plush carpet, I can only imagine how the original owner felt as they climbed these ornate treads. The thick duck-egg-green runner and dark oak twisted-barley banisters ooze longevity and heritage.

The walls, painted in pastel greens and creams, are adorned with pictures of local Gloucestershire landscapes, which lend a calming country air to the surroundings.

At the end of the first-floor corridor, I push my key-card into the door latch. A little lamp flashes green and the lock clicks open. I walk in, look around, and smile. I love this room – my room.

Not only does it have a double aspect, but there are French doors that open onto a small balcony, which has a magnificent view across the lawns, and on to the ancient oaks framing the distant, rolling Cotswold Hills.

From the window, I can see my car in the front car park, and the driveway as it meanders down to those massive stone entrance pillars.

I unpack my overnight bag, hang my suit and shirts in the wardrobe, and put my toiletries into the bathroom. Then I sit at the desk and boot up my laptop, which immediately sets up a high-security connection through the hotel's WiFi, with the final check requiring insertion of my unique Yubikey.

Emails checked and everything tidied away, I eagerly grab my trunks and towel, and go down to the spa – a little personal luxury to revive me before dinner at nine.

****

Sitting in the restaurant bar's snug, refreshed from my swim and now in my smart casuals to comply with the restaurant's dress code, I knock back a couple of glasses from my bottle of Bodega-Norton Malbec, and, looking at the label, I smile.

At ten to nine, Nicky, the maître d', finds me and we exchange the usual cheek-kiss and a hug. She apologises for the dining room being so busy this evening. Our chitchat will have to wait.

Then, with the food and wine menus under her arm, she escorts me to my reserved table.

As I sit, she smiles at me knowingly. "The usual, Lucas?"

"Yes please. I've been looking forward to one of your steaks for what seems like an age."

"Rare? A good vet?" She grins at our shared joke.

"Indeed. If a good vet can't save it, then it's overcooked." We both chuckle as she gently unfolds the white swan-shaped napkin and places it across my lap.

Fifteen minutes and another glass of Malbec later, Nicky and one of her waiters return with my sumptuous dinner.

"Bon appétit," she says, refreshing my glass, and then silently disappears once again to attend to other guests.

The medium-rare buffalo steak, from F1 driver Jody Scheckter's farm, is as usual divine, as is the remainder of the accompanying Malbec. I'd been hoping to savour the restaurant's speciality ice cream from Winstones at Rodborough Common, but alas, the twelve-ounce sirloin left no space.

However, back in the snug, a couple of large Rémy's and an Illy double-shot coffee round the evening off nicely. When she appears, I have a catch up with Nicky, who is being promoted to assistant manager here next month.

My evening of treats complete, I go back to my room for an early night, as I really want to fit in a swim before breakfast.

Sitting in bed, I check the morning's alarm on my mobile, and, seeing my calendar for tomorrow, I'm reminded of the course: Memory and Associated Neurological Advances. How on earth does this come under the province of GCHQ, or indeed MI5?

'Oh, shit!' I exclaim to myself, noticing the time. It's 11.30pm, and I've not called Helen.

I grab my mobile and phone home.

Having woken Helen, and after a very brief exchange of views, mostly hers of me and my job – not dissimilar to our earlier skirmish – I have apparently been upgraded from being in the doghouse to being in the shit-house! I must confess I probably deserve it, and admit that to her – but it cuts little ice.

Helen also says she has decided to keep Daisy and Molly at home tomorrow. So all is definitely not well in the Norton household. But, having plied Tim with Peroni and a midnight snack, and after he checked all doors and windows, she at least feels safe for the night.

With still no word from Suzi or Coops on the sniper's backers, I am still uneasy about my girls being home alone, even with two of my teams guarding the estate.

If this doesn't give me nightmares, then nothing will.

SIX

As predicted, I've had a fitful night's sleep, what with worrying about Helen and the girls, about who's behind the sniper, and why. But the early-morning swim clears my head, and the hotel's superb full English breakfast, complete with Jody Scheckter's bacon and sausage, fills my stomach.

Having grabbed my computer bag from my room, I go to my car, lock my laptop and iPad in the boot, and start the ten-minute journey to the "doughnut", as GCHQ's main building is known.

As I drive into the site's main entrance, just before 9am, I recall my arrival here a few months ago. I was on a bicycle in horizontal sleeting rain. This time, it is a little more dignified.

The sign next to the somewhat bland entrance states: Authorised Persons Only Beyond This Point.

The tarmacadam road surface is billiard-table smooth, and it covers advanced electronics that analyse the underside of vehicles entering the site. Every automobile and truck in the world is built to a detailed specification, and every one of those specs has been imaged and stored in the memory of this monitoring system. When a vehicle enters, it is laser scanned, and checked against its registration and manufacturer's spec. Any variance and it's directed to a manual inspection area a few hundred yards away, the other side of a bombproof wall.

In my case, the scan clears my car, the hidden wireless ID is okayed, and then the CCTV's facial recognition system authorises me. Only now does the outer barrier's tiny red flashing lamp change to green and the full-width road-blocker ahead descend into the ground.

This allows me to drive ten yards up to the next pillar-mounted stainless-steel panel. I look at the pinhole camera where my retina is scanned, proffer my contactless ID card, and press my thumb on to the sub-dermal scanner.

This last one is our latest tech: Finger Vein Authentication Technology (FVAT), more commonly known as VeinID. As ever, when I think of this technology, Carly Simon's You're So Vain plays in my head.

Basically, VeinID reads the sub-dermal patterns of a person's finger vasculature, which is done by using near-infrared LED lamps and monochrome CCD cameras. As the haemoglobin in blood absorbs the near-infrared light, veins appear as dark lines on the resulting image – making a pattern as unique as a fingerprint. Also, VeinID is impervious to human skin cell-shedding, and, morbidly, requires a finger attached to a living body.

Anyway, I finally get to enter my ten-digit keycode, which is the last opportunity for me to raise an alarm, should I need to: changing the last digit of this code to that diagonally opposite on the keypad initiates a silent alarm. The site's SAS response teams would be here within minutes.

On this occasion, my last key-press turns the red flashing lamp green, and the six huge stainless-steel tubular road barriers sink down into their tarmacadam burrows. I proceed at the prescribed 5mph speed limit to my designated parking space, take my laptop bag from the boot and start my short walk to reception.

During this hundred-yard stroll, various systems monitor my physical dimensions and gait. Then, when I walk through the marble-floored entrance, my weight, heart, breathing rate, emotions and full-body magnetocardiography are analysed. Again, this last one is a new technology, which measures the magnetic fields produced by electrical activity in the body, mainly emanating from the head and heart.

At the reception desk, my iris is again scanned, and my hard-copy credentials checked. I am now officially an approved, if temporary, resident.

The receptionist tells me which building and room is hosting the training course – right next to a small cafeteria. As I'm fifteen minutes early, I make my way straight to that café. Plenty of time to grab a latte before I report to the course tutor, Pete Skinner.

I carefully remove the piping hot coffee from the dripping machine, but as I turn around I bump into Alex. "Bloody hell," I exclaim, both at seeing him and at the shock of the spilt coffee, which I lick off my hand. "What are you doing here?"

"HR manager called saying she had a spare seat," he replies, grabbing a serviette from the nearby shelf and mopping my slopped coffee from the floor.

"Anyone else we know on the course?"

"A young woman you may know." Alex grins. "Coops."

"Well, blow me! I'll text her."

I quickly select Coops from my mobile's contacts and start typing. But before I finish, it rings, making me jump, and I hear a very excited voice burst from the handset.

"Helloooooooooooooo!" screeches Coops. "How are you?"

There's a strange echo on the line, but before I can answer, I am tapped on the shoulder. I turn, and there she is. Five foot nothing of overactive adult, beaming from ear to ear!

We chuckle as we hug; typical prank from this minx.

Alex smiles and introduces himself; although he has spoken to Coops a few times, they have never met. "You must be the irrepressible Coops. Thanks for your help on that last case – remarkable!"

"Why, thank you, kind sir," she replies with a small curtsey, and then turns back to me.

"It's brilliant to see you, Lucas," she says with the cheekiest of grins, "and I understand Tony and Alex will be joining us for dinner this evening – wicked."

"I presume you've confirmed this with the hotel?"

"Of course." She smirks like a child expecting a treat. "You promised dinner weeks ago!" she says with big cow-eyes and a butter-wouldn't-melt smile.

"Don't you dare change, Coops – you're priceless."

We're totally absorbed in chatting when someone sidles up beside me and boldly introduces himself. "If you lot are here for Memory and Associated Neurological Advances, I'm your lecturer. Pete Skinner."

It amuses me how even the "firm's" lecturers fall into a Cambridge shabby-chic style, and Pete is no different. Long, grey-blond hair, small goatee, check-pattern country jacket with leather elbow patches, corduroy shirt with threadbare collar, and orange elephant-cord trousers. But, always, those immaculately polished, brown Charles Church brogues. He jokes about having had the same pair of shoes for twenty-odd years, but admits they've been re-soled at least ten times! This always makes me think of Trigger's broom from Only Fools and Horses – he had the same broom for twenty years, and said, "It's had seventeen new heads, and fourteen new handles."

Despite the world-worn appearance, Pete is a man with erudite manners and believes in good etiquette at all times. Accordingly, he insists upon proper introductions from each of us, except me; we go back a few years.

Everyone else introduced, Pete turns to me and shakes my hand as if testing its connection to my wrist.

"So, Pete, I guess with all the new faces you've forgotten mine?"

"Oh Lucas, how could I forget that face, like the love child of Worzel Gummidge and Nanny McPhee," he laughs. "Or indeed our last late-evening discussion, lubricated with the occasional glass of Ribena!"

"You say the sweetest things, Pete," I grin at him. "Indeed, a good evening, and if I remember correctly that last bottle of Ribena was in fact a 2009 Malbec?"

Pete smiles and nods, and then makes a gentle herding gesture with his arms. "Okay then, let us go to the training room."

We enter the classroom and take our pre-assigned seats, which are suitably placed to ensure we mingle. There are already four unfamiliar faces in the room, making a neat class of eight.

Pete covers housekeeping: start/finish times, loos, fire escapes, lunch. Then we go round the room and get our personal introductions out of the way.

"Okay," Pete says earnestly, "this is a fundamentals morning, followed by a few team activities this afternoon." Then with a smile: "The mainstay of the course is tomorrow, with Wednesday morning being a practical session, which is followed after lunch by a written assessment."

I pipe up. "What's the pass mark, Pete?"

"Eighty-five per cent. If you don't pass, then you re-sit the course in three months' time."

The whole room sits in silence for a moment, glancing at one another.

"Really?" I say in disbelief. "Seems a bit steep."

"Serious subject. Serious assessment!" says Pete, straight-faced. The message is crystal clear: "Take this course seriously."

Strangely, I start to feel nauseous, and whisper to Alex sitting next to me: "Is it me, or is there more tension than normal?"

"Yeah, I feel it. I've not had butterflies like this since my Sergeant's exam."

I whisper to Coops two seats away, "You feel it?"

"What?"

"Nervous?"

"Always, but more than normal today. In fact, I could throw up," she grumbles. "I hate courses… well, exams, damn things!"

Not just me then, I think to myself.

Pete checks his notes, and after politely covering a near-silent burp with the back of his hand, looks up over the top of his half-moon spectacles.

"Let's do a quick questionnaire," he says with a smile, "just to baseline your awareness of the subject."

Coops and I look at each other, raise our eyebrows, shrug, and accept our fate. Back at school!

SEVEN

It's now 4.30pm, and, thankfully, the first day is finished. I'm not sure we covered all the intended subjects, as Pete went off at a tangent, theorising on human instinct and gut feelings, and, to a lesser extent, the human soul.

But worst of all, and everyone felt it, was the *intense* nervousness.

We put it down to magnificent staging by Pete, who at sixty-four has served some twenty-plus years producing and running training and development courses. I invite him to our evening meal at my hotel, but he politely refuses, saying it was his evening for baccarat with his mother.

As we're strolling towards GCHQ's front desk to sign out, Coops pipes up, "Lucas, I've arranged our table for 8.30."

"Excellent. You and Tony staying over at the hotel?"

"Nah, we're getting a taxi home, booked for 11.50, just before their cab rate doubles!"

I smile at Coops. "Crafty as a barrel-load of monkeys!"

There's a gentle chuckle at my dear departed dad's saying. I don't know its origins, but he used it to emphasise someone's shrewdness; it always caused a giggle. The research I did gave the earliest use of the phrase as 1840, though later in London's Docklands it moved to being a barrow-load of monkeys.

We sign out at reception, and make our way across the car park.

I've no sooner sat in my car than my mobile rings. It's Helen.

"Hi, how're things?" I say, stifling a yawn.

"Not good," she says bluntly. "Okay to talk?"

"Of course."

"Grace bit Casper this afternoon. The cat's okay but Grace has never done that before." Then, with a little sob: "What the hell's happening, Lucas?"

Grace is one of our retrievers, and Casper is my boy cat. I emphasise *boy* as we are the only males in the household.

"Don't worry, this sort of thing can happen occasionally. Are they okay now?"

"They are, but I'm not!"

"Look, have a cuppa, let me get back to the hotel and I'll

phone you in fifteen minutes from a landline."

"Fine!" The phone immediately goes dead. Obviously, she's still pissed at me – but God knows how this is my fault.

As I put my mobile on the passenger seat, there's a rap on my driver's window. I turn my head to see an immaculately dressed agent standing a foot from my door, and pointing a Heckler and Koch MP5 machine pistol at my head. He shouts, "Window down. Hands on the wheel. Do it now."

In my peripheral vision I see another armed agent standing to the rear offside wing; his MP5 is also shouldered and aimed at me. I immediately comply; only an idiot wouldn't.

I put my left hand on the steering wheel and slowly move my right hand to press the window button, and then place that hand on the wheel.

After the window is fully down, I offer my ID, which the agent inspects, whilst his colleague, statue-like, keeps aim on me.

He then questions me through the window. "You've sat in your vehicle for ten minutes, and not responded to our text."

Uncharacteristically, I feel a near-uncontrollable urge to tell these guys to just fuck off. This must have been a more emotional day than I thought.

But that response, or indeed any protest, will only result in a protracted and uncomfortable interview.

I keep eye contact with the officer whilst both hands remain firmly on the steering wheel. "Sorry, Captain," I say in a humble tone. "Urgent call from the missus. Married twenty-five years, and being out of the shackles for a few days still makes her nervous!"

Seeing my lapel pin, an SRR (Special Reconnaissance Regiment) gift, he smiles slightly and after a few silent seconds lowers his weapon. "No problem, been there myself." He briefly turns his head and nods at his colleague, who likewise lowers his weapon. "But please move along now, sir. Have a nice evening." I thank him and drive off sedately.

These guys have a tough job, and it bugs me that I felt such animosity. This has been a strangely emotional day.

Oh well, back to the hotel, freshen up, quick swim, shower, and then down to the restaurant with Alex to meet up with Tony and Coops at about 8.30.

Once back at the hotel, as promised, I phone Helen. She's calmer this time, but she still blames my job for Daisy nearly being assassinated – and I remain the target of her anger.

I can't stop her feeling this way, but I really don't know what to say; I just need to be home more. And find the perpetrators.

EIGHT

I've had my swim, and am now sitting in the spa hot tub, eyes closed, legs outstretched, floating on a mass of bubbles; perfect relaxation after a difficult day.

Hearing footsteps, I open my eyes to see Alex strolling along the side of the pool toward me. I hit the 'bubble' button for the fifth time.

"Hi Lucas, sorry I'm late."

"No probs. What's the time? Did you nod off?"

"It's about 7.30. And yes, when I got back to my room I felt dizzy and lay down. Woke up nearly two hours later!"

He drops his towel next to mine on the adjacent lounger. "Sit back and relax," I suggest as he steps down into the hot tub. "I've lined up a couple of bottles of Malbec for interrogation later." That makes him smile.

We chat generally about the day until eight o'clock, and then make our way to our rooms. Twenty-five minutes later, on the way down for dinner, I knock on Alex's door, number fourteen, to pick him up.

When we get to the lounge area, it's crowded, but Tony and Coops have already ensconced themselves in a couple of huge winged armchairs, quaffing a couple of drinks.

Tony clocks me as I start to cross the room and, much to the surprise of the other patrons, kicks off our usual repartee.

"Hi Lucas, you old fart, lovely to see you. How is the incontinence and memory loss these days? Still hiding your own Easter eggs?"

"Lovely to see you too. You're starting to look quite grown up, but still the blond kiss-curls. Have you started to shave yet?"

"I'm naturally blonde."

"Well, you're definitely not as stupid as you look."

"Wish I could say the same for you!"

A couple at the next table are looking quite alarmed until we start to laugh, and then give each other a bear hug. As usual, although he releases, I hold the hug just a little too long, testing Tony's lack of tactility.

Coops knows this banter of old and just looks at us, shaking her head: "Come on guys, get some new material!"

"Sorry," I stutter, distracted by Tony's gesturing of L for loser. "Been waiting long, Coops?"

Coops glares at me, then Tony, and replies, "Nah, about ten minutes. Enough to get first drinks and buy a couple of mispriced bargains blogged on Money Saving Expert. Now you're here, you can get the next round?"

"Okay." I look around the table. "What's everyone having?"

"Same again," says Tony, gulping the last mouthful. "Large Glenfiddich."

"Handmade snowball please," says Coops.

Alex says, "Pint of Directors for me, boss."

"Right." I turn to Coops. "Can you check we've got a decent table?"

"Already done, Master," she beams. "Your usual corner seat!"

"Good, but a bit tight?"

"Would have been, but when Nicky realised it was you she moved in a larger table!" With a suggestively cheeky grin, she adds, "I think she *likes* you, Lucas!"

I shake my head and make for the bar, and Alex comes with me to help carry the drinks.

When we get back, we continue chatting and laughing. Not long after, Alex gets the next round – on my contactless card, of course.

Just before 8.30, the maître d' arrives to escort us to our dining table. Unfortunately, it's not Nicky, but instead her understudy, Susannah, who, with the menus and wine list, guides us to our table, where we take our seats. I've got my back to the corner wall, with a view of the entire room, and the two means of exit; if nothing else, I'm predictable.

We order our various mains, which arrive only fifteen minutes later. There is ample food, which, despite the efforts of the skin-removing white-hot plates, nonetheless becomes cold as we chatter about the day's training, politics, "the company", and of course why we don't get together more often.

Time flies and suddenly it's 11.50pm, and the maître d' walks over and quietly advises that there's a taxi waiting for Miss Cooper. Alex and I go with Tony and Coops through reception to the main entrance, and the waiting cab. There I get another ribcage-crushing hug from Coops as we say our farewells.

Alex and I return to the winged armchairs and have a large nightcap before we toddle off for the evening.

An hour later and I'm back in my room making sure everything's ready for the morning.

Lastly I check my email, scrub the fangs and, finally, dive into my pit.

As I lie here admiring the original oak-beam ceiling, my mind wanders back to the charged emotions in class earlier today, and how strange I should get so nervous.

Maybe tomorrow will shed more light. It certainly needs to if I am to come away with anything other than a raging headache!

NINE

After my swim and breakfast at the hotel, I finally arrive at five to nine and sign the training room's register on Pete's desk, and then swap pleasantries with Tony, Coops and Alex as I squeeze past them to my seat.

"Sorry I missed you at breakfast, Lucas," says Alex.

"No problem, I was running a little late myself, trying to find some paracetamol for my headache." To which Alex gives a knowing smile.

The rest of the attendees are already here. Now we just need our lecturer.

The room gently buzzes with chitchat, but it's now ten past nine; much longer and the paper planes will be flying around. In fact, I can already see Alex surreptitiously chewing a small piece of paper from his large milkshake straw, no doubt purloined from the café!

Finally, at twenty past nine, a casual but smartly dressed chap enters the room.

He wears beige elephant-cord trousers and a pale yellow check shirt with blue Oxford cravat – Man at Dunnes, I think to myself – definitely a member of the lecturing team.

He looks around the room with solemn eyes. "Good morning. I am Elliot, Principal Lecturer. It is–" he swallows, and looks at his shoes before continuing, "–it is my duty to inform you that Professor Peter Skinner will not be attending today's lecture due to a severe migraine." And, swallowing again, "As there is no one else suitably qualified, I am afraid I have no option but to cancel this course."

Concerned for my friend Pete, I pipe up. "Hi," I say, and gently straighten my name card. "Lucas Norton." I sit forward, gesturing with open hands, "I've known Pete for years; I had no idea he suffered from migraines. Any idea what caused it?"

"I'm afraid not, and it's a bit of a surprise to me as he was in fine fettle yesterday evening," says Elliot, "but he has been burning the candle both ends recently on some newfangled project. I guess it's caught up with him."

He advises that our departments will be reimbursed the course fees and expenses, and he will arrange for us to be rebooked on this course in a few weeks.

We ask that our best wishes be passed on to Pete and then pack away our stuff, wander out of the room, and head along the corridor towards reception.

After a few steps Coops nudges me and smiles.

"Fancy a coffee before you shoot off?"

"Yeah, good idea." I turn and invite the others, who nod, and we all head for the café. We sit and chat for an hour before we decide it's time to get some lunch from the main cafeteria.

Then, before I know it, the café clock's displaying 2.30. "I really must get Alex back to London, and me home."

As I'm whizzing down the M40, Alex dozes in the passenger seat. Apparently, his earphones are providing him with "mellow mood" tunes coming from his iPhone.

Meanwhile, I can't help reflecting again on yesterday's events and my overwhelming feeling of trepidation. We all had a deep feeling of nausea and disorientation, to a greater or lesser degree, and I wonder if that is what caused Pete's migraine.

I only hope it's not something more serious.

TEN

Having dropped Alex off in central London, I get home just after 6pm. The white gates either side of the road display a sign: Downlands Private Estate – 20mph – No Through Road.

Twenty yards further and I get a single green flash from the undergrowth. The guys are still here, and their camera will have scanned my number plate.

I drive half a mile through the narrow and winding privately-maintained roads before pulling up on my drive.

As I look up from applying the handbrake, two retrievers, front feet on the windowsill, stare at me through the lounge window. Their golden heads gently sway as unseen tails wag.

That's the best of the welcomes, as no doubt Helen will give me the third degree.

No sooner am I in the kitchen, with two fluffy faces nuzzling me as if I'd been away for months, than her voice reverberates from the lounge.

"Dinner's on the side – nuke it."

As I lift the glass pan lid from the plate, the condensed water drips off onto the already languid fish fingers, overcooked baked beans and slightly burnt, yet soggy, chips.

"Thanks. I love fish fingers!" My expression, if she could see it, would give the game away.

"Yeah," she replies, "Tim liked them too!"

Her tone implies another evening of verbal swashbuckling.

Having nuked the food, I plonk a dollop of mayonnaise on the plate, put that on a tray along with a spoon, and then wander into the lounge.

I've barely sat down, having side-stepped the two dogs, who have one eye on me, and the other on my dinner.

"So." I look at Helen. "How was your day?" I ask, putting a spoonful of near-liquid fish finger into my mouth.

"Fantastic," she replies sarcastically, frowning and tut-tutting at my spoon.

"The girls okay?" I try to keep the mood light.

"Fantastic." Repetition only emphasises the sarcasm, and she returns her gaze to a Downton Abbey repeat, her preferred escape from the harsh modern world with no manners. "*They* don't use a spoon for every meal!" She glances over and again tuts at me.

"Would make their table-laying a lot easier, not to mention the washing-up!" But my attempt at humour is completely ignored.

After a couple of mouthfuls, I continue. "I presume Tim and the guys have remained unobtrusive?"

"Not seen any of them," she replies flatly. Then adds, "Except for Tim," which seems to make her eyes smile, and she softens her tone. "He's been popping in for supper, bless him."

"That's… good," I reply, as an unexpected gentle ripple of concern goes through my mind.

"So, when is this shit going to end?" she jibes.

"Thought you liked Downton, isn't this–"

"Don't be a prat!" Her glare could sour milk at fifty paces.

"As soon as we can catch the bastards. We've a couple of leads, but nothing concrete."

"Great," she says sarcastically, "that'll help the girls and me sleep at night."

"The guys are doing their best "

"Well, their best is bollocks!" She cuts me short. "Tim says they should never have got this close in the first place."

"True," I reply flatly, whilst thinking to myself that I need to have a little word with Tim.

As the lounge clock ticks past nine o'clock, we say our goodnights. She makes her way to bed, leaving me to deal with the dogs.

Like my dad would say with a smile, "Married life, son. Always in the shit, it's just the depth that varies."

As I walk upstairs I give Tim a quick call, just to let him know I'm home.

He will receive my talking-to at some point tomorrow. I'm too bloody knackered now.

ELEVEN

A few days have gone by, and it is now Monday, mid-morning, and I'm sitting at my desk in Thames House.

I have been on the phone to Coops, discussing if she's heard anything about Pete Skinner, when Tony's voice bellows in the background: "Coops! Check out your PC, bloody unbelievable!"

"Sorry, Lucas. Call you back." And she's gone.

I get on with my daily pen-pushing and deal with a few urgent emails. It's only been about fifteen minutes when my mobile buzzes again; this time it's Tony.

"Hi, you managed to sort Coops' PC?"

"That's why I'm calling. We've had a couple of those weird messages, like a few months ago, to the Rome mobile!"

"Oh shit. Thought we'd put that one to bed."

"Yes, me too."

"Same team, or a copycat? I bet Coops is hot on their trail!"

"She's mad as hell," he says, feigning fear. "I'm ten feet away and throwing chocolate at her until she calms down!"

We chuckle, and I gather my thoughts.

"Email me the details, and I'll discuss with Suzi."

"Will do. Speak later when I know more."

My mind darts back to the sniper, and my family's clifftop shooting – Italian mafia? Russian mafia?

Half an hour passes, and I've returned to my office from briefing Suzi, when Tony's name again pops up on my mobile.

"Hi Lucas. No real news I'm afraid," he says, frustrated, "other than the destination of the call was definitely Rome." He sighs. "The origin could be anywhere, as it went via literally dozens of ISPs. Coops should be able to trace it but not as quickly as last time."

"Keep me posted."

I close the call, grab my folio and leave for my Monday budget meeting with our Finance Manager. My gut grumbles about this new comms, don't know why, but I sense this is going to get big, and quick.

It's just before noon and I'm still in the budget meeting when a text vibrates my phone – it's from Tony: *Urgent. Call SOONEST!*

I immediately give my apologies to the Finance Manager, walk out into the corridor and phone Tony. "What's happening?"

"We've double-checked the trace, and… oh shit, this is unbelievable!"

"What is?"

"If this gets out we'll be a laughing-stock, and I'll be on the dole – if I'm lucky."

"Christ, Tony, if *what* gets out?"

"It's here!"

"What's there? You're making no sense."

"GCHQ – the source of the message – it's bloody here!"

"Oh bollocks!"

"Exactly. And probably mine. *I'm* responsible for the security of *all* GCHQ comms."

"Where on the site? Precisely?"

"Don't quote me until I've got irrefutable fact–"

"Come on!" I cut him short. "This is like pulling teeth!"

"Pete Skinner's PC."

"No, no… not Pete… you sure?"

"As sure as I know my bollocks won't hold my body weight!"

"Bollocks!"

"Don't keep saying that," he says, sounding terrified. "Get down here, Lucas… please. And bring Suzi!"

"We'll be there in two hours."

TWELVE

Suzi is driving us in one of the Audi RS6 pool cars, and I'm telling her Dr Peter Skinner's life story.

He's a veteran of the Gulf War (1990/91), having been a Tornado pilot with XV Squadron, specifically supporting the insurgence-leading SAS into Iraq.

The technology back then allowed the SAS on the ground to light up a target with a long-range laser rifle, and call in Pete's Tornado with its LRMTS (Laser Rangefinder and Marked Target Seeker) to guide the missile to that exact spot.

The SAS guys doing this certainly had balls of steel, as it was often just them, the rifle, water and a Land Rover, and they were often within one hundred yards of the target to get "eyes-on".

It was also a nerve-jangling combat role for Pete as he flew twenty feet off the deck under cover of darkness.

Pete was shot down twice by ground-to-air missiles, but remained flying for three more years. He was never shot down again, and took out a further eight enemy fighters, and dozens of ground-based targets.

Pete describes his exploits modestly: "Most of the time a pilot, occasionally a parachutist."

He always jokes that if he ejected once more, he would have been invalided out of the service, as each time it takes nearly a quarter-inch off your height.

I remember one of his stories about testing the Tornado's twin 30mm cannons. The pilots would fly out in pairs and the lead plane would cast a shadow on the sand dunes, thus giving a target for the second plane's guns. This second aircraft would shoot at the silhouette, with the subsequent flying sand marking each successful "hit".

On one of these training sessions, it was Pete's turn to play lead and cast the shadow. Sure enough, his comrade in arms made sand fly up from the silhouette on the desert, as suddenly did debris from a small building.

"Bloody hell, Pete, what was that?" shouted his buddy.

"Swindling bastard of a bar owner won't be derogatory about my wife again!" replied Pete calmly.

A gentle man, but with unbending morals, and definitely not

a person to cross.

In 1992, he spent two years with the Red Arrows before going to GCHQ at the end of 1993 due to back problems. "Too many ejections," he used to quip, unless he'd had a few beers, in which case the last word would be modified slightly.

He later moved into training and eventually got his doctorate, but I'm not sure in which science subject.

The long and short of it is he's a senior, thirty-year-plus career servant of the realm, who now appears to be involved in a most serious breach of GCHQ security. I find it impossible to believe it's him, unless he's under severe personal duress.

Suddenly my iPad beeps – an email from Pete, dated two days ago.

I think the first thing to come under scrutiny will be his research, and here's an email outlining it.

Apparently it's a laboratory-based theoretical study, which revolves around two core elements: zepto-bots, and infrasound.

THIRTEEN

Suzi and I walk into Tony's office, just after 2.30pm, and as I shake one hand, he uses his other to mute the TV.

"Afternoon Suzi, Lucas. You made bloomin' good time; caught me on a coffee break – had brain fade."

"No problem. Six Nations?" I ask as a rugby fan. "What's the latest?"

"22-8 with ten minutes remaining. Ireland's indestructible this year! Scotland doesn't stand a chance."

"Oh well, benefit of you being half Irish; shout for them or England!" says Suzi.

"Indeed." Tony smiles as he turns off the TV. "Let's go find Coops."

We walk around the corner into her office, to find she's kneeling on the floor, with the computer's side panel lying next to her. No doubt she's cajoling it to run faster than designed. I can see she's wearing earphones, and I gently tap her shoulder, so as not to startle her.

Removing her miniature, bright pink earphones, she turns around. "Lucas!" she squeals, grinning, and she jumps off the ground to give me a long hug. Then she holds me by my shoulders at arm's length. "I'm so sorry to hear about Pete," she whispers, staring at me with sullen eyes. "I know you are great pals."

"Don't worry, nothing's proven," I say as she releases me from her koala grip and sits at her terminal.

"What have you found?" I ask, dragging over a spare chair, and sit looking over her shoulder at the monitor.

"Where shall I start?"' she grumbles, pulling up list after list of files on the screen. "It's like this–"

Suddenly, there is a SILENT ALARM warning flashing on her monitor: six-inch yellow capitals on a red screen. This is immediately replaced by: SITE LOCKDOWN. SILENT ALARM FROM MAIN GATE. RESPONSE TEAM DISPATCHED. And then, almost immediately, our mobiles vibrate and flash the same message.

I look at Tony: "What was the trigger?"

"Main gate keycode," he replies as we watch Coops flick from screen to screen, scrolling through the alarm software records.

"Which resident?" I ask. Presumably someone has been forced to enter GCHQ under duress and, unknown to their abductors, they have raised the alarm.

"Yes. Last digit changed from seven to three," Coops shouts, jabbing her screen with an index finger.

Then Tony asks, "But who is it?"

"Hell," gasps Coops.

"What?" we say in unison.

"It's Pete!" replies Coops, confused, as are Tony and I.

"What's on the SAS feed?" Tony chirps again at Coops.

She expands the video output from a slightly unsteady Land Rover dashboard-mounted cam onto one of her desk monitors. This image sits next to those feeding from the main gate and secondary gates, as well as reception.

In addition to GCHQ's visible guards, a twenty-strong SAS team in five armoured Land Rover Defenders are seconds away: two vehicles (Alpha team) to the main gate and one to each of the secondary gates (Bravo, Charlie and Delta). They're authorised to use deadly force.

From the super-high-res still photo taken at the main gate CCTV, we can clearly see it is Pete, flanked by two innocuous-looking guys in plain charcoal business suits.

Coops' face recognition system instantly confirms our man Pete. But it's still comparing millions of images, which momentarily flash on screen, to identify his "abductors".

I turn to Tony. "Get hold of the leader of Alpha team. We need to let these goons get into the premises, find out what they're up to."

Then, looking at Coops, and tapping her shoulder: "Get his personal bodycam onto my mobile, and put the site's CCTV up on your wall monitors."

We have no idea what influence these goons are exerting over Pete to get him to comply, and I need to know how the hell this relates to his work. A thorough investigation into Pete's PC earlier gave no clues, but it's still being monitored by Coops.

My iPhone beeps. *Enter surveillance code,* its screen demands. I enter my seven-digit code and the SAS team's AV stream bursts on to the screen of my handset.

"Thanks Coops."

"No probs." She glances at me, nodding at the wall of monitors. "All CCTV up there now. Just gesture to zoom in."

"Gesture?"

"Like your iPad; stretch and squeeze."

"Reminds me of the cycle of a four-stroke engine – suck, squeeze, bang, blow!" I grin at her. She merely shakes her head in mock frustration at me but chuckles nonetheless.

The SAS team leader immediately requests confirmation of my last command, as their initial order is *not* to allow Pete onto the premises.

I activate the hands-free on my phone, and give them my name, rank and ID code. Their voice recognition system gives a two-second lag before it confirms my authority to them, and so I advise, "SAS team leader. Allow progression into the building and monitor. Do not, repeat *not*, intercept, but be ready to take down immediately upon my command. Lethal force remains approved."

An impassive voice replies, "Team leader, understood… confirm Peter Skinner remains a friendly."

"Yes. Confirmed. Pete is a friendly." I reply with a hint of angst in my voice.

Watching my phone's screen, I can see Pete stroll over to reception where his pass is scanned and cleared. He then hangs the blue-corded ID around his neck.

I gesture at the CCTV on the wall and zoom in to the reception's feed. He declares the two with him are consultants from a company called IT Russe Né, whereupon temporary access cards are printed and slid into clear plastic ID wallets, which the two hang round their necks from the bright orange visitor lanyards.

So, they're definitely not French, nor do they speak it, as Russe Né translates as 'Russian Born'. Good clue Pete.

There is no diversion from the normal visitor procedure, other than an invisible tracking spray, which is automatically released on to the shins of these goons' trousers as they pass through the revolving barrier.

This spray of holmium microspheres only has a half-life of 48 hours, but that's ample for tracking by satellite. Strange to think that in a more sustained application these microscopic beads can kill cancerous tumours in the liver.

We continue to watch the wall monitor CCTV, and my mobile, to track the progress of the goons as they and Pete casually navigate a few corridors until, after only ten minutes, they enter his office.

A couple of minutes later, we see them and Pete take something small from their inside jacket pockets, and then put their hands momentarily to their ears; wireless headphones?

I react immediately. "Alpha team leader. Can you see what they're up to?"

"No." There's a brief pause. "It could be audio but our systems aren't registering any signals."

What comes next is totally unexpected.

Literally, all-embracing silence.

I can't hear anything but I feel a sudden, ferocious earache, an incapacitating headache and nausea, and I crumple to the floor.

****

Suzi, Tony and Coops are on the carpet next to me. We all have our hands over our ears. Eyes screwed up, we're immobile, barely able to talk.

I look at the SAS AV on my phone and stutter into the mic: "Alpha one. Don't engage. Repeat, don't engage. Monitor and report. You got headaches too?"

"Understood. Don't engage. Yes, headaches." Then after a second's pause, "Team, do not engage, I repeat, do *not* engage." Then, at seeing one of his men go down on one knee, "Suck it up, boys!"

The team again respond in sequence confirming their compliance.

I can see from the AV feed that they too are struggling with the same agony as us, but they remain standing, holding their positions – how the hell do these guys cope?

Glancing at Coops' sixty-inch wall monitor, which shows all of the site's CCTV images, I can see everyone else in this building is reeling with the same debilitating symptoms!

One of the goons points at the desktop computer, and then

prods Pete sharply in the ribs, making him wince. He immediately complies with their unspoken demands as we see him push what looks like a thumb-drive into a slot of his PC.

Almost simultaneously a message comes onto Coops' PC screen.

> *Coops, your screen only. What you guys feel now is only pain. The threshold is controlled with a micro-sensor strapped to my chest, which monitors my heartbeat. If my heartbeat stops, the systems output will jump to a lethal level; your death will occur within two minutes. This control system is wireless, but if it gets interrupted for more than ten seconds then again it will assume I am dead. Several miles away there is an array of sensors monitoring your transmissions. Any attempt to contact persons outside the base will turn the systems output to the lethal level. When we've finished here, and are satisfied you are not tracking us, my chest strap will be removed, and the source will self-destruct.*
> *Hit Enter to continue.*

She taps the Return key on her PC's keyboard, and another message flickers on her monitor.

> *We will now leave this felicity. Make sure we are left alone. You know my abilities; you must comply, sit back and enjoy the rugby, Tony. Message ends.*

Coops nudges me: "He needs to use his spell-checker!"

"What?" I wince at her.

"He's typed *felicity* instead of facility – numpty!"

I speak into my mic, "Alpha one and team. Allow these guys to leave. Do not, I repeat *not*, radio or use any other comms outside the boundaries of this site. Understood?"

"Alpha one, understood."

After a brief discussion I get Tony to prepare a global GCHQ email:

> *Hi all. There has been a problem with one of the extract fan bearings vibrating and emitting infrasound. This unit has now been isolated, and will shortly be replaced by a standby fan.*

This will be quite believable, even if Googled, as there was an instance back in the 1960s where a professor in his lab, after observing apparently ghostly images, discovered that he had a faulty extract fan. The sound could not be heard by the human ear, but did register on his acoustic equipment as a 19Hz frequency: the resonant frequency of the human eye. Hence the false images. If the sound had been at a higher volume and prolonged, it would have caused him major and permanent sight damage.

We have no choice, and, in every sense, have to watch in agony as Pete and the goons leave the site.

It's only been five minutes and we hear a dull bang from the direction of Pete's office – no doubt the self-destructing transmitter.

Tony sends his email.

FOURTEEN

It's 3.30pm and there's frantic chatter as I enter the Situation Room just down the corridor from Coops' office. Everyone is here – well, those who know what really just took place: Tony, Coops, Suzi and me.

I go to the front of the room and join the others sitting at the large oblong table, which stands below a massive flat monitor.

Pete will have left us clues, so the first thing we need to do is analyse those messages on his computer, and everything else in his office.

I break the ice and kick things off. "Okay. This is what I know." With a sigh of disbelief, I begin. "Pete Skinner and two 'visitors' entered this site today." Then, leaning forward and gesturing at the image on the huge monitor: "Pete did trigger the silent alarm, but from replaying the CCTV we see one of the goons nudge him as he hesitates over the last digit – I reckon they probably knew about the silent trigger."

Coops leans back in her chair, the wireless keyboard on her lap. "Agreed," she says, gently nodding. "They must have seen the SAS presence, and were unfazed when they went to Pete's office."

"There," I continue, as Coops scrolls through the log on Pete's PC, "a pre-prepared message was displayed by Pete on his computer, accompanied immediately by a massive burst of infrasound, causing our incapacity, and discomfort to most staff in nearby buildings."

Coops fast-forwards through CCTV footage, going into slow-mo at a scene showing the open door of a cleaner's cupboard in the adjacent corridor. "When they left, we know Pete took a small box from his desk, probably a controller," she says, then, glancing at the monitor: "and the goons pick up something from the janitor's room."

This thing the goons grab looks like an electronic drum top. It's about four feet in diameter and four inches thick – a speaker? We reckon this is a second "kit", with the first being responsible for damn near making our ears bleed!

Sitting upright, I bang my fist on the table. "Worst of all, we had to let them leave, and are now struggling to track them!"

Coops gives me a quizzical glance. "What gets me is the last bit of the message from Pete."

"What do you mean?"

"Well, all of the messages are done in Microsoft PowerPoint. So, why was the word *understand* in the last message somehow blurry?"

"Can you pull it up on the monitor?" I ask.

"Yep, no probs," she says happily, and a few seconds later the message is on the massive screen.

I smile at her. "Looks okay to me."

"Here… look," she says, looping the cursor around the word *understand*. Then, in a seamless action, she zooms in, making it six inches high.

Tony chips in: "The T is in a different font. Just means Pete was sloppy prepping the slides; he must have been under tremendous pressure!"

"The last thing Pete is… is sloppy," I snap protectively. "This is deliberate. He's trying to tell us something."

We sit perplexed, staring at the screen, willing it to shout the answer to us.

Suddenly Coops breaks the silence. "It's no good, I'm not getting anywhere with this," she shrugs, "but it's definitely a clue. Changing the font of one character is *so* deliberate."

"I have an idea," I say tentatively.

This causes Coops to spin round. "What the hell have you spotted?" she says with a frowning grin.

Tony and Suzi look equally exasperated. "Yeah," he adds, "come on, out with it!"

"I think he's splitting the word into two–"

Coops excitedly finishes my reveal: "Yes, *under* and *sand!*" But then, shrugging her shoulders, she exclaims, "But what the hell does it mean?"

I continue following my gut's guidance, brain racing through millions of slivers of information, recalling and assimilating facts from decades of friendship. Then, in a similarly haphazard fashion, I start verbalising my mind's output.

"Something to do with Pete's time in the RAF… in the desert… something relating to the sand, or under the sand."

I know I have to be patient while my brain frantically glues disjointed memories together. Then, in my mind's eye, a distinct image of a framed picture on Pete's desk.

"Got it!" I shout. "Something to do with Pete's Jag! That's the key to this puzzle."

"Jaguar?" Coops says. "I thought he was an Alvis man?"

"Elvis?" Tony frowns.

"No!" says Coops, smirking. "Alvis car – he's got a 4.3-litre, short-chassis tourer!"

"No! You've both got the wrong end of the stick. I mean the flippin' jet fighter! There's a photo of it on Pete's desk."

Coops immediately logs off the PC, and we all scamper off to Pete's office to find the picture. And, hopefully, the key to the events of the day.

****

As we rush down the corridor, the photo image in my mind becomes clearer.

It is a very young, skinny Pete, looking barely old enough to drive, but with a wispy moustache, which unfortunately makes him look more like Twizzle than Biggles.

He's standing next to his desert-camouflaged fighter with a look of pride and apprehension in equal measure. First day at battle readiness, one day before his first kill, and two days before his first premature ejection, as he laughingly called them.

After a few beers, he'd occasionally joke that the worst thing in combat was the sand. "Gets into every sodding orifice – bloody uncomfortable for humans, but deadly for engines." Apparently, the ground crew's half-dozen "sweeping" trucks repeatedly cleared the runway. Otherwise it could disappear in a matter of hours.

It's only taken a couple of minutes for all four of us to get to Pete's office. Here the heavily armed and humourless guard checks our credentials, before begrudgingly allowing us into the locked-down room.

We are only a few feet in when we stop dead in our tracks.

The room looks like it's been ransacked by St Trinian's year two. Pete's right, chaos theory does exist; it's here!

The room's disarray is reminiscent of Coops' desk, and

heaven help anyone who moves anything there. Obviously the same goes for Pete's fiefdom.

To many, Coops' and Pete's chaos is an enigma. We are merely left to stare in awe at the way they interconnect the seemingly meaningless dots in the world.

I go over to his desk and pick up the photo, the left third of which is bleached from the sunny window it faces. In a trice I have the frame apart with its four pieces lying on his oxblood-red leather desk blotter in front of me: frame, glass, picture and back-board.

We offer round the photo, staring at it, slowly turning it this way and that, willing a clue to jump out at us.

Nothing.

Just a date, and a simple phrase on the reverse of the photo, "Transport to Felicity". His nan, passed away now. He believed she was "up there" looking over him.

****

We return to the Situation Room, empty-handed from Pete's office, save for the poorly reassembled Jaguar photo.

What are we missing? Does the phrase on the back of the photo mean something? Or am I just grabbing at straws?

Maybe there's some other clue in the screenshot, so I get Coops to put it back up on the monitor. Again we all stare at the image while Coops unconsciously makes slow loops around the word *understand* with the cursor.

Suddenly she sits bolt upright in her seat, making the rest of us jump. "Hell, talk about missing the flippin' obvious!"

"What do you see?" I reply excitedly.

"Watch when I run the cursor over the second part of the word – *sand!*"

"Christ, it's a hyperlink!" I shout. "Bloody brilliant. Come on, Coops – where's it take us?"

She clicks on *sand* and the computer whizzes off and offers a single folder. Coops double-clicks on it.

Immediately, flashing red in the centre of her screen: "Restricted Access – PASSWORD".

Coops starts typing like she's possessed, loading different

words and numbers into her self-programmed password cracker.

These snippets relate to Pete. Bits of passwords she has accidentally seen him enter, his date of birth, parents' names. At the same time she's researching his mother's maiden name, dogs, cats, house numbers, NI number, schools, colleges, etc. When she's finished she sets off her program, which rapidly tries the millions of combinations of the information she's just entered.

This way of breaking passwords is called a brute-force attack. It can take time, because an eight-character password can have 1.6 quadrillion variants. (For those interested, that is based on 80 guesses for one character: two alphas of 26 characters each, ten numerals and 18 symbols. Theoretically, there are 127 characters available, but in practice fewer are used. Therefore, for an eight-character password, 80x80x80x80x80x80x80x80 combinations, or 1,677,721,600,000,000.)

But, after a few minutes, still nothing. The same message keeps reappearing, relentlessly blinking on the screen: "Restricted Access – PASSWORD".

Then I get a brainwave. "Coops! Bring up the message where we laughed about his spelling error. The one where they're leaving and want to be left alone."

"No problem. This is it I think?"

The message comes up on screen; we read it again and chuckle.

We will now leave this high security felicity. Make sure we are left alone. You know my abilities; understand you must comply, sit back and enjoy the rugby, Tony. Message ends.

"What are you thinking?" asks Coops.

Looking down at the back of the Jaguar picture, and then back at Coops, I smile and exclaim excitedly: "Felicity… *Transport*… try that as the password, replacing 'a' with @ and 'o' with zero!"

Nine clicks, and then the Enter key.

This time the computer is happy and goes searching, only to come back with a long list of file names, all kept in a folder entitled Memory_Instinct_Genes.

"Bloody hell, what is *this* all about?" Coops bursts out, staring at the list. "I know everything that's on our systems but I've never seen this directory before. Pete's either kept these private somehow, or…" She stops talking, mesmerised by her screen as she taps away at the keyboard.

She sits back in her seat, plonks the wireless keyboard on the table, turns to Suzi and me and, raising an eyebrow, announces: "These files are deep in the archives of MI5, Thames House!"

We sit stunned for a second.

I glance at Suzi. "Get hold of Jeff in London and–" But she's already on her mobile, and mouths at me, *Jeff*.

Then, to Tony, "Find out about Pete's work." And then to Coops, with a smile: "And you, liddle lady, have a crack at getting into those files."

"I can do that," she grins back at me. This is the sort of challenge she relishes.

I stand, slide my iPhone into a pocket, pick up my iPad and turn again to Suzi, saying, "You and I need to get back to London. Do some serious digging."

We all leave the Situation Room and go our separate ways at the landing lobby: Coops and Tony back to their offices, and Suzi and I take the lift down to reception.

As soon as we're out of the main gate, I put on the engine grille's 'blues' and floor the Audi toward the A40 out of Cheltenham, toward London. Suzi calls the local Bill's headquarters at Quedgeley and politely requests they leave us alone as we scream through the villages of Northleach, then Burford, skirting the towns of Witney and Headington, towards the M40.

Glancing at the satnav, it looks like we'll be back at Thames House just after teatime.

FIFTEEN

After nearly an hour of fighting our way down the M40, the M25 and A4, we walk into my team's open plan office at Thames House.

Everyone has their back to us and I can see they are being addressed by Jeff, who, on seeing me, gives a small nod to acknowledge my arrival.

As he finishes, he makes steady eye contact with me. "Okay, that's it for now… I see Lucas and Suzi are back from GCHQ, and they would like to say a few words before you all disappear." He then gestures for us to join him at the front of the gathered throng.

"This will be short and sweet," I say sombrely, looking around the room at the expectant faces. "We have a man down, Peter Skinner, and I cannot overemphasise that getting him back takes precedence. However, if any other high-priority work comes in, then check with Suzi; just in case something needs to run in parallel with finding Pete."

Jeff gently taps my shoulder, and whispers, "Lucas. I know you'll want to continue with a formal team-briefing, but first *we* need to speak."

Looking back at the dumbstruck, silent room, I continue: "Okay. Grab a coffee, and meet me back here in fifteen minutes for a formal update. After that, liaise with Suzi to get live-case priorities agreed."

Turning to Suzi, I say softly, "Jeff wants a private word. Shall I grab you a coffee on my way back?"

"Brilliant, thanks."

Jeff and I stroll briskly along the corridor, chatting as we stop at the whirring bean-to-cup contraption. We double-cup our near-scalding coffees, grab some cold milk sachets and stir sticks, and start back to his office.

As Jeff slides behind his desk into his chair, he quickly neutralises the desktop monitor and wall screen, before "Fenella", the AI (Artificial Intelligence) secretary on his wall monitor, has a chance to introduce herself. I sit in the slightly lower visitor's chair, and Jeff insistently pushes a coaster toward me just before I put my coffee down.

He leans forward, chin balanced atop his clasped hands. "Lucas, there's been a development in the last half hour, and I wanted to tell you in person."

"Sounds ominous."

Jeff breathes a frustrated sigh. "The stuff Pete's working on is eyes-only classified, and unknown outside of MI5. Including 6 and GCHQ, and obviously the colander we call Government."

"That explains why Coops had trouble getting hold of the information."

"What?" he shouts, jumping back in his seat, face rapidly turning crimson with embarrassment. "She's got copies?"

"No, no, but she traced it here."

""Good," he gasped in relief. "At least for now." His cheeks fade to pink. "As far as anyone else here is concerned, we are focusing on getting Pete back, not what he was working on."

"Unless I deem his work relevant to his disappearance!"

"Of course, Lucas, of course."

This is not the first time a person's work is more valuable than the person – but Pete's a mate.

"So, how do you want to proceed?" I ask flatly.

"You go to the meeting room, bring the team up to speed, and set them to work. I'll join you and Suzi later for a separate briefing, and arrange for Coops and Tony to conference call."

"Okay, will do." Then, staring at Jeff: "So, come on, what is this stuff Pete's working on?"

Jeff looks at the ceiling, and takes a few moments as he ponders my question, which obviously has ramifications.

"Basically, it's gene manipulation, one being the reloading of a person's memory or instinct… and the sexing chromosome."

"What, their entire memory?" I ignore the second reference.

"No, just the deep, quiescent stuff. It's what our brain calls on when we react automatically to a new situation, sometimes giving a sense of déjà-vu, or a gut feeling."

"Bloody hell! That's actually possible?"

"Zepto-technology. It can be implemented remotely. The trigger is ingenious – an inaudible, untraceable, infrasound burst of digital code!"

After the briefest pause, Jeff continues, "We made sure no one got wind of it. But obviously, somehow, the cat is now out of the bag!"

I wish I could call my pal Mike at the FBI's New York HQ. But even if they have it, he'd have to deny it, and if not, they'd then know about it, and they would try to recover it before we could.

I recall Pete's love of back-up plans. "So what back-door did he put into the system?"

Jeff's brow furrows. "That's between him and me."

"But you know they'll break him. They already coerced him to get inside GCHQ!"

"Indeed." The anxiety in Jeff's voice is audible, and he takes a long breath. "Okay, you need to get back to the meeting room. I'll join you in twenty minutes." He adds with a grin, "I'll get some more coffees and cake."

This will give Suzi and me time to brief the team, and get them off and running. Then we can get the secure conference call to Coops and Tony online.

After briefing the team, and whilst waiting for Jeff, Suzi and I sit here, swapping chitchat with Coops and Tony on the conference call speakerphone.

****

Jeff taps the door closed behind him with his foot, as he enters the meeting room balancing three coffees. Then, whilst distributing the drinks, sugars, stirring sticks, and, more importantly, the pastries, he quickly says hi to Tony and Coops.

"Okay," Jeff says with a sigh. "We need to find Pete and damn quick, both for his own security, his family, and this project."

The speaker in the middle of the desk crackles, and gives Tony's frustrated tones a metallic echo. "Jeff, given that the hardware was here, why was this project not known to GCHQ?"

"It was felt to be of such a sensitive nature that no one outside of MI5 could know of its existence… no one!"

"Well, in the end, Coops found its scent on Pete's PC," replies a triumphant Tony.

Knowing Coops is sitting next to Tony, Jeff replies: "Praise indeed to Pete's efforts if we managed to keep it from you,

Coops, until now."

As usual, and we'd have it no other way, Coops has none of his bullshit. "Thank you for the platitudes. Shame you weren't so successful with those who've stolen it," she grumbles. "I presume you now want us to herd the cats back into the bag?" And, with a sigh, "Mop-up duties as usual!"

Jeff knows better than to confront her, especially when she's right, and so he glances at me with a nervous smile. "Exactly, Coops. I can only apologise," he says, which immediately defuses the situation.

He looks around the room and then continues, "The team here will focus on locating Pete, and getting him back. But I need you, Coops, to check the security on all the project's data and files. I will open up access to the relevant server for you; just search on iGenus."

"Okay," replies Coops flatly. "Exactly what should I be searching for?" Still a barb of sarcasm.

Jeff again glances at me. "This is an 'eyes only' project, and you know who may be listening–"

We sit in silence, waiting for Jeff to continue. Concerned, I look at him, as I've pretty much been staring at the conference pod, enjoying his jousting with Coops. He's sitting stock-still, seemingly dazed, staring back at me.

Then suddenly he clasps his head, apparently in pain, but only mouthing near-silent words. I lean over and put a consoling arm around his shoulders. "Jeff – Jeff – you okay?"

His eyes widen, and, with a mix of gasping for air and trying to speak, he collapses with a thump, face down on the desk.

"Shit!" I shout. "Jeff's passed out. Speak later."

I close the call whilst simultaneously hitting the emergency pressure pad circling the underside lip of the table. Immediately the building's tannoys, on every floor, repeatedly belt out the words: "Lock Down. Secure Perimeter."

No one enters. No one leaves.

SIXTEEN

After searching for a pulse on Jeff's carotid artery, I turn to Suzi: "Fuck, he's dead!" My eyes are moist. "Get the defibrillator and then call forensics!" She runs out of the room and along the corridor to get the wall-mounted defibrillator next to the lift, whilst dialling Ruth Hare on her mobile.

Dr Hare works at the Forensic Science Service (FSS), a grim concrete bunker in south London on the site of what was once an abattoir; how apt. She's one of only a handful allowed to enter this locked-down site, and she'll be here in minutes.

For the second time in just over a fortnight, I hold down the Fingerprint Scanning On button on my iPhone. Keeping it depressed for five seconds puts the Personal Alarm – Armed Assault option on screen, and then in a further five seconds it activates. But this time I am within Thames House, in central London, so the software presumes there is a terrorist attack on the building.

The tannoys now alternate their authoritative commands: "Terrorist Attack. Deadly Force Approved" and then "Lock Down. Secure Perimeter."

As I gently manhandle Jeff down onto the floor, putting my rolled-up jacket under his head, Suzi runs back into the room with the defibrillator, advising me that Ruth's en route, and our resident techie James is on his way to me with the Faro Focus X130 3D laser scanner. Also, his team are now monitoring Jeff's and my vitals through the microchips in the napes of our necks.

Following the graphical instructions on the defibrillator, I stick the paddles onto Jeff's now freshly alcohol-wiped chest. The first goes three inches below his left nipple and under his arm, with the second centrally above his right nipple. This ensures the shock goes directly through his heart.

The defibrillator's electronic voice advises, 'No pulse. Charging.'

My mobile rings. It's Dr Ruth Hare, so I take the call.

"Hi Lucas. With you in ten. Ambulance same. Jeff's status?"

"Unconscious, unbreathing. Defib attached; no pulse, and charging."

"Okay," she continues, "just follow the defib's instructions until I get there."

The phone goes dead.

It's down to me.

After twenty seconds, the defibrillator's electronic voice says, 'Stand back. Press green button when clear.'

Just as I go to press the button, Suzi grabs the pendant from Jeff's chest. "Thanks, Suzi, he'd have looked like Ironman." I try to smile, and press the green button.

Jeff's torso leaps into the air as if kicked by a horse.

After ten seconds the defib's staccato voice states, 'No pulse. Charging.'

Another twenty seconds, and the defibrillator instructs, 'Stand back. Press green button when clear.'

Seeing a tear roll down her cheek, I lean across to Suzi, who's crouched the other side of Jeff, and gently pat her arm. She's holding it together, but, like me, only just.

After the third attempt the defib senses a faint pulse, and states, 'Pulse detected. Not charging. Not allowing shock treatment.'

I leave the sticky paddles attached, just in case, and start CPR with thirty compressions to two breaths. The Vinnie Jones TV advert and Bee Gees' Stayin' Alive keeps my rhythm. But after only a few minutes, again the defib's staccato voice warns, 'No pulse. Charging.' And, a little later, 'Stand back. Press green button when clear.'

It repeatedly goes through its one-minute cycle of belting shocks into Jeff's body as it tries to get his heart going again.

Another few minutes and paramedics run into the room and take control, confirming we've done a sterling job. But after only a few minutes they look at me, shaking their heads: it's over.

They close Jeff's eyes, pull the pads from his chest, and put a blanket over him, covering his face. They advise the central monitoring team he's gone.

Some ten seconds pass and my phone beeps. I look down at its screen: *Jeff TOD 17:48hrs,* which comes from the central computer system monitoring his microchip neck implant.

Within a few minutes, James runs into the room, stopping in his tracks just inside the door. The blood drains from his face as first he looks at the blanket on the floor covering Jeff's lifeless body, and then at me, and my sweat-soaked shirt.

Suzi, seeing the mood spiralling downward, immediately takes charge and gets me, the paramedics and herself out of the room, first instructing James to set up the 3D scanner and plot from four positions around the room. Still looking down at Jeff, James nods sombrely and complies with her instructions.

Dr Hare arrives, countersigns the TOD as 17:48, and predicts the forthcoming autopsy will corroborate her theory of a massive stroke.

Having received a text on my mobile that all data has been downloaded from Jeff's implant, I authorise Ruth to remove it from the nape of his neck and hand it to James, and arrange for the body to be taken to the basement mortuary. It's only been 25 minutes and James has uploaded the room-scan data to our servers, and a fully rendered image is streamed onto my iPad.

Meanwhile, London's two omnipresent Typhoon Eurofighters circle overhead at twenty thousand feet, with heat-tracking and facial-recognition cameras focused on Thames House and the surrounding area. Four more fighters are scrambled from 3 Squadron, RAF Coningsby, with two racing to GCHQ and two coming to London.

SEVENTEEN

It's now quarter to seven; nearly an hour since Jeff died, and the tannoys finally belt out the all clear – "Lock Down Rescinded".

For everyone else, all is now well inside Thames House.

I'm back in my office, cogitating on the events of this afternoon, particularly Jeff's passing; coincidence?

'No such thing!' I hear Jeff's voice in my head. He always said that everything has a cause and effect, and occasionally quoted Aristotle: "*Excellence is never an accident. It is always the result of high intention, sincere effort, and intelligent execution; it represents the wise choice of many alternatives – choice, not chance, determines your destiny.*"

We must also presume Jeff's death is linked to Pete's disappearance. The timing alone stopped him giving us the password.

At least Coops has tracked down the files, but the real problem will be their encryption. All codes can be broken, some in hours, but some can take months, or even years; certainly the ones Coops uses! I doubt Pete's will be any less challenging.

My mobile vibrates into life. "Hi Coops, how's it going?"

"Good news," she replies, slightly subdued. "I've found the specific project files. All I need now is the encryption key!"

"Easier said than done."

"There must be something Jeff or Pete shared with you. They wouldn't allow this situation." She emphasises, "Always a backup!"

"Nothing comes to mind, Coops. Not even sure where to start looking." My mobile vibrates. I glance at its screen: Ruth. "I'll have to call you back Coops."

I switch to the waiting call. "Hi, Doc, what's up?"

Ruth often walks the FSS corridors munching a carrot, and with her surname, even in such sombre surroundings, the 'What's up Doc?' quip occasionally pops out. But she pays no heed.

"I'm looking at Jeff's emergency talisman neck chain," she says, distracted. "It's engraved on the reverse with 'pie vestle', and inside there's just one allergy listed – 'nuts' – with the owner named as *Pete*. But neither Jeff nor Pete have allergies!"

"This must be some kind of clue," I reply, smiling to myself. "He used to joke with Pete about who ate all the pies!"

"Well, he's spelt vessel wrong."

"What?"

"P…i…e…V…e…s…t…l…e." She pauses while I repeat the characters and scribble them onto my notepad. "Then n…u…t…S."

"What, the last 'S' is capitalised?"

"Yes. Strange, huh?"

"Thanks, doc. Let me know if you find anything else." And I close the call.

"Holy shit!" I say under my breath, looking down at my scribble. It stands out like a sore thumb!

"Pie Vestle" is an anagram of Pete lives.

And nuts backwards, indicated by the oddly placed S, is stun; the definition of which includes "to shock with noise".

My gut does its happy dance.

****

I pull Coops' number up on my mobile, and call to give her the good news. "Hi, how's it going?"

"Good until fifteen minutes ago," she replies tersely. "Then it all went Pete Tong."

"Anything I can help with?"

"Not unless you've got the bloomin' encryption key!"

I keep quiet for a moment.

"You sod," she says abruptly, "you bloody well know the password, don't you!"

"Might do."

"Come on!" Her voice rises an octave. "Don't be an arse all your life; take a day off!"

"Very ladylike." She is certainly not a happy bunny, and so I immediately spell out the clue. "Here you go. Two words, P… I…E and then V…E…S…T…L…E." Then after a slight sigh, "Not sure what's upper and lower case or if any alphanumeric transposition."

"Sorry for being grumpy," she says quietly, "but I've been racking my brain on this blasted thing. Wait a second."

After listening to a lot of frantic key-tapping from her end, I can wait no longer. "Come on then, Coops, you're in aren't you?"

"Might be." She returns my tease in a smug tone.

"Fair go. Give me a call later, and let me know what you find."

I close the call and, stomach rumbling, decide to get some fresh air and something to eat, as I seem to be surviving on caffeine and precious little else.

Taking the easy option, I go out through reception, turn right, and head west along Millbank Road a hundred yards to Pizza Express. I would prefer The View at Skyloft fifty yards further, but can't justify their prices just for my dinner.

Once I start eating, I realise I am ravenous.

As usual, the food is lovely, but most of the time my mind is elsewhere; thrashing through a million things to do with this case, and my marriage.

But nonetheless it is a respite from my office.

EIGHTEEN

At just gone half eight, just as I've sat down at my office desk, my mobile rings. It's Coops. "Hiya, what ya got?"

"This project is bordering on science fiction. I've seen some strange stuff, and–"

"Do not say any more," I interrupt, "if you have any concerns over the security of this line."

"This line's fine, but I'll send you a pair of new 4k public encryption keys, before I email the link to this file."

"So – give me a summary."

"There are several strands, but the main project name is iGenus. Scarily apt for the subject matter."

"And what is the subject?"

"Gene modification. This first bit's about mind control, based on our memory gene, our instinct, controlling our very soul."

"Bloody hell," I say, incredulous, and slump back into my seat. "Is it viable?"

"I'd say so," She takes an approving breath. "Pete was… sorry, *is* a very smart cookie!"

"Okay. Don't say any more now." I sit back upright. "Email Suzi, cc me, and ask her to meet me, with a printout, in the Situation Room in fifteen minutes. And you and Tony be available for another conference call."

I close the call and start scribbling some notes, when for some reason, the Hitler mind control and the sodium fluoride (NaF) conspiracy buzz around my head.

The latter hits a chord as at home we are trying to get rid of a vermin problem, and NaF is used in large concentrations in rat poison!

Anyway, better grab a couple of strong coffees and make my way to meet Suzi.

NINETEEN

It's quarter to nine, and I am sitting in the Situation Room waiting for Suzi when my mind wanders, trying to recall anything Pete or Jeff said about iGenus.

Controlling a population has been a dream of dictators, kings and governments for centuries. A few have achieved it through fear, religion or cult following, and, on very rare occasions, a general belief in the leader concerned. Never, though, has it been through absolute control of a person's soul. That's unthinkable, let alone achievable. But now, apparently, it's here?

Finally Suzi strolls into the room, and pushes the door closed with her heel. She is distracted, a little out of breath, and has an expression of total disbelief.

"Suzi, you okay?"

"What can I say – this summary from Coops reads like an Isaac Asimov novel synopsis." She drops two printed copies onto the table.

After a gulp of the double-shot lattes, we both start to speed-read our copies, underlining minor points and circling major ones. After ten minutes my paper looks like it's been attacked by a red-ink-footed spider performing Holiday on Ice.

"So… zepto-bots?" Suzi stares at me with a look of trepidation. "Is this possible?"

"It would appear so," I sigh. "Hopefully, they're just at the laboratory stage."

"And these zepto-bots can be used to make nano-bots!"

My mobile rings. "Yo, Master!" shouts Coops, sounding excited to the point of implosion.

"I guess this stuff's right up your street?" I say with a smile.

"You bloomin' kidding, this is better than chocolate, better than sex!" Only Coops could put those items in that order.

"Steady, young lady–"

"Okay, it's not better than chocolate." She quickly continues, "Have you read the bit about the size of these things, and how they power themselves, and–"

I interrupt, as her voice is now reaching a pitch only dogs will hear. "Slow down, liddle lady." But even the mimicking of her hero does not distract her from her line of thought.

"Zepto-bots – atom-size devices." She gasps a breath. "It's all too incredible. A *nano* is a billionth of a metre (10^{-9}m). In layman's terms, one inch equals 25.4 million nanometers, and a human hair 75,000 nanometers." By this time she's nearly hyperventilating with excitement. "And zepto is a billionth-billionth of a metre (10^{-21}m)!"

Coops finally has to stop talking to get her breath back, which lets Suzi chip in. "Okay, okay, my brain's fizzing and to be honest I'm more concerned with these things being used against us, and *how* they could be delivered to a target?"

"That's the thing," Coops replies, slightly calmer. "Five years ago, I would have said water supply. But at this minuscule scale… they could be inhaled! The aerosol would be invisible!"

"Bloody hell," Suzi exclaims. "Has this been trialed?"

"Yes," says Coops. "It's all in this report. And the other amazing thing is how they are powered–"

"But," I interrupt, "how can they be neutralised?"

"Ah, thought you'd want that bit first, Lucas," says Coops. "They can be killed with a terminate command in their software, which is delivered using infrasound. Unfortunately, I've not found the code for it yet."

Suzi jumps back in: "I trust you're going to be able to work that out, Coops? I mean how to kill them?"

"Sure. But there's also mention of a batch going rogue during human trials which couldn't be shut down."

"Bloody hell! What happened?" asks Suzi.

"Female test subject died," Coops says. "Massive stroke and heart failure. Cremated the poor student."

"Millions of quid's worth of zepto-bots up in smoke!" states Suzi flatly.

"Suzi!" Coops says, surprised at her lack of sympathy.

"Sorry, didn't mean…poor girl," replies Suzi.

"We need to find the likeliest method of delivery," I say in the pause. "I'm guessing most accurate is water supply, and least aerosol. Target choice is probably a major city."

Coops agrees to search for some "soft" water-supply targets, whilst Suzi will map out some easy-access high-rise towers.

Meanwhile, I go back to my office and ready myself for the last train home – I need sleep.

TWENTY

I 'm running to the station to catch the train to Eastbourne when my mobile rings, and *Home* pops up on the screen. "Hi." I answer, a little out of breath.

"Where are you?" says Helen in her *you're bloody late* tone.

"Got held up at the office. Just running for the 10.25."

"Great. Plate's in the fridge."

"Okay. Thanks for making me dinner–" but the phone's already dead. Maybe it's the signal, I think to myself, but probably not.

Giving Helen the benefit of the doubt, I call her back. "What?" she answers sharply.

"Thought we'd been cut off. So I–"

"You never bloody think. Not about us. Your family!"

"Helen…I can't help occasionally being late and–"

"You're *always* bloody late!" she interrupts.

I try to hold back, but the lack of sleep causes a brief lapse in focus, and the floodgate momentarily opens. "Jeff's dead, and Pete's been kidnapped!" I blurt out.

Silence.

"I'm so, so sorry Lucas," she says, adding quickly, "We're all fine. Just come home now, and be careful."

"I will. Better run, see you later… I love you."

"Me too," she says softly.

I pick up my pace and get to Clapham Junction just in time to jump on the last carriage of my train as a kindly woman struggles to hold the closing door. Smiling, I thank her, and lean up against the glass partition to catch my breath.

At least it's not rush hour, so I get a good seat. I love London, especially the buzz, but I loathe the hygiene-challenged, who always seem to stand next to me on the Underground.

Nonetheless, right now on this near-empty train, I smile to myself, recalling Jeff's story about his Japan holiday and its Underground. Their travellers wear elasticated paper face masks, and are stuffed into rush-hour trains by official pushers known as *oshiya.* He said we could do with the masks here for the BO problem! And I can hear my mum saying, "A bar of soap is cheap enough! Cleanliness is next to godliness!"

As the train pulls away and I watch the quickening concrete sleepers turn into a blur, I reminisce about the times I dined at Jeff's and Pete's homes, and the times they'd been to mine, with Helen always remarking on them having such lovely families.

It's sad, but maybe it will help Helen and me refocus on the positives of our rocky marriage. And, selfishly, I know it will certainly lessen the discord when I get home.

In minutes my leaden eyes are closed.

****

After an hour I stir at Lewes station, with only a dishevelled copy of the Metro next to me sharing the carriage; just thirty minutes left to Eastbourne.

My eyes close again.

The next thing I feel is the gentle bump as we stop at Eastbourne station just before midnight. The few dozen commuters totter sleepily out of the front carriages.

Having passed through the platform's wide-open electronic barriers, I look back and see the near-empty train traverse back out of the station, to continue its journey on to Hastings. Only the truly hardened commuters take on that final trek!

Walking through the marbled 1850s train station foyer, I swap pleasantries with one of the waitresses from the Thai Brasserie before going out into the balmy night air. It's only a short stroll to where my car is parked in the Avenue, one of the many squares of the "Superior Seaside Resort of Eastbourne" – so named by the developer, and landowner, Lord Devonshire.

I find my car and sit stationary for a minute, letting the engine warm, and the windscreen and side windows demist. I find myself, as usual, admiring the white, four-storey Victorian properties with their black doors and matching cast-iron street lamps. They have wonderfully corniced high ceilings, and mosaic tiled entrance hallways. I wonder what it must have been like for the Bobby on the beat back in those days – with only a billy-club and a whistle!

Windscreen clear and daydreaming over, I drive out of Eastbourne via the coast road, and then negotiate the twisty Upper Duke's Drive. These z-bends, which climb out of the village of Meads on the western edge of Eastbourne, are magnificent, and they zigzag up the 500ft rise like an Italian mountain road. Midway up the steep hillside, between these narrow strips of tarmac, snuggle forty pristine allotments – level at their entrance, but with the loop-back road towering 150ft above. Only a thick flint wall prevents cars plummeting onto the immaculate rows of unsuspecting vegetables.

This stretch of road is a cyclist's dream when descending, but a lung-buster to climb – as those on the Tour of Britain found one Saturday afternoon in 2014.

Once the ascent is finished, it is then out across the first of the Seven Sisters chalk downs to Friston. Less than ten minutes later I'm parked on my drive. The dogs give a welcoming bark from the lounge on hearing the turn of my front door key.

In the hallway, I kick off my shoes as Helen comes out from the kitchen, closing the door behind her. With soulful, wet eyes, she gives me a bear hug. "So sorry to hear about Jeff and Pete."

It's the best embrace we've shared in months. Shame it's on such an unhappy occasion.

We chat briefly before going to bed – both shattered.

TWENTY ONE

This morning, bizarrely, I am running a little early, no doubt due to a sombre, if smooth-running, breakfast routine. The loss of Jeff, and Pete's abduction, have certainly focused the mind.

I'm sitting in my car on the drive, having clipped my mobile into its rubber-suckered windscreen mount, as it completes its Bluetooth connection to the vehicle's sound system. Almost immediately it rings, making me jump.

(I say ring, but my car interior reverberates with the "bee dah, bee dah, bee dah, bee dah" of the Minion who believes he is a fire engine.)

Coops–Home the car's dashboard screen informs me, and, grinning, I answer. Note to self: don't leave your mobile near Coops unattended.

"Morning, Lucas," she chirrups excitedly. "I've been working on this all night, and finally, I've just got into the–"

The call goes dead.

I speed-dial her back, but all I get is, "This number is unreachable. Please try later."

"Sod it!" I shout as I beat a fist on the steering wheel.

I dial Suzi, who, after five rings, answers sleepily, "Lucas? Bit early, I'm on a day off." And yawning, "What's up?"

"I'm in the car on my way to Eastbourne station. I'll be in the office just before nine, but in the meantime I think something may have happened to Coops."

"When and where?" she replies, immediately awake and focused.

"At her home. I was literally just speaking to her. Line went dead, and now it's disconnected. She called me about the case. I sensed she's found something!"

"Okay, I'll get a team to her and an eye in the sky." She adds, with authority, "Don't worry, I'll keep her safe."

"Let Tony know what's going on. He may be in danger too!"

"Will do. See you in a while."

"And, Suzi–"

"Yes," she interrupts, "I will keep you informed."

She's definitely the one to have around in a crisis, reassuringly in control, even when she's half asleep.

I reverse off the drive and whizz down through the estate and out onto the coast road towards Eastbourne.

After ten minutes I'm in the station's concourse, too preoccupied by Coops' predicament to engage in my usual banter with the staff. I go to the platform and find my seat, and redial Coops, but get the same out-of-service message.

TWENTY TWO

I've been on the train no more than ten minutes when my phone bursts into life – "bee dah, bee dah, bee dah, bee dah."

"Thank God. You okay Coops?"

"Yeah, I'm fine. Just had Suzi on the phone."

"What the bloody hell happened?"

"When we were talking, I noticed a shimmer on my screen, and realised my router was being hacked. I immediately killed our call, pulled the SIM out of my iPhone, and then the mains lead and battery out of the laptop. Then finally killed the power to my desktop, and the router."

"Well, thank God *you're* all right – you scared the life out of me!"

"Sorry, Lucas, didn't mean to frighten you, but time was of the essence."

"You're safe – and that's what matters. What now?"

"I've changed passwords and firewall settings, and everything looks fine. I'm certain they didn't actually breach my home or office systems."

"So they were trying to piggy-back off your WiFi?"

"Yep. They really know what they're doing, and must have been close by. Suzi's sending a team over to have a look around."

"You know the drill now. Anyone coming to you will have the agreed password from Suzi; anyone else, shoot if you need to, if your bodyguard hasn't already. You have agreed a password, haven't you?"

"Yes."

"Okay, well, you take care, and we'll speak when I get into the office… eight-fifteen-ish."

I sit back in my seat and smile to myself, knowing the little scamp is safe. Time for forty winks – I'm knackered.

****

In what seems like no time at all, I wake to the clatter of half a dozen sets of points, and then, after the doors beep open, the frantic train-hopping of commuters at Clapham Junction.

I join the throng of impatient and ill-tempered travellers as I cross the platform and jump onto a train to take me the last ten minutes to Vauxhall station. From there it's across Vauxhall Bridge and then just a ten-minute walk along Millbank to Thames House.

Finally, I arrive at my office just before eight twenty. No sooner am I easing myself into my office chair, balancing a piping hot latte and pastry, than Suzi comes flying through the door.

"Morning, Lucas," she grins. She turns to shut the door and inadvertently catches my elbow with the corner of a manila folder, which in turn sends a massive slug of near-boiling coffee onto my lap. The hot latte soaks through my trousers to my nervous nether region, which has barely recovered from my Fiery Jack experience a week ago.

"Jesus fucking Christ!" I leap up and, fumbling at my double button and zip fly, nearly tear off my trousers to try to stop the excruciating pain.

"Oh Lucas, I am so sorry, I didn't–"

"No you bloody didn't," I wail at her, as I grab my swimming towel from my gym bag to cover myself whilst removing my steaming pants. "Well shut the bloody door at least!"

"Sorry, Lucas," she says over her shoulder, scurrying out of the room. As the door swings shut with a clunk, I just hear her shout, "I'll be back with some ice!"

With the bathing towel around my waist, and legs akimbo, I sit gingerly back in my chair, Jim and the twins recoiling at the cold leather. Luckily they didn't suffer further damage.

I am grateful when Suzi returns after a few minutes with ice wrapped in a teacloth and a couple of hand towels.

"Thanks, Suzi. Apologies for the outburst."

"No problem. I'm sorry for the… well, the…"

"It's okay. We'll be fine." I smile.

"Well," she says, trying to keep eye contact, but flicking occasionally to my barely covered groin, "call me if you get any swelling. I mean–"

"Certainly will," I say, cutting her short and winking.

She goes bright red, and we start laughing.

"I'll go and get these trousers dry for you. I presume you've still got your shorts in your sports bag?"

"Certainly have. See you later."

She scuttles off, and I replace the towel with my neon orange swimming shorts.

Garish, but nice and baggy.

TWENTY THREE

It is now quarter to nine, and finally I'm back into my freshly sponge-cleaned, hand-blower-dried trousers, when my phone again bursts into "bee dah, bee dah, bee dah, bee dah" – Coops, and she's still at home.

"How are you doing, liddle lady?"

"Not bad, hot rocks." She giggles.

"Very droll. You've obviously been speaking to Suzi!"

"Nah, watching it on YouTube!"

"What the…" Then I realise, as usual, she's pressing my buttons. "Again, very bloody droll."

I still have a grin on my face as I ask, "So, what have you found?"

"IGenus focuses on two specific areas of human gene manipulation: chromosomes and the memory gene, using zepto-bots."

"Okay. Pretty much what we thought, but any more info on what controls these bots?"

"Definitely a low-frequency signal, using the infrasound electronics they stole from GCHQ."

"The bots are definitely pre-programmed then?"

"Yes…" She drags out the word and pauses.

"Go on. What else, Coops?"

"Well, there is some good news. If they get into fresh air, they are zapped by the sun's UV."

"What? I thought that's only in the event of a solar storm?"

"Believe it or not, they deliberately use really old tech: UV Erasable Programmable Read Only Memory (EPROM). These things were around way before my time – invented by Frohman who had the patent in 1972 – more your era?"

"Cheeky… but you're right. I remember those, they were massive: over an inch long and storing just 1KB."

"Well, these new beauties are obviously minuscule and store 10GB, but the data erase process is the same; just put them in the sun and they're dead!"

"Okay. So, we need to find them before they get into human hosts, and get them into daylight!"

"Yep. But, if they burn in UV, then the goons must be

keeping them in some sort of container or liquid until they can get them inside the body."

"Rules out airborne distribution then?"

"True."

There's a brief pause, then in near unison we say, "Water supply!"

"Easier than monitoring tall buildings," I say, almost grateful.

"And they'll go for major distribution points."

"True again. I'll speak to Suzi, and you get yourself escorted to work."

"Okay, hot rocks." And I hear her giggle as the line goes dead. I have a feeling this joke could run for a while – thank goodness she doesn't know about the Fiery Jack.

I call Suzi and ask her to come to my office in thirty minutes.

TWENTY FOUR

This time, Suzi's entry into my office is more restrained. She sits in the chair at my meeting table, and leans forward on her elbows, hands clasped – eager as usual to "just get on with it", as I often hear her tell colleagues.

"Okay, so what's the plan Lucas?"

"Well, Coops' ferreting into Pete's files leads us to believe these zepto-bots will be distributed in the UK's tap water system."

She looks at me quizzically. "Almost psychic! Alex, who's been following the two goons and Pete up the M4, says they lost them at the services."

"How is that psychic?" And, grimacing: "More to the point, how the bloody hell did they lose them?"

"Well," she frowns, "losing them and psychic sort of go together."

"Okay, now you've totally lost me."

"Well, they lost them because they swapped their fancy suits for three sets of builders' overalls."

"What… why on earth–"

"They told the builders they were on the TV reality game show Hunted, and needed to lose their surveillance."

"Bloody game show!"

"Yep. Corny, I know. But you can't blame the builders. They swapped ten-quid overalls and trainers for Armani suits, shirts, ties and shoes!"

"So… psychic – how?"

"Well, when Alex interviewed the builders, they remembered glimpsing the lanyards the goons were wearing. Their cards showed the logo for Thames Water!"

"Okay, now I get it – lucky break."

"Sort of. The strange thing is, they've been spotted parking in Praed Street, and entering Paddington District Sorting Office in west London."

"So, they've been picked up?"

"Ah. There's the problem. Alex's team's been right through the sorting office but there's no sign of them, and neither CCTV nor our drone saw them come out."

"So they're still in there then!"

"That's what I thought. I got Alex to go through the whole building again."

"And?"

"Still no sign of them."

After throwing my arms in the air in frustration, I slump forward and put my head in my hands.

"You're absolutely sure they went in, Suzi?"

"One hundred per cent: it's on CCTV." She takes a frustrated breath. "They parked at a meter outside, and then strolled through the main gate – waving a pass the guard happily accepted." She pauses for a second. "Alex and his team went in very shortly afterward, and covered the only two other building exits."

"Shit. Where the hell are they then?"

"Don't know, Lucas, but our team has been running around in there for an hour now, and I'd bet your pension the goons are still in there somewhere – probably waiting for us to leave!"

We sit, deep in thought, and then suddenly it comes to me. I had a dear pal, Dave Jeal, who retired from Post Office HQ, back in 1995. He'd worked there for near-on forty years, and he knows everything about their London offices – of which there are over a dozen in the square mile alone. In fact, they own nearly as much land in London as the Duke of Westminster.

I need to give him a call.

TWENTY FIVE

Trawling through my contacts, I finally locate Dave's mobile – just hope it's still current. I dial, and a phone starts ringing; that's a start. It rings half a dozen times and then goes to voicemail. I end the call and redial three more times.

He may be retired, but it's nine forty-five; he must be up and about by now.

I'm just about to give up when he answers. "Hello!" he bellows angrily, no doubt looking at the *number withheld* message on his mobile. "Whatever it is you're selling, either I've got one, or I don't bloody want one, so just sod off!"

"Hi Dave. How's your power boating?"

There's a few seconds' silence before he twigs it's me. "How's it hanging, young Norton," he sniggers. "Long time no see, matey."

"Indeed it is, and even now it's because I need to pick your brains."

"No problem. Cost you lunch, though, and somewhere special – near your new office at Five – The View at SkyLoft?"

"Deal. But how the hell do you know I'm at Five?"

"I still keep an eye on you – benefit of being my protégé; you get a friendly follower." Again he gives a lovely gravelly chuckle: many years of whiskey, filterless fags, and screaming along to ZZ Top.

"If you can help with this one, you can have lunch anywhere you damn well want!"

"Go on, Lucas – fire away matey."

It's great to hear Dave's voice, and it'll be even better when we meet up. It must be nearly ten years since we last shared a curry.

"Paddington DO," I say bluntly.

"Bloody hell, Lucas, not been there for a while. It's a huge Royal Mail sorting office."

"I know, and we've got three suspects holed up in there somewhere."

"I guess you already emptied the building with the fire alarm."

"Yep. And we've got a dozen guys around it. But we know

they're in there."

"What about the old viewing gallery?"

"The what?"

"Surely you remember that?"

"We're not at the bloody opera, Dave!"

His gravelly laugh rumbles again, "Good one."

"Come on Dave, spill," I say with a tinge of impatience.

"You must recollect the POID (Post Office Investigations Department)?"

"Indeed. Some of them seemed to think they had a Met badge," I say sarcastically. "But anyway, what's that got to do with anything?"

"Don't mock, matey, they've done some fantastic unsung work, even on the 1963 Great Train Robbery," he says defensively. "In fact they are the oldest recognised criminal investigations authority in the world and can trace their origins back to 1683. Now they're part of Royal Mail Security."

"Apologies. I'd forgotten you'd worked there."

"Well, anyway, before the days of matchbox-size wireless cameras costing twenty quid, we had to watch any suspects eyes-on."

"Go on." Dave likes to tell a good story, and it's been a while.

"Well, we watched them from the viewing gallery. It's a high-level enclosed corridor, with just the occasional black glass, one-way window, and a stool. Now and then there's a red pygmy bulb at floor level, but you can barely see where you're going. It's a tight fit, but you choose your vantage point and sit there with your flask and sandwiches during the posties' shift!"

"Blimey. So how do we enter these hamster-runs?"

"Near the front offices on the first floor, look for a door with a large yellow sign. It'll be a triangle with a lightning bolt in the middle, and text below: 'Danger – High Voltage. Isolate elsewhere before opening.' And in the lower right corner is a reference number, 'Sign N°: VG1'."

"Okay. I'll get the team on it now. Thanks."

As I close the call, I hear some unintelligible comment from Dave, which I ignore. I need to get this info to Alex, who I redial. "Alex? You need to find a doorway near the front offices on the first floor. It will have a yellow triangular sign warning about high voltage, and, importantly, a code at its bottom right corner saying VG1."

"Okay Lucas. Where's it lead?"

"It's an old viewing gallery the PO security guys used back in the day."

"Oh, okay, I'll call when I find it."

The phone goes dead, and I call Suzi and give her the same update. Whilst we're talking, my phone buzzes.

A quick glance at the phone's screen shows 'Dave Mob'. I ignore it, but almost immediately he calls me back; again I ignore it. But when it buzzes a third time, it says Alex. I close the call to Suzi and pick up Alex: "Hi Lucas. This is amazing!"

"Go on."

"Well, it's only a couple of feet wide, and barely four feet high!" Then, after a bit of coughing: "It's not been used for a very long time. Half an inch of dust, filthy blacked-out windows, and only one working pygmy bulb halfway down its 100ft length."

"Wouldn't fancy staying in there for long."

"Definitely not. And once they'd found their spot they didn't dare move. It's made from pressed steel panels, like ventilation ductwork; anyone below hears every step!"

I can hear Alex scuttling down the tunnel, with the occasional expletive as he hits his head. But after a chuckle he replies, "Bet their farts echoed!"

We both laugh before closing the call.

After ten minutes, Alex, having traversed its length and that of its sister tube the other side of the sorting floor, calls me. "No one's been in here for a very long time, Lucas."

"Bloody hell, where are these bast–"

But before I can finish my cussing, my phone buzzes, and again it is Dave. This time I tell Alex to hold, and, a little frustrated, I answer Dave: "What is it?"

"Steady, just trying to help, matey."

"Sorry. We've been down the dusty tubes – nothing!"

"Shame." And, after a long pause, "Remember the underground?"

At this point my heart sinks. Somehow, Dave's lost the plot and thinks I'm talking about the London Underground.

"Dave. We're in Paddington DO – *sorting office*, not tube station."

"What?"

"Sorry, Dave, but I've got to go. Thanks for your help but I really must dash."

Luckily, just as I take the phone from my ear, I hear him shout, "I know where…"

And so I listen again. "What do you know?"

"There's a Post Office underground railway. Runs, or used to, from Paddington to Whitechapel."

"Bloody hell. How do–"

But he keeps talking. "At the southwest corner of the sorting floor are a set of horizontal concertina doors – probably padlocked. Sign next to them says 'Station Switch Cabin'."

"Thanks Dave. Speak later."

Immediately I switch back to the waiting Alex, and bring him up to speed on the train system below him.

I then ask, "Have you got a head-cam?"

"Yes, I'll put it on–"

And, interrupting him, "Get Coops to put the AV feed through to my iPad," and I hear him race off to find the station's doors.

"Will do. Bye."

TWENTY SIX

My iPad flickers into life with the image from Alex's head-cam as he runs the last few feet of the sorting office.

Out of breath, he finally reaches a set of concertina doors. To the right of them at head height is a small, bland sign with black lettering: Station Switch Cabin. Dave was right.

The image on my iPad swivels around, stopping at the door handles. "Okay Lucas," says Alex. "The doors are secured with a massive steel belted nylon cable tie." His hands *mime* as they slowly probe the route of the strap as it wraps around the polished-brass handles, "This looks odd."

"What do you see exactly?"

"There's a remnant of what looks like hundred-pound fishing line, knotted through a pinhole on the end of the cable tie."

"Is the tail pointing toward the closing jamb?"

After a second Alex answers, "Yes."

"It could have been used to pull the tie tight through the slit of the closing door. They *must* be in the station!"

"Okay. I'll cut this and get down there."

"Be cautious, Alex, we need them alive." My mind flashes back to Jeff lying cold on the floor. "Well, communicative!"

Alex snips the cable tie, and with two colleagues, Glocks drawn, sets off down the dark, narrow concrete steps. Their intense, narrow-beam headlamps cast sharp-edged shadows, which dance around like miniature lighthouse beams.

Whispering, Alex gives a running commentary. "I can hear something in the distance, and there's a dim light." He takes a slow sniff. "It smells of paper dust, hessian, oil and old paint," he says, with a smile in his voice, "just like being in the steam train shed at the Bluebell Railway."

I also speak in lowered tones: "Yes, I know you love trains."

Suddenly the image on my iPad stops moving. "Are you okay?" I whisper.

"Fine. But… did you know this line was built in 1927, and runs all the way from Paddington to Whitechapel?"

"Yes, I can read the plaque you're staring at, but right now you need to focus on getting Pete back!"

The image starts bobbing around again as Alex continues off

down the stairs.

After a seemingly never-ending 97 steps (Alex counts), he whispers, "Opening out into a corridor." It is still dark, but now, like Alex, I can see that the light comes from a distant doorway.

Suddenly there's a crunching noise. "Bastards have dropped broken lightbulb glass on the floor – definitely expecting us."

"Okay," I say softly.

The team and Alex check every side door as they go down the corridor, and I hear a repetitive 'Clear' as each room is declared empty. Finally, they reach the lit doorway. It's a large, dirty, cream double door with frosted, wired safety glass.

Alex goes through the door and the room opens out into a large, brightly lit workbench area.

"Lucas. I can hear something mechanical in the distance but can't see any movement."

"Okay," I respond flatly.

"This must be the train workshop. I'm gonna look for the lighting switchgear. Have you got the schematic?"

"Just got one from Coops, but it's twenty years old. You're looking for a large panel, the size of a door, over to your right on the north side of the room. It's labelled–"

"Lighting: Platforms & Workshop?" Alex interrupts. And, with a noisy clack of the main circuit breaker, the room is pitch dark, and I lose the image on my iPad.

"Night vision on," informs Alex. The picture returns, albeit in a lower definition and with a spooky green glow.

I watch nervously as Alex and the team proceed cautiously through the room. They've gone no more than thirty feet, when the room suddenly widens into the main train workshop. It must be eighty feet wide and a couple of hundred feet long, and with half a dozen sidings. Everything is in miniature for this two-foot narrow-gauge railway line, including the carriages.

At one point Alex stops and is obviously having a good look around.

"Alex! You're not on a bloody heritage tour!"

"I know, but look at this!"

The image on my screen gets bigger and I can now see the little carriage. It's twenty feet long and has two rows of old maroon Austin Mini car seats.

"Yes, I can see, Alex," I reply, frustrated. Whilst he's been "clearing" the room, I've Googled the train station. "The carriage was for the kids' Christmas party train journey – a track loop below Mount Pleasant Sorting Office." And, with a sigh of annoyance, "Now, for Heaven's sake–"

"Okay, okay. I'm on it."

He picks up the pace and I see a sudden funnelling of the room as it reaches two nine-feet-wide tunnels, each with a sign above – one saying eastbound and the other westbound. I watch Alex grab a two-foot-long metal rod, place one end on a rail and the other to his ear. "The sound is definitely coming from the eastbound tunnel."

"Nice one Tonto!"

"Very bloody funny," he says tersely.

"Get your team down there. I'll get Suzi to arrange cover for the other stations."

"I'm gonna see if I can get one of these train engines going. Where's the control panel?"

"Give me a minute, Alex."

I pull up an indexed electrical schematic on my iPad and quickly trace the pen lines to a major supply panel : Control Room, Mount Pleasant.

"Alex, the control room's in Mount Pleasant Sorting Office, which is miles away. Just test the live rail and then use the controls on the train itself – hopefully all's fine."

"*Test* the bloody live rail? You bonkers?"

"Just grab a thin piece of copper wire a few feet long and throw it across the rails: there's so much electrical power it will vaporise. Just watch your eyes!"

"Okay," he says doubtfully. "I presume this is another insight from your chequered childhood?"

I daren't tell him the stories I heard as a kid from one of my dad's signalman friends. One was about a guy who was waiting for the last train. He'd probably had too much to drink, and he unintentionally pissed on the live rail. He lived, but Jim and the twins weren't happy.

Alex wanders off to a workbench, finds a piece of electrical cable, strips off its insulation, and then wanders back to the rail lines. With some hesitation he lobs the wire across the tracks.

With a blinding flash, and a bang like a shotgun, the wire disappears.

"Shit. That was fun. Definitely live!"

He goes back to the City of London loco, with the kids' carriage attached, and he and his team jump in. After a minute or two, and with a chuckle, and no doubt a huge grin, he starts off down the eastbound line, ducking as he enters the tunnel.

Knowing they are in a radio dead zone whilst inside the tunnel, I slide my iPad onto the desk, grab my mobile and call Suzi.

"Hi, Lucas," she answers in a jolly tone. "How's it all going on the Toytown railway?"

"Pretty sure Pete and his babysitters are down there. I presume you've already covered the exits."

"Indeed. I've checked surveyors' drawings and there are nine stations along the twenty-three-mile route: Paddington, Bird Street, Wimpole Street, Rathbone Place, Oxford Street, Mount Pleasant, King Edward Street, Liverpool Street and finally Whitechapel. I've sent an armed two-man team along to each of them."

"Okay. Let's get together in the Situation Room to sort out our next move. See you there in ten mins."

TWENTY SEVEN

En route to meet Suzi, I go via the canteen, as it's ten forty-five, and hence a lot quieter between the rushes of noon and one o'clock. When I meet her in the Situation Room, she smiles. "I think we're spending too much time together, Lucas?"

Looking at the table, I see we've each bought two lattes and two chocolate croissants.

For a second, looking into her eyes, everything is still: her pupils slowly dilate.

Suddenly, my mobile bursts into life.

Un-looking, I grab at it a couple of times before it slides off the table. I pick it up from the carpeted floor, and glance at the screen as I put it to my ear. "Alex… hi… how're things?" I say, preoccupied.

"Just a quick update as we go through Bird Street station. Everything okay there? You sound distracted."

"Oh, fine thanks. I'm in the Situation Room with Suzi. Sorting out our next move… direction."

"Well, nothing here so far. No doorways out of the tunnels, just the stations. Speak later, just going into–" Alex is cut off, no doubt going into the next stretch of tunnel to Wimpole Street.

I look back at Suzi, who smiles. "So… nothing?"

"No. Bloody infuriating," I try to focus on matters in hand. "Right, where do we think they're going?"

We stare at the wall monitor showing the MailRail map.

"Looking at the Water Board sites," Suzi says, aligning the images, "I would say maybe Coppermill Lane in Walthamstow."

"That's the nearest Thames Water distribution site." I tap its details into the PC. "But it's currently closed for refurbishment!"

"Bloody hell, Lucas!" she says, waving her hands in frustration. "What are they up to?"

We spend the next few minutes offering decreasingly likely scenarios, none of which seem credible. Luckily, it's not long until I get a call from Alex, and I put him on speakerphone.

"You're not going to like this," he says.

"What?" I say, taking the bait of his long pause.

"We're at King Edward Building station right behind their loco. It's still warm… but no exit – everything's padlocked from this side."

"There must be a way out! Why else go there?"

"Sorry guys, but no exit – doors are barred, bolted and padlocked from this side. We've checked every square foot of the place – nothing. Looking at their loco's switches and regulators, I'd say it's remote controlled, and I'd say it's a pukka retrofit by MailRail; done some years ago."

"Shit!" I shout. "Where the bloody hell are they?"

"Sorry, boss, but I'm going to break out of here to street level. Suzi, can you get a car to me pronto?"

"Sure can."

I stab the red call-end button on my mobile and look straight at Suzi.

"Okay, if these bastards never went down onto the MailRail, then where are they?"

TWENTY EIGHT

It's just after eleven fifteen and I'm back at my desk, having left Suzi with her team to work out where these sods could have gone. We still believe they are heading for a major domestic water distribution point – but not a clue as to which one.

No sooner have I sat down to trawl through a list of waterworks lat/long references on Google maps, than I get a call on my mobile from Coops. "Afternoon, Master."

"Hi Coops, how's things at the doughnut?"

"Still a bit shaky down here, with those out of the loop wondering about the fan bearing, and those in the know worrying about poor Pete."

"Indeed. Same here."

"So, my illustrious leader, have you tracked down the perps?"

"Thought we had, but somehow they gave us the slip."

"Hey, you remember a few years ago you dropped some papers off at an old friend's home in southwest London?"

"That narrows it down, Coops," I say with a hint of sarcasm.

"Very funny," she says, giving a huff. "All I remember is some oddly named island in the Thames – Eel Pie?"

"Oh yes, you kept asking how it got its name."

"Yep. Never did get a sensible answer out of you!"

"That was Alistair. Moved now, but he lived in Hampton."

"Yes, Alistair, lovely Scottish chap, insisted on us having coffee and cake in a nearby tearoom."

"Okay Coops, but what the hell has it got to do with this case?"

"Well, after we left, we drove past a *huge* waterworks."

"Hampton Water Treatment Works, right next to the Thames. But it's miles from central London."

"True, but it supplies water to nearly all of west London, especially with Coppermill Lane being out of action."

"You *have* been doing your homework!"

"Always."

"So, any untoward activity at the Hampton site?"

"Well, apparently there was a security scare this morning after a couple of guys were found walking around with fishing gear."

"What?"

"Indeed. But that's not the weird bit. When I checked the CCTV footage, all they had was a couple of fishing rods and what looked like a cool box. No wellies, waterproofs or brollies, just blue overalls and trainers."

"Like our guys."

"Yep. And when they were confronted by Thames Water security guys, apparently the cool box only contained sandwiches and some sort of fish bait, wrapped up in silver foil – which would keep zepto-bots safe from sunlight!"

"True! Good one, Coops."

"I'm fast-forwarding through a shedload of CCTV. Give me twenty minutes."

"Nice work, Coops. Let me know, and in the meantime I'll bring Suzi up to speed."

TWENTY NINE

Sure enough, just before half eleven, my mobile phone rattles and again Coops' name comes up on its screen. "Told you I'd find something, boss. But good and bad news again, I'm afraid."

"Go on," I say nervously.

"Well, the goons were thrown out, but not before they got inside one of the process plants."

"*Inside*? I thought the guards reported everything was secure?"

"It is to humans, but not to fishing rods. By the looks of it, something from a foil container was dropped into the final filtration pond."

"Oh, hell! They've got the zepto-bots into the domestic water supply?"

"Seems so." She pauses. "And there's no sign of Pete, not anywhere on the footage. Including the van cab and rear. Maybe a good sign?"

"It is," I say hopefully, "but at the moment I'm more concerned with these things being in the water supply. Check with the Thames Water laboratory what, precisely, are the next stages of treatment."

"Okay, speak in a bit."

I'm clutching at straws here, but there must be something we can do; we urgently need a break in this case.

THIRTY

Still at my desk, I call Alex.

"Hi, Lucas. I just got an update from Coops on my mobile. What's happening at Hampton?"

"Not good, I'm afraid. It definitely looks like the bastards got the zepto-bots into the water supply."

"Shit. Fait accompli?"

"Maybe." Then I remember something. "Actually, did you have a friend who works for the Water Board?"

"Yeah, Elin. Don't know if she's still working there, as she was looking to move down to Worthing. I'll ping her on WhatsApp."

"See if she knows about the final filtration process. Say it's part of our Disaster Recovery strategy for water services."

"Will do, Lucas. Presume you want me and the guys to get our backsides over there?"

"Spot on. Keep me updated."

He's gone, no doubt relishing the drama of thrashing the arse out of his RS6 over to Hampton.

I decide to go and grab a coffee, and on a corner halfway down the corridor, I nearly get side-swiped by Suzi… again!

"Whoa, sorry Lucas – close one!"

"Do you ever *walk*?"

She looks fleetingly at the ceiling, pretending to consider my question, and then, with a big grin, "Nope!"

"Come on, let's chat en route to the coffee machine; it's my two-hourly caffeine feed. What's the latest?"

"Well, the big news is that Coops has a location for the perps, and it's not far from Hampton. In fact only a few miles."

"What about Pete?" I ask, concerned about my dear friend.

"Still nothing. No sign of the poor sod."

"Well, he can't just vanish!"

Just as I pick up my cardboard beaker, my mobile sparks into life. I hit the green button. I wave a finger at Suzi to wait a minute, and then put the phone to my ear: "Lucas."

"Good afternoon, Mr Norton. This is Giles McWade, director of Thames Water Laboratories. I've been asked to call you directly; one of your colleagues is also on the line."

A familiar voice pipes up. "Hi, Lucas. I've been explaining to Giles about this bug." It's Coops.

"Hold on a second." I put my mobile on speakerphone, and gesture at Suzi to follow me into an empty office. "Okay Giles, you're on speaker with me and my colleague Suzi."

Coops jumps in. "I thought it easier to do a conference call, as Giles wants to shut down the whole water supply immediately."

"What!" I shout, startled. "We must avoid that if at all possible. The last thing–"

Giles interrupts me. "We cannot take the chance of poisoning three million Londoners, and goodness knows how many foreign holidaymakers." Then, after a blustering huff: "We must shut down the water supply with immediate effect!"

I'm pleased Coops used the ruse of a possible poisonous bug rather than gene-altering invisible robots.

"There *must* be an alternative. What treatment takes place after the pond where the product was introduced?"

Giles stutters slightly, seemingly unaccustomed to his demands being questioned. "I insist my–"

I don't like bullies or arrogance, and so now I interrupt him. "*No*. And unless Queen Elizabeth herself joins this conference call, I hold sway here. Please just answer my question!"

"I do apologise. Um, how to explain in layman's terms," Giles replies, flustered, but still patronising. "Mainly filtration, sedimentation, and finally the black lamps."

"What?" I say, still frustrated with his tone. "What the hell are black lamps?"

Coops chirps in, "UV lamps, like you had when you went to the disco in the 70s, Lucas." She's trying to lighten the mood.

"Ah, UV lamps. Lit up white clothing like it was fluorescing." I smile to myself at the thought of Saturday Night Fever. "But Coops, wasn't that the one thing your colleague said neutralised this poison?"

"Indeed it is. Until now, I didn't know they were used in filtration."

Giles explains further. "These ultraviolet lamps are very high-powered. They kill any living organism in the water. Far weaker ones are used in domestic fish-pond filtration systems."

"Thanks, Giles, sounds like between us we've found the answer." I finish with a plaudit. "No need to terminate the water supply. But I will be sending a team in with yours just to verify all is well with these black lamps; they'll be on site at Hampton in ten minutes."

"Okay, Mr Norton. I'll tell my site manager not to isolate supplies, and I'll text you his number now."

Coops says her goodbyes and drops Giles off the conference call. "He's gone, Lucas."

"Okay Coops. Liaise with Suzi and get our science officer on site. Alex may be able to pick him up on route. I want absolute confirmation these bloody zepto-bots are dead."

THIRTY ONE

I use this lull in proceedings to call home. Hopefully everyone's relaxed after lunch.

"What?" answers Helen abruptly.

"And good afternoon to you," I reply calmly.

"It would be good if the bloody college hadn't just called."

"What's the problem this–"

But before I can finish, she breaks in. "Always the same. I'm left here to cope with everything, and now with my arm hanging off!"

"But I–" She cuts me short again. My input only seems to alienate.

"I got a call from the principal," she huffs. "Bastards are charging us £120 *per day* for non-attendance by Daisy, and it's now twelve days. That's £1440!" She gulps a breath. "But apparently they are being *'oh so kind'* in offering to halve it if we pay within seven days!"

"Surely they can't–" I try to prise a word in.

"Oh, and if we don't pay then they'll start a fast track prosecution under section 444 of the 1996 Education Act!"

"Darling, I'm sure it–"

"Well, they can bugger off. And so can you! You should be here dealing with this shit, instead of swanning around London being sodding indispensable!"

"I'll call them, and–"

Again she cuts me short. "And don't forget Daisy's recital this evening!"

She ends the call.

Just as well I wasn't give the chance to reply: I had forgotten, and it's at eight-thirty this evening!

I stand bewildered, looking down at my mobile, and thinking to myself, *That went well – not.*

THIRTY TWO

I'm still staring at my mobile, trying to decide whether to call Helen back, when it rings.

"Hi, Alex," I answer sombrely.

"You okay, Lucas?"

"Yes, I'm fine. Just had strips torn off me again by Helen."

"She not dealing very well with being shot?" he says mockingly, highlighting my lack of understanding.

"Well, when you put it like that."

"Just be supportive, she'll deal with it. But make sure you get her flowers and dine out a few times, and include your girls."

"You're right, but I'm bogged down with this case–"

And now even Alex interrupts me. "Family comes first!" he states, letting the words hang.

"Noted. So, what's up?"

"I'm in the on-site canteen, which is the first water take-off for this supply. Their lab are carrying out on-site tests as we speak; results in ten minutes apparently."

"Impressive."

"They say it's just a simple test?"

He sounds distracted. "What is it, Alex?"

"Gut feeling after talking privately to the site engineer. He reckons the power of those UV bulbs would definitely have roasted our bugs."

"But he thinks it's a living organism – we're not talking about the same thing."

"That's just it, Lucas. The UV exposure power level he's talking about is a thousand-fold what Coops said will kill a bot! I reckon this is a red-herring."

My phone vibrates, "I see what you mean. Hang on a tick," and I check my phone's screen. "Coops on the other line, Alex. Speak later."

I hit the red button on my phone, which closes Alex's call and switches me to Coops. "How're things, liddle lady?"

"Bollocks!"

"If I want abuse, I can phone home."

"Not you, Lucas, eBay. I just lost a bid for a 'Magic Cube' and it's in its original box from 1977!"

"Why the call?" I ask, listening to a load of keyboard clacking in the background.

"Oh, yeah, CCTV footage from Heathrow – dodgy painters!"

"What are you on about?" The keyboard clicks seem to slow down a little.

"Sorry, one second. Yay! Got the cube, just had to give the winner a few bad ratings so the seller switched to my second-place bid."

Some would question her ethics, but, after John Wayne memorabilia, Rubik's cubes are her great love – she must have dozens in various incarnations around her home.

"Okay Coops, back to national security – dodgy painters!"

"Indeed, oh great one. Perfectly clean overalls and £600 limited-edition Nikes!"

"What the hell has that got to do with this case, for Christ's sake?"

"Their arrival mainly, then their vehicle – same reg as the one at Mount Pleasant! Two vans, same plates," and, after a second's pause, "also, my face recognition software identified Pete, briefly, but it's deffo him!"

"For heaven's sake, why didn't you start off with that snippet?"

"Good news is worth waiting for and their plane's not taking off for an hour."

"Okay, get Suzi to have a team pick them up pronto!"

"Will do, over and out from *Broke Ruin*!" The line goes dead. The minx has set me an anagram, a pastime of hers when I was her tutor many moons ago.

No sooner have I put my iPhone back in my pocket than Alex calls. "Results of the tests: the water's clean. No bots."

My mind races back through the day's events, and I keep reminding myself of Suzi's mantra. Stick to absolute facts – irrefutable facts. Then it dawns on me.

"Alex! There are no bots at the water works."

"Where else could the goons introduce them?"

His words make my gut churn: it's not happy.

"We have *two* vans. Coops has found one with the same plates at Heathrow!"

"Two teams of goons? They're taking bots to the States?"

"Possibly, or decoy, but the water works was definitely a red-herring." I pause a second. "Either way, you and Matt get over to Heathrow?"

I say goodbye to Alex and redial Coops, but all I get is her phone's engaged signal.

THIRTY THREE

Finally, nearing one o'clock, I get hold of Coops, who apparently, was arranging recorded delivery of her new cube!

"I got your anagram – Erno Rubik?"

"Yay! I knew you would. But do you realise that as of 2009 there were 350 million sold worldwide – isn't that incredible!"

"Coops," I say, more concerned. "Where are the perps? And tell our guys at Heathrow to hold off. There's a situation."

"Wait a second," she says bluntly.

For a minute I can hear part of her conversation on another line. "Stand down. Now… I don't know… order direct from Lucas… stand down now." She's back on the line. "Okay, the team's been called off, they are eyes-on but out of sight. Apparently the goons are just checking in their hand luggage."

"Monitor them boarding the plane. I'll call you back in a tick."

"No problem, great one."

I dial Suzi, who answers immediately.

"Status?"

"Good afternoon to you too, Lucas."

"Sorry, bit of a panic to get on to the plane."

"Do you want me to call Mike, FBI?"

"Yes, and tell him I'll call in ten minutes. First I have to tell Helen I'm off to New York again." And, after a deep sigh, "Wish me luck!"

"You don't need luck… more like a cricket box."

"Indeed."

THIRTY FOUR

I rack my brain trying to think of a way to sugar-coat this news to Helen, but whatever I say, I'm going to get a bollocking.

I pull up "home" on my mobile and hit the green button. I can almost feel my testicles shrivel and try to hide in my pelvis.

"What is it this time? Running out of people to piss off?"

"Yes," I reply, and, trying to jolly the mood, "I think they've put me on their call-blocking list."

Silence.

"Well?" she jabs. "What's the problem this time? Don't tell me you're going to be late *again*." With a heavy sigh, she adds, "and I need you to call those little Hitlers at the college."

This time I'm silent, and take a deep breath. "I've got to fly out to–"

She cuts me short "You shit!" she snaps. "You're jetting off *again*." She can barely draw breath. "You utter shit! Why don't you stay there this time, or in London with your playmate Suzi!"

The line goes dead.

"Bloody hell," I think to myself, and where did that "Suzi and me" stuff come from? I try a few redials but the phone's engaged – no doubt she's comparing notes with her friend Annabel. That's not going to help matters, because Annabel's husband has just departed with his rugby team buddy. Definitely didn't see that coming!

Yet again I find myself staring down at my phone, shaking my head in disbelief.

I'm certainly sinking further into the brown and smelly, and right now I don't know how to fix it.

THIRTY FIVE

I've been picked up in one of our Audi RS6s and am being rocketed over to Heathrow. Whilst the bucket seat holds me firmly in place, I can still feel my innards being bounced around like jelly in a basketball.

When we hit a straight bit of the A4, I call Coops. "Hi, how's it going?"

"Not bad," she says cheerily. "I keep rolling back through the CCTV timeline and it won't be long before I get a fix on when the goons arrived at Heathrow."

"Brilliant. Let me know how you–"

My phone vibrates with an incoming call. I look at its screen. "I've got Suzi on the other line, call you back."

I switch to the waiting call. "Hi Suzi."

"All boarded. Only business class left, so Jeff's card's going to take a beating – but your boys are well chuffed!"

"Oh hell, they'll bring the neighbourhood down," I say only half joking.

"Indeed. Let's hope the galley is well stocked!" Suzi knows Alex's reputation as a trencherman.

"Did you get hold of Mike?"

"Yes, I've briefed his team over at the FBI. He's getting Dan to meet you at the airport."

"Holy shit!" I scream, pushing hard against the dashboard.

"What, what's happening?" Suzi shouts back, alarmed.

"Arsehole jumped a red light." And, with a sigh of relief: "My driver's emergency stop missed him by a fag-paper, but I'm now peeling my nose off the sodding glove-box airbag."

Suzi laughs. There's nothing like a colleague's near-death experience to bring a smile.

"Suzi?" I say in my *favour* tone of voice.

"What do you want?" she replies in mock desperation.

"I'm in the proverbial at home, yet again, and wonder if you could organise a treatment day for Helen, Daisy and Molly at the Reading Room day spa in Iford, near Lewes. Tim can play chauffeur for the afternoon."

"Okay," she replies begrudgingly, "but you can book me in there one day as well, and Coops!"

"It's a long way to come for a spa day."

"Not if you're paying, and we could come to yours for a BBQ in the evening."

"We'll see. Just book it for Helen and the girls for now."

"Okay, no problem. I'll check a date with Helen."

I hope she'll have a girlie chat with Helen, but that's probably in vain after Helen's recent insinuation.

THIRTY SIX

I'm dropped at the main entrance to Heathrow's Terminal 5 customs building, where I'm ushered through to the boarding gate for my American Airways flight. I'm cheerily informed I'm the last to board, and now the plane's departure is running some twenty minutes late.

Once I've crossed the access bridge to the forward door, an immaculately dressed man shakes my hand "Hello, Mr…" He gives a cough of suspicion. "Smith." And, after a slight pause, "I'm Craig, the senior steward for business class." With a hint of sarcasm, he continues. "Welcome aboard. It's a shame you're not in economy dear, as you would have been clapped on board."

"Last thing I need is the clap," I reply, tongue-in-cheek.

"Oh, very droll sir," giving me a tight-lipped, pouting smile, "Please go up to your seat, where Sara will look after you, and arrange a complimentary drink – maybe a sour-mash whiskey?"

"Thank you. But please don't rush. I didn't." I give a cheesy grin and go to sit down.

As I find my seat in business class, a very pretty blonde smiles and ushers me over to the starboard rear seats. Sara, as indicated by her shiny lapel badge, looks at me whilst gesturing towards two men. "Here we are, Mr Smith. As requested, I have put you, Mr Jones, and Mr Brown nearest the exits."

They look up from their menus, smirking – Alex and Matt, already comfortably seated.

****

I've no sooner sat down and buckled my belt than Sara returns and pats my shoulder. "Mr Smith. Just to let you know: you can use your mobile on this flight, but only when the seat belt signs are off."

"Thank you Sara. And I do apologise for being late."

She smiles. "No problem, sir." Then she moves down the corridor, reminding other passengers about their mobiles.

Some men's heads turn and follow her as she walks model-like to the forward galley.

Matt nudges me in the ribs. "We thought the same." His

smirk turns into a full-blown grin. Honestly, sometimes I wonder about these guys. Mind you, it's not a bad thing, since she distracts most men, and probably some of the women, from their flight nerves.

"So," I say, looking at Matt, "any news?"

"No change. We got here as quick as possible, made sure the targets boarded, and then waited for you." After a brief pause, he adds, "Result, in business class, boss."

"Indeed. Only problem is you won't get cheeseburger, chips and beer here."

"Don't you bet on it," Alex pipes up. "On the dinner menu they have a wild boar and chorizo burger!" I shake my head as Alex and Matt grin at each other like kids, and then simultaneously start looking at the drinks menu.

On glimpsing Sara in the galley getting her mask and flotation props ready, I'm reminded of a family trip a few years ago. Helen, the girls and I were flying off on an Italian holiday, when Daisy started to get anxious on seeing the stewardess prepare for her routine of exits, oxygen mask, lifejacket, etc. To calm her down, Helen started to hum the "birdie song", which included miming the arm movements. Remembering this tune from her grandpa playing the original vinyl, Daisy started to smile, and then mimic Helen. Ever since, when a flight attendant starts her advisory procedure, that tune pops into my head and I chuckle to myself.

Five minutes later, Sara returns to take our dinner order.

"Hello. Did any of you order your main course online?"

In unison we reply, "No."

"Never mind," she says, smiling at Alex. "Tell me what you would like?"

"The burger and a lager, please."

Sara then looks in turn at Matt and myself and takes our orders. We choose the same main as Alex, but share a bottle of Malbec.

The final instructions regarding the plane's departure come over the tannoy from the captain. "*We've been cleared to taxi, and from there it's only a couple of minutes before being cleared for take-off. Thereafter please just sit back and enjoy the luxury of this new Boeing 777-300ER for our eight-hour flight to New York JFK.*"

Just as he finishes speaking, my mobile bursts into life. I look at its glowing screen, which advises "caller unknown". This never happens to an MI5 phone – *all* callers are known!

"Hello," I reply, non-committal.

"Hi you ol' limey, how the feck are you?"

"Mike! What the hell?"

"Look, I'll be brief as I'm just rushing into a meeting at our London Embassy. I need to see you urgently – like now!"

"Impossible, I'm afraid, I'm off–"

Mike cuts me short. "I know, you're on an American Airlines Boeing at Heathrow. Well, it's not going anywhere. In fact, any minute now you should–"

"Wait a second, Mike."

Sara runs over to me and explains that the captain has just received an urgent message. Apparently I am needed back at the office. She looks a little shocked. "This has never happened before. You must be important to stop a flight?"

"It would seem so. Sorry about this, Sara."

Then I return to my phone call. "Okay Mike. I've got the message. Where do you want to meet?"

"At yours in an hour."

"See you there."

I close the call and get up to retrieve my case from the overhead locker. As I turn back to Alex and Matt, Sara leans between us.

"The captain advises that the passenger bridge is re-attached, and passenger door open. He asks all three of you to kindly leave the plane as quickly as possible."

"Come on, guys, let's get going. This must be bloody important if Mike's arranged these shenanigans!" Having now grabbed our bags, we head back to the exit.

Sure enough, standing at the door, and grinning like a Cheshire cat, is Craig the senior steward. "So sad to see you leave, it's been *such* fun."

"Indeed it has," I retort, "but the service just wasn't up to much I'm afraid, so we're going with Ryanair."

This takes the wind out of his sails as the three of us bundle past and off up the tunnelled walkway.

I call the driver who dropped us off. He's already on his way back, with an ETA to our original drop-off point of ten minutes.

As we're running through the customs hall, my phone rings; it's Coops. "Hi Lucas," she greets me cheerily.

"Hello Coops. I presume this is all your doing?"

"Oh yes, but it's amazing what effect Mike's and Jeff's authority gives."

"What? You used Jeff's name?"

"Well, sort of."

"Could end up being… well… *embarrassing*?"

"Maybe," she chuckles, "anyway, Mike and Dan say that some new intel has come to light."

"Okay, I'll be back soon."

"I think it's to do with something I was working on," she says, concerned, "and I bumped into the FBI doing the same thing. It all got a little confusing."

"What?" I say, frustrated. "You're making no sense."

"Exactly. It made no sense – really weird day!"

"Okay. Well don't worry. I'm just coming to the exit door for my ride. Let's touch base after I've been briefed."

THIRTY SEVEN

After being dropped off by Matt and Alex, who will shoot off to a local café, I run up the steps into Thames House main reception, where I'm met by Suzi.

"What the hell's going on?" I ask her as we hurry across the marble floor of the lift foyer.

"I honestly don't know, but it's all a bit odd. Jeff calls me, which obviously is a sick hoax, then Mike at the FBI, and then Coops."

"Well, it'd better be worth it. We've left the goons on a plane to New York!" We stare at the changing floor number indicator as we wait for the lift.

Getting out at the sixth floor, we rush along the corridor to the Situation Room. As I walk through the open door, I'm completely taken aback by Jeff's outstretched hand.

I stand, staring at him, legs turning to jelly and shaking my head in disbelief. After a minute, and with immense emotion, I hug him like a long-lost brother. I whisper to him, "You fucking arse! You were on the floor in my arms – dead! I knelt next to you, I even–"

He cuts me short, speaking softly. "I know. I've got two cracked ribs courtesy of your resuscitation!" Then, chuckling, he adds, "And your rendition of Stayin' Alive was apparently near fatal!"

I stand back and look at him quizzically. "How did you survive the defibrillator?"

He looks apologetic. "Ah, sorry, that was a replacement, just before the meeting. Just a static shock, like you can get from a filing cabinet, courtesy of James's boss in technical."

I shake my head at being fooled. "So, technical were in on it?"

"Well, yes, and our chief of medical, for the minute dosage of Tetrodotoxin to drop my heart rate and breathing."

"You could have really died – arse!"

Then, with a smile, we turn our attention to those waiting.

Mike frowns. "So, you guys always this cuddly?"

THIRTY EIGHT

We sit around the large oval table, which has half a dozen plates of M&S finger food; sandwiches, wraps, small fruit kebabs, and a large cafetiere of coffee.

"Okay." Jeff takes a sip of water. "I know this is all a little strange, as thirty-six hours ago I was pronounced dead."

"Christ," exclaims Mike, "so this is some kind of resurrection – praise be!" He does jazz hands at the ceiling.

Jeff gives an almost apologetic smile as he looks at my gently shaking head and expression of exasperation. "It was a necessary decoy as we thought our security was compromised, and being dead would allow me to work in the background. Turns out it didn't help, so here I am!"

We all smile and gently applaud his joking bow.

"So." I look sternly at Jeff. "What the hell is going on?"

He in turn looks to Mike. "Would you like to bring us up to speed on your side of things?"

"Sure can, pal." Mike says, leaning forward. "I think both our teams are acting on the same intel, except your side of the pond is where the action is." He pauses. "It seems both our companies are being led to the clue of 'track 61'."

"News to me," I fire back grumpily.

Jeff gestures for me to stop goading Mike. "I think what Mike's about to share will help give a little insight."

"It's like this," Mike continues. "We've been monitoring you guys, and we think track 61 must be here, in the UK."

Mike looks past Dan, who appears as confused as me, to Jeff who nods for him to continue.

"That's where your delightful Coops comes in. You there, hun?"

"Always!" she chirps from the conference unit in the middle of the table.

"Please elaborate, Coops," asks Jeff.

"Well, I was backtracking through a load of mobile transmissions, and several bumped into one another at near-identical times." She pauses for the merest breath. "The voices were matched by our systems across multiple burner mobiles, and the one phrase that popped up several times was 'track 61'. Mike, over to you."

I turn to Mike. "So, come on, what is track 61?"

"Coops called me," he says smiling, "because she remembered a US TV programme from some time back, which mentioned the mysterious track 61 in New York."

"Exactly," says Coops excited. "Can I?"

"Go on, liddle lady," replies Mike in a very passable John Wayne drawl, obviously remembering Coops' and my little joke.

After a polite giggle, Coops continues. "Well, track 61 runs south from deep under the Waldorf Astoria, New York, straight down Park Avenue and into Grand Central station, and then on below Broadway, and down to the FBI HQ at 26 Federal Plaza, and then on again to the City Hall, in City Hall Park." She has to pause for breath.

"What's that got to do with our case?" I ask, confused.

"Well," Mike replies, "my team in New York got straight onto it, at which time you guys were running around MailRail tunnels." He sits back in his seat, gesturing in frustration. "But nothing. We literally hit the buffers at City Hall."

"May I?" interrupts an overexcited Coops.

"Please do," confirms Mike.

"Well I overheard Tony doing his crossword," Coops says, pausing as if waiting for a question.

But again, silence. I think we were too puzzled to know what question to ask.

"Anyway," she continues, "Tony was muttering about a crossword clue: *'6D, one word, five letters, Principle Held True'*."

"Tenet," I reply without thinking, "but what the hell has that to do with train tracks?"

"Oh, nothing," says Coops, and then, after a second's pause: "Well, everything, actually."

"Please, Coops," I frown. "Explain now. This is giving me a headache."

"Well, I got our polyglot, David, to listen to the voice recordings of the goons and he said it wasn't sixty, as we all thought, but rather it was definitely two words – 6D!"

David is our verbal communications specialist and a truly hyper-polyglot. He dresses like a 1930s professor, but with a receding hairline, ponytail and neatly-bordered two-day stubble.

"Still not with you, Coops," I say, still frowning.

Mike smiles and nudges me in the ribs. "Lucas can't keep up, hun."

With a slight snigger, Coops continues. "After a fair bit of research, I've tracked down a disused train tunnel that runs from the Western Central Sorting Office station, on the MailRail line, down to Waterloo station." And, after an excited breath, "Its nomenclature derives from Track No 6 at Waterloo to Destination No1 (D1)."

"Where is Destination No1?" I ask, trying to keep up.

"Oh," Coops says excitedly, "It's the old WWII government bunker deep in the North Downs of Kent, just east of Faversham."

Finally, the penny drops. "Bloody hell. But why are they taking the…" I tail off as I look questioningly at Jeff. It strikes me that not everyone present may know of the zepto-bots.

"It's okay, Lucas." Jeff smiles. "Mike and Dan are aware of what we're chasing."

"So then," I continue, "why take them there?"

"I don't know!" says Coops, matter-of-fact.

Mike sits back in his chair. "It could be they are just re-grouping. Their first attempt failed and they're probably trying some kind of plan B?"

We all sit in quiet contemplation for a few minutes. Then it strikes me. "No one's mentioned Pete. What's the latest?"

"Well, there's the thing," answers Jeff sombrely. "His swipe card was used at the D1 secure entrance. And according to our monitoring, it's the first time the site's had a company visitor in over twelve months."

"Why Pete?" I ask.

After a slight pause, Jeff says, "Don't know, but that's not the primary question, I'm afraid. Go on Coops, what else do you know?"

"Well," she continues, "he accessed the site within four hours of Alex starting down the MailRail tunnel!"

"Bollocks!" I say angrily. "They definitely have two teams! One to the waterworks at Hampton, and the other down to D1."

"That's my analysis of it," states Coops confidently.

"Shit," says Mike, rubbing his brow. "I presume they've got the other zepto-bots?" He looks at Jeff, who just nods.

Again we are sitting silent, contemplating. *Why?*

THIRTY NINE

With them having been fed and watered, I sent Matt home and Alex down to Faversham, just north of Destination No1, over half an hour ago; he's useful backup should I need him. And he's now on my mobile as I jog down to Thames House underground car park with Mike and Jeff.

"How the bloody hell are you going to get into D1?" says Alex, perplexed.

"Dunno yet," I answer. "But Coops and Suzi are on it, so it'll be sorted by the time we get there."

The certainty in my voice stems from my unwavering confidence in that irrepressible duo. They are brilliant at determining the credence in the intelligence they gather – credibility and confidence. I call it my gut feeling, but it's the same two variables. Their methods, however, are somewhat more scientific.

"Hope they do," he says. "The damn place's first design rule was to be totally impregnable!"

"Indeed," I sigh, "and they can certainly match our technology following its last refurbishment, but they don't have a Coops. In any case, Pete's credentials worked, so worst case she can ghost his identity."

"Yeah, but the D1 systems will already know he's inside and the alarms will start blaring."

"If he's still there," I say, unconvinced. "Let's see what Coops and Suzi come up with."

I confidently close the call, but privately I am worried about getting inside the place unnoticed.

Yet again we rely totally on Coops and Suzi, and far more than we should, or than I like to admit…

FORTY

It's just gone ten past four as Mike, Jeff and I barge our way through the inner London traffic, trying to make our way south-east to Destination No1. Our driver, John, is something of a veteran behind the wheel; he trained some seventy percent of the advanced/VIP drivers back in the 80s. Having recently returned from early retirement, he's normally found moving the MI5 hoi polloi around London. So for him, today is like a trip back in time, with a licence to drive as fast as he damn well likes. Apparently he's been to D1 before – but he keeps pretty tight-lipped about those days.

I gather from Jeff that literally less than a dozen people know about D1. In fact, once an earwigging civil servant reported to the Ministry that D1 was a disgusting waste of taxpayers' money, which could be redistributed to support a modern hospital. His findings were quickly quashed, as the place is not on any map or satellite image, and subsequently believed to be an administrative error. Needless to say, the loose-lipped civil servant found himself serving elsewhere – Prêt à Manger, I think.

The guys who maintain it love the technology, as, like GCHQ, it is completely self-sufficient, including standby generators, water purification, air-con and air scrubbers. In fact, there is a team of rotating staff who look after the site, which is protected by the most sophisticated electronic surveillance this side of the "doughnut".

And where exactly is this place, you ask?

Courtenay Road, Dunkirk, in the county of Kent – the "Garden of England" as it is known, epitomised by the TV programme The Darling Buds of May. It's found down a small country road, just off the Boughton bypass, east of Faversham.

Anyway, here I am, having just gone around the Elephant & Castle roundabout at forty miles an hour, in the front of an RS6 with Mike and Jeff clinging to their seatbelts in the back, as we start storming down the A201, New Kent Road, on our 51-mile jaunt to Dunkirk.

The Elephant & Castle derives its name from an old coaching inn, which was a staging post for horse teams for stagecoaches and mail coaches.

Unlike the roundabout, at least the name of the road gives comfort that we are going in the right direction.

As we leave London, the Old Kent Road becomes the New Cross Road, and the thinned-out traffic and straighter roads allow greater speed – John's in his element. My iPhone's satnav tells us that if we choose the fastest route, the trip will take an hour and twenty minutes. Shame they don't have an option to choose "raging lunatic": according to John, "We'll be there in under forty minutes!"

Just over ten minutes have passed and we slow a little to negotiate the traffic lights at the junction on Deptford Bridge, before picking up the pace again down Blackheath Road. Then it's a mix of flat out and emergency braking as we surge across Blackheath and then on down Shooters Hill.

Seeing the road sign for Shooters Hill always makes me smile, as it was believed to get its name from archers in the middle ages. Then later it was attributed to highwaymen and the many gibbets from which those felons hanged. Even as late as WWII, its name was apt, because it was both the "Last Line of Defence" – the site of a massive array of anti-aircraft guns that protected London – and "London Stop Line Central", the last line of defence from a German land invasion.

But already it's now in the rear-view mirror as I look to my left across the open patch of land called Greenwich Park, with its maze of tree-lined tracks leading down to Greenwich Royal Naval College and the Royal Observatory, the latter being ground zero of our navigational longitude world and birthplace of Greenwich Mean Time. Right now, if I were in New York, my PC's clock would be set to (GMT) UTC-5.

My daydreaming is abruptly halted when we traverse the roundabout at the junction of the A2 with the A102 in a four-wheel drift. Finally we are on the open road, and John blasts the Audi up to a steady 120 miles per hour, with the speedo occasionally red-lining at 160. Even at these speeds, I feel totally safe with John at the wheel – he's had nearly twenty years as an advanced driver, which for him peaked when driving for Her Majesty the Queen.

In less than thirty minutes we will be at RAF Dunkirk. Well, we still call if RAF but in recent years it changed hands to USAF.

Anyway, if we don't make it in time John's buying the Krispy Kremes, and not only does he hate doughnuts, but "£1.50 each! Bloody ridiculous!" he grumbled when accepting the wager.

FORTY ONE

It's 4.35pm and time is flying by, as have hundreds of blurred lampposts, hedges and ignored road signs, when again my mobile rings. I press the green button and before it's at my ear I get the soft and precise tones of Suzi. "Zepto-bots found in pre-filter."

"And hello to you."

"Sorry. Hi Lucas."

"What pre-filters?"

"The lab guys at Hampton have found zepto-bots in the pre-filters, way before the murderous high-powered UV lamps."

"So, the little blighters are still kicking and screaming?" I reply with a nasal chuckle.

"No. Dead as doornails!"

"What? How?"

"That's exactly what I asked Coops to look into, because at least some, if not all of them should be alive – their battery power lasts about ten days."

"So what's Coops' take on it?"

"Not a clue, same as me. So she's reviewing the CCTV footage of the villains at the water works, and she'll call you as soon as she knows more."

"So." I pause. "It could be they were all dead even before they got to the UV lamps?"

"Highly probable, the techies think."

"If we're right, then these slippery bastards cocked up?"

"Abso-bloody-lutely," says Suzi, "but we need corroboration from Coops."

"Okay, I will await her call."

FORTY TWO

Impatience gets the better of me and I call Coops.

"So, what have you found?" I ask eagerly.

"Good morning, Master," she says with a knowing tone.

"Come on, you will have found something by now."

"Nope."

"What? Nothing?"

"Hah, got you!" she says with a chuckle.

"Smarty pants!"

"Well," she continues, "following Suzi's call I reviewed the section of CCTV where the goons prepared the zepto-bots, before putting them in the main supply pipe behind the access panel."

"And…" I say impatiently.

"I must have looked at it a dozen times before I saw the simplicity of their error."

"Yes, yes…"

Then there is silence, as if the call had dropped out.

I smile to myself at her game, and recall the term "dropped out", which harks back to the manual telephone exchanges. A telephone operator would connect caller and recipient by plugging a patching cable from one line to another. Occasionally, when the operator wasn't paying attention, the plug would drop out of the socket – hence the phrase.

"Coops… Coops… Coops?"

"Lucas, Lucas, Lucas…" she replies, teasing, but quickly continues. "The numptys took the zepto-bots out of the plastic cool box and laid the aluminium-foil-wrapped plastic Tupperware pot on the floor in the shade. Then they opened the foil to look at the bots."

"Okay?"

"Look around the image, particularly the pavement kerb where their plastic box sits – two sharp-edged shadows: the sun's being reflected off the stainless steel access panel they removed."

"Reflected, sun-powered UV! Bloody hell, Coops!"

"Exactly, Lucas – lucky for us, they're a load of dumbasses!"

"Bloody well done Coops. This confirms the credence of Dunkirk – it's the real deal."

"Understood. I'll get as much intel as I can. Good luck."

No doubt, like me, Coops is wondering why RAF Dunkirk.

FORTY THREE

It's been twenty minutes since the Krispy Kreme wager and only forty-ish since leaving Thames House. Lewis Hamilton would be proud of this bit of driving – and not once did we run into a teammate's car!

Just before five o'clock we four-wheel drift around the last roundabout of the M2 at near sixty, then take the third exit down the A2, signposted to Dover and Canterbury. It's only a few hundred yards until we take the narrow slip road left onto the Old Canterbury Road, designated Dunkirk and Boughton Only. This is a tree-lined B road, which runs parallel with the A2 dual carriageway – yet we are soon doing over a ton and leaving the adjacent dual-carriageway travellers standing.

We peak at just over 150mph before John slams on the anchors and slithers the car up to the T-junction with Stocker's Hill Road. He then floors the RS6 again, and we fly off left for Boughton-under-Blean and Dunkirk.

At this point we glimpse, in the distance, RAF Dunkirk's remaining WWII mast, standing proud at the peak of the rise, 260 feet above sea level. But we are at the bottom of the legendarily steep Boughton Hill.

Again my thoughts are drawn back to my youth, and my dad's love for his old AJS350 combination: motorbike and sidecar. He occasionally regaled us with stories of how it barely made it up this hill, which always elicited a grimace from my mum. She was the one who would walk, since it couldn't propel both of them, and she was only four feet eleven… and a *half*… inches, and eight stone!

The dazzling setting sun strobes through the trees and brings me back to reality. Seemingly in seconds we're back over the ton, and approaching the top of Boughton Hill, screaming past a 30mph sign, as we turn left into Courtenay Road. We continue for one third of a mile along this C road before turning down a farmer's track. This unmade road will take us through the adjacent forest, and up to the rear entrance into RAF Dunkirk.

FORTY FOUR

As we drive the last 200 yards of the chalky, flint-strewn, hardened-mud track on these North Downs, the ruts made by the farmer's tractor make me feel queasy. This RS6 is a hard-core semi-track car and the low ground clearance causes it to bottom out more than once, making John mutter, "If this carries on much longer the sodding exhaust will be ripped off, and that'll bollocks our silent arrival!"

Nonetheless, after 200 yards of this space-hopper ride, we reach the unassuming and somewhat diminutive entrance to this village-size, underground bunker. The large grey door looks like any other rust-brown, mottled, paint-peeling industrial roller shutter that has seen far better days. Even the massive padlock is rusted closed.

Any self-respecting locksmith would tell you it's a cheap padlock, and probably protecting only a few bits of decrepit farm equipment.

The thing you can't see, which is all part of the design, is that the door, frame and hinges are one-piece, carbon steel. Even the cheap-looking "antique" padlock is again high-carbon steel, with its clasp micro-welded closed.

Twenty feet behind this near impenetrable dummy shutter are two more outward-opening doors, which are nuclear bomb proof. And, just like at GCHQ, and the offices of MI5 and MI6, we are surrounded by security we cannot see, nor detect: but that's how good security works.

In fact, the first thing to pick us up would be one of the 360° 8k Ultra HD cameras atop the mast we passed on the way in. Even before we turned into the unmade road, the site monitoring systems will have checked out our Audi and found it registered to a keeper with MI5 clearance. Phone calls by the guards will have been made, and the appropriate response obtained, sanctioning our presence.

As Mike, Jeff and I walk to within a few yards of the shutter door, it smoothly moves inward a few inches before quickly sliding into the left-hand wall.

Once we're a dozen steps into the inner area, followed by John reversing in the Audi, the outer door closes as quickly and quietly as it opened. John switches off the ignition, jumps out and joins the rest of us; he doesn't bother to lock the car.

The ceiling lights come on and then the bombproof inner doors slowly swing open and clunk as they reach the sidewall. All around are bare concrete walls, with the occasional large bright yellow sign warning of immediate dangers, such as the fact that standing behind an 80-ton door when it's opening is a "crushing risk" – no shit Sherlock!

We are greeted by a couple of heavily armed guards and escorted to the "reception" desk, as the bombproof doors close behind us – again giving a gentle but powerful thump as their meeting-stiles make contact. Just at that moment my phone rings, startling me as it echoes around this concrete cavern.

Coops' name pops onto the screen, this time with a photo of her in a white Stetson; she must be one of the good guys – as depicted by old westerns.

"Hi Coops, what's with the cowboy hat?"

"Ha, thought you'd like that. Just checking your phone's security settings, and thought I'd update my profile pic."

"So, what's happening then? I thought we'd have a harder job of gaining access."

"Yeah, me too." She gives a frustrated huff. "I got into their systems a little too easily, and so I've fired off an email to their IT director offering a couple of improvements."

"The goons have come here for a reason. They must have triggered something?"

"Agreed, and all systems and controls look fine – if anything, a little *too* fine."

"You've lost me now."

"One of your old mantras: 'If nothing looks out of place, then assume *everything* is out of place.'"

"Ha, I'll give you that one."

Whilst we're talking, Mike, Jeff and I are cleared by the guards, follow each other through the Johnson doors, and start our way down the corridor toward the main reception area.

The Johnson units may be old, but still formidable, as they have obviously been upgraded over the years.

The basis of this type of security door is one tubular door inside another. The unmoving outer tube, which has two opposing doorway cut-outs, is fixed into the wall. There is also an inner tube with only one doorway cut-out; this rotates to align with one of the outer tube doorway cut-outs.

If the system determines a problem, then the inner door stops between the outer doorway cut-outs, thus preventing egress, and raises an alarm.

I smile, recalling a guy locked inside one of them early in my career – due to the extra weight of an ankle plaster-cast!

"So, Coops, what have you found?"

"Bad news I'm afraid." She pauses as if trying to find the right words.

"Come on, spill the beans."

"Well, I've gone through the whole building's sensor records, and CCTV, and it appears Pete – well, his swipe card – was used by two USAF maintenance engineers. Apparently they did a health and safety spot check on the station's 'environmental services'."

"What?"

"I've checked phone records, and the guardroom were given clearance from their USAF contacts. The annual check wasn't due until next week, but they were passing by from another job, and the contractor would give a thirty per cent discount. They also blathered on about staff off sick, and putting off next week's job for a month…"

"What exactly did they get up to while they were here?"

"Nothing really. They went to the electrical switch room, the AC plant room, water purification plant room, air scrubber's plant room, and the standby generation and UPS rooms. All in all they were on site for about fifty minutes, and left over an hour ago!"

"So why here? What the hell are we missing?"

Coops sighs, as do I, and we close the call with her pledging to find "something", and me vowing to find a decent cup of coffee!

FORTY FIVE

The one good thing about this bunker is that it has absolutely everything, with no expense spared – it would have to last for two years after a nuclear attack.

As we stroll, chatting, towards the café area, one of the American guards taps Mike on the arm, having picked up on his accent, and grins. "Would you like a cup of joe from the best Naffy in the world?"

"Sure would, buddy… but Naffy?"

"Just what the Brits nickname this kinda military café."

I can't help but chip in, as it's another gem from my dad. "It comes from the acronym NAAFI – Navy, Army and Airforce Institute."

"Like a walking library!" Mike nods at me, and pats my shoulder, whilst smiling at the guard.

I continue, "NAAFI was set up back in 1921, but over the years it got bent into Naffy. It was only for junior ranks, as officers had their Mess."

"Officers' Mess?" Mike declares with an American version of a B-movie Oxbridge accent. "I can guess where that term originated!"

We all laugh a second, and then I reply, "It's actually from the old French 'mes', meaning 'portion of food'. And then a lot later, in the 15th century, a group of officers eating together were called a 'mess' and the term stuck."

"Can we just get a cup of coffee?" smiles Mike.

When we get to the Naffy, it's more Starbucks than Dad's Army. There's a corner with half a dozen cream leather seats around two circular coffee tables, and even four chrome barstools below a breakfast bar. But most importantly, behind the counter, there is a shiny red – and rather fabulous-looking – vintage Gaggia 3-group coffee machine from the 1960s. And it is currently applying its 15-bar pressure to our freshly ground coffee.

I wander across and sit in a leather chair, looking back at the Gaggia. Mike sits next to me, and, pointing at it, he says, "Jeez, will you look at that ancient piece of junk. Hope the joe's okay!"

"What!" I gasp. "It's a classic… a 1950s model!" I say in

disbelief. "The first commercial one was in London's Soho Moka bar – opened by none other than the Italian actress Gina Lollobrigida in 1953!"

"Hell, Lucas, I know you drink too much coffee, but I hadn't realised it was a religion!"

We laugh, and I continue. "In fact the inventor, Giovanni Achille Gaggia, got a patent for his coffee machine in September 1938 – at the age of forty-three!"

"Okay." Mike grins. "Enough already."

One of the guards brings over our drinks. We pick them up and sit back in the armchairs.

"So, what next?" Jeff looks at me expectantly.

"Almond croissant?" I say with a grin.

Jeff shakes his head, and I continue. "Okay then, let's get the building's plans and find out what the hell's been fiddled with here and why."

FORTY SIX

The cappuccinos were, as expected, superb. If only we had time for another, but it's half past five and we need to crack on.

We sign out four radios from the on-site security team and then split into our pairs. John and I will go to the plant rooms at the west of this underground chasm, whilst Mike and Jeff go east.

Another good thing about this bunker is that its directional signs and the colour-coded wall lines make it almost impossible to get lost. It's a bit like a building-wide London Underground map. Mind you, with a footprint 300 yards square, and twenty-four-hour man-made daylight, it's very easy to lose track of time, let alone your bearings.

We walk for fifteen minutes through zigzagging corridors before we finally make it to one of the two massive double doors to the Restricted Access plant area. There are several warning signs, but the one with "Danger 11,000 volts" particularly catches my eye.

The temporary swipe cards and associated, memorised, ten-digit access codes are accepted and the doors' latches release, allowing us to enter. Once inside, we can see the corridor we're now in stretches some fifty yards, with at least a dozen doors leading off into specific plant rooms.

We go for the first door, signed as "High Voltage Switchroom – Danger of Electrocution", supplemented with a lightning bolt and the text 11kV. I shudder as I recall one of my electrical engineering tutors, many years ago, saying 11,000 volts is not a *danger*, it's a *certainty* – it *will* kill you! Then I allow myself a guilty smile at his accompanying story.

It was an incident at an 11kV substation whereby one of the switches exploded and blew the two power engineers through the open doorway, and ten metres across the car park. Luckily it was a sweltering hot day and, against protocol, they'd not closed the doors.

The guy shielded from the blast by his colleague had minimal injuries, but the poor chap in front had quite severe burns, and spent a few weeks in hospital. Friends and workmates visited regularly and made sure his wife and young family were fine, but even so, it didn't prevent him getting a new nickname when he returned to work: Cinders.

Anyway, the first thing that strikes me about this place is the cleanliness; it's spotless! But again, every surface, ladder-rack, cable, and cabinet is battleship grey.

I walk over to the room's log and check attendance. As expected, no one's been here for nearly a month – or so says the book.

In the corner is a small office and I make my way over while John checks if any cabinet doors are unlocked.

When I get into the office, I go to the engineering PC and, moving the mouse, bring its monitor to life with the usual message demanding Username and Password.

I call Coops on my mobile, which piggy-backs onto the building's WiFi; there's no phone signal 80 metres into the earth. Three rings and Coops answers with a flourish, "Hello fearless leader."

"Hi Coops. I need to get into the Engineering Manager's PC, which is in plant room EL1."

"No problem. Give me a few seconds." I hear again the clatter of her keyboard, and after about twenty seconds, "Okay, try it now."

"What? No Username and Login?"

"Just move the mouse to wake the screen up."

I comply, and sure enough the opening screen of Windows *XP* comes to life.

"Hell Coops, XP!"

"Yeah." I can sense the smile in her tone. "Probably due to the Building Management System (BMS) having to link to old plant monitoring software."

"Thanks Coops. I think another letter to their IT director?"

"No problem," she says with a giggle. "Okay, I'll leave you to it. Oh, and don't let John walk on the glass plate–"

But I've closed the call and completely miss her last comment. I'm already busy going through the logs of the BMS software. This one is a Trend system, which controls and monitors every engineering system and links to the security access systems.

What I'm looking for are the lighting control logs. It's a trick Coops came up with on our last case, whereby she tracked someone's movements around a building as they triggered the automatic lighting. The same should be true here, and with luck, some records of door locks and CCTV as well.

FORTY SEVEN

As I suspect, the BMS logs tell me that no one has been in here for weeks.

John finishes his walk around and doubts his wife could get it any cleaner. "So, Lucas, you found anything?"

"No one's been in this plant room for over a month, but I'm just checking the other plant rooms on the lighting control system logs."

"Neat trick," John replies, impressed.

"To be honest, it's one of Coops' brainwaves."

"Smart cookie that one, must get it from her mum," he says, smiling. "I knew her dad, and he struggled to help with her homework when she was eight!"

We chuckle, as I have the same problem now with my daughters. This thought takes my mind straight home and for a few moments I stare unseeing at the computer screen. Once I've finished here, I really must phone home.

The monitor flashes as it returns to its opening menu, and my mind is back on the task.

I've been through all the logs and the only one where the lighting has been triggered today is the air scrubbers plant room.

Glancing at John, who's been watching the screen over my shoulder, I wonder, "Why would they tinker with the building's air scrubbers?"

"You're asking the wrong person, Lucas; I'm a driver – and definitely no engineer – 13A plug is my limit!" He smiles and raises his eyebrows.

"Oh, and Coops said for you to watch out for a toughened glass panel over a well or something."

"No way!" John says with a look of fear in his eyes. "Sod that for a game of soldiers. I'm not walking on glass!"

I just grin at him and make a mental note of the air scrubbers plant room AS1, and turn off the PC. Coops assures me it will reset and ask for the Username and Password next time someone logs on. She is indeed a smart cookie.

Locking the door behind us, we start off for AS1.

FORTY EIGHT

Again I use my card and code, and we enter AS1. There are no immediate signs anyone has been in this southwest corner room, which has also turned out to be the furthest from the site's entrance.

Following me in, John goes south and I split off to the north.

Within two minutes I hear a bloodcurdling scream from John's direction, and instantly spin round and run towards him, shouting his name. But there's no answer.

As I round the last floor-to-ceiling cabinet I see him, facing me, only a few metres away. He's standing stock-still, staring at the floor, and physically shaking.

"I… can't… move!" he says without lifting his head. "I heard it crack. I know I did."

As I get close I immediately see his predicament.

He's standing plum in the middle of a sheet of glass some three yards in diameter.

"It's okay, John." I walk up to him, and, bending down to look up at his face, I see his eyes are scrunched shut. "It's perfectly safe."

"It's fucking not! I heard it crack for fuck's sake!"

To me it's irrational, but then so is people's fear of spiders, or the dark; but nearly everyone I know suffers from one, or in some cases more, of these phobias. Mine is small spaces, and it gives me the shivers to see people potholing – really, what is the point?

"John, it really is okay. Look, I'll get on it with you and–"

He cuts me short, and, with eyes still shut tight, he looks up and throws me a grimace that would curdle milk at fifty paces. He then slowly takes his Glock from its holster and waves it in my general direction. "Any closer and I will fucking shoot you!"

"Okay, okay, just trying to lighten the mood."

"And don't fucking say lighten!"

The sweat is pouring off him as he lowers, but doesn't holster, the Glock.

As I look down at the pane of glass I notice one of the retaining bolts stands a few threads proud, and the sound he heard was probably just the glass rubbing against the thread.

"John, John – at least look at me."

He grudgingly opens one eye and then the second, staring straight at me. Holding his gaze, which is a mix of crushing fear and absolute fury, I say, "John, hold out your left hand, grab mine, and, eyes fixed on mine, slowly walk towards me."

He gulps several times, latches on to my outstretched hand and tentatively takes the first step, barely the length of a pencil, then the next, and then half a dozen more before he's finally on concrete.

He breathes a massive sigh of relief and immediately sits on the floor, holstering the Glock.

Looking at me with thankful eyes, he gasps, "Shit. I'm really sorry, Lucas. I know it's crazy but I just can't control it."

"Don't worry, it's over now." I pat his shoulder. "At least I didn't tell you about the loose bolt."

His eyes flick down to the edge of the glass. "Fuck!" He takes a deep breath. "If you'd mentioned that I probably would have passed out!"

I sit next to him. "Next time I'll say. It's a lot easier to deal with a person holding a Glock when they've passed out." And we grin like a couple of kids.

He nudges me. "What the hell's that?" he asks, pointing to a McDonald's-straw-sized copper tube, equidistant between two bolts, the loose one and another. "It appears to go under the glass."

"Dunno, but it looks odd." I take a photo of it with my mobile and email it to Coops and Suzi.

"While I'm doing this shall I post a pic of you levitating onto Facebook?"

"Just remember, I can still shoot you!"

We both laugh and get up, and John walks away toward the exit, but I just can't resist walking on the glass to see what all the fuss is about.

Fascinating. I am looking down a brick well. The spotlights facing downward from the stainless steel rim of the glass surround flood its red-brick walls with light, and at the bottom, I swear there are ripples in the water. I snap a mini video on my phone and send that to Suzi as well.

My phone rings after some five minutes – it's Suzi. "Hi

Lucas, one of our building services engineers reckons the tube may be some kind of pressure equalisation, something to do with the glass sealing the top of the well and changes in water table height."

"Ah right. Did you ask him why the water at the bottom is moving?"

"Hold the line, he's still talking at one of the pods just outside my office." The call goes completely silent; she must have pressed the mute button. A few seconds later she's back. "He reckons it could be an underground stream, and says they're generally in chalk downland and *very* deep below ground. Where the hell are you?"

"I'm in a plant room at Dunkirk RAF base. The goons have definitely been in here but there's no sign of them touching anything." But even as I say it, my eye returns to the loose bolt. "Actually, ask your guy to look into where the underground water flows from here."

"He's gone now, but he's given me a number for an expert on groundwater, so I'll follow that up and get back to you shortly." She adds with a snigger, "A *diviner* gut feeling Lucas?"

"Very droll… could be, or just the call of the amazing coffee in the Naffy."

She laughs, but knows my gut is reliable, as is hers.

FORTY NINE

John and I return to the Naffy, meeting Mike and Jeff there at just past 6.15pm for a coffee.

We have barely sipped our lattes when Suzi calls me. "Lucas, you need to get back down to the plant room!"

"Why the urgency?"

"Long story short: the underground stream ends up in the Sevenoaks aquifer!"

"Bloody hell, Suzi!" That causes Mike, Jeff, and John to stare at me, as I put my phone on speaker. "What do you want me to do?"

"It's possible the goons fed the zepto-bots into the well through the copper tube, and so you need to get a swab sample."

"Right, on our way, and then what do–"

She interrupts: "Get them back here to the lab. Oh, and Coops said to tell Mike to give you the bird."

Which causes Mike to nearly choke on his latte.

"Not sure Mike needs any encouragement… Speak later."

Looking straight at me, Mike prepares the one-fingered gesture, but his hand remains at waist level.

"Come on then, give it to me!"

"Nah." He puts his hand down to his side. "She's winding you up."

"What?"

"She's discovered the Black Hawk we keep below ground – to get your samples back to London!"

I grin from ear to ear. "Now that's a windup I happily accept!"

Leaving John and Jeff here to hold the fort, Mike and I run back down to the air scrubbers plant room. This, as I knew it would, turns into a race. I just beat Mike into the plant room and run down to the far south corner with him still hot on my heels.

At just before 6.30pm, we are next to the well's massive glass cover, looking down its vast depth. The flowing water at the bottom shimmers under the downlights.

We both stand stationary for a minute, bent over with hands on our knees, catching our breath, before Mike turns to me with a look of frustration. "How the feck are we gonna get samples from in there?"

"Not a clue!"

Still puffing, but now upright with hands on hips, I hear my phone buzz. It's Suzi and I stick it on speaker. "Hi Lucas, how's it going?"

"I think we can get a sample from the tube; just need something small to take a swab."

We're silent for a few seconds, then Suzi shouts in my ear excitedly, "First aid kit!"

"What?" I reply with my left ear ringing.

"Cotton bud, first aid kit!!"

"Brilliant."

I jump up, as does Mike, to track down a first aid kit. All plant rooms must have a decent kit, and electrical switch rooms even have a defibrillator. Mike spots the green box with a white cross, runs over to the wall where it is mounted, and snaps it out of its bracket. He runs back and kneels down beside me, adjacent to the glass panel, next to the little copper tube.

Mike opens the kit and tips its entire contents onto the floor between us. I grab the hermetically-sealed pack of ten cotton buds and tug one out. I then open a 20ml eyewash pod to moisten the bud, and poke it as far as I dare into the tube.

Meanwhile, Mike tears open a pack of rubber gloves, removes one and folds the wrist down, exposing the openings to the fingers and thumb. I drop the first cotton bud into the forefinger. This is repeated with three more cotton buds, as I take more swabs of the tube, filling all fingers of the glove.

He then folds the wrist of the glove back, stretches it and, just like you would with a balloon, ties it in a knot.

Mike smiles at me. "Right, let's get back."

"Indeed. I'll call Suzi and get our lab team ready."

As we again start running back down the corridor, I turn to Mike. "Your chopper's going to be a lot quicker than the Audi."

"Sure thing. I'll lay claim to the one here, and get a replacement flown in."

Mike gets on his radio to the guards: "Get our bird out, cos we're leaving in fifteen minutes!"

There is obviously a question, as Mike then commands: "Just get the bloody thing ready immediately or you're transferred to the Afghanistan office!"

When he's finished, I smile and click the transmit button on my radio, calling for John or Jeff.

Jeff replies immediately, "I'm in the café with John. What's up?"

"Going back to our labs with Mike and–"

I'm interrupted by an incoming call, and, glancing at my phone's screen, I see it's Coops. "Jeff, call you back in a tick, Coops on the other line… Coops, what's up?"

"I've got the goons going south, down the A21 – totally illogical."

"Bloody hell! What are they up to?"

"I don't know and I need to get back onto my tracking them, but suggest you get Mike's chopper in the air and I'll get back to you with directions."

"Okay, update me soonest."

I drop the call and radio Jeff, whilst still trying to keep up with Mike running along the corridor.

"Jeff, change of plan."

"Fire away."

"Mike and I will now be using his chopper to follow the goons, who, for some reason, are heading down the A21."

"Okay, no problem. I'll go back to the office with John in the Audi with the swabs."

"Cool. And call Suzi and she'll get the Old Bill to clear the route."

"Will do," Jeff replies. "What's your gut feeling on this then?"

"Not sure, and to be honest my gut is doing somersaults – something's seriously out of kilter."

"Shit," Jeff replies nervously.

FIFTY

When Mike and I get back to the café with our samples, Jeff and John have finished their drinks and are bidding farewell to the guards, one of whom strolls over to Mike and introduces the pilot. They swap pleasantries while I chat with Jeff and hand him the gloved swab samples.

Jeff and John shake hands with Mike and at just after 7pm they are let out through the bomb doors to the Audi. Once the guards are happy there are no Joe Publics around, the outer door does its magic.

Mike turns to me and says, gesturing at the pilot, "This is Scotty, he's got the chopper ready." With a wink to Scotty, he slaps me on the shoulder. "Come on me ol' china, let's go find the whirly-bird!"

"Dreadful!" I shake my head at Mike and his cockney accent. "It really is like sharing a stage with Dick Van Dyke." And then, smiling, "I know where I want to shove the sweep's brush."

I shake hands with Scotty and follow him into a small hangar. Well, I say small, but it's probably 100 feet square, with a Black Hawk sat centre stage.

"Hell, Mike, where does this come out?"

"We're plum in the middle of the forest, directly below a water reservoir."

"Don't tell me – the lid of the reservoir slides open and we fly off into the sunset, like James Bond in You Only Live Twice?"

"Sort of." He grins.

"You are joking?" I stare at him and shake my head. "Someone will see us, and we'll be on Facebook before you can say Ernst Stavro Blofeld!"

"Ha… we released a malodorant!"

"A what?"

"Think of it as a stink bomb, but military grade – we generally use them for crowd control."

"Brilliant," I chuckle. "Reminds me of when Matt thought it would be fun to tie an orange signal flare onto my car's exhaust pipe, on my thirtieth!" I remember it was a hot, sunny, humid and virtually still summer's day. "It took half an hour for the near-choking orange smog to finally clear the neighbours' gardens."

"I'm really liking Matt," Mike smiles. "Anyway, there's no one within 500 feet of the woods at the moment. Gotta be quick though, last time a few locals got curious – thought there'd been a sewage spillage!"

"Indeed." I smile. "Don't want any nosy parkers to come sniffing around."

At this point we both start laughing and firing off double entendres like a couple of kids.

What is it with boys – well, men – and fart jokes?

FIFTY ONE

A few minutes later, our extremely skilled pilot slowly raises the engine revs, lifting us very gently out of the hangar, with seemingly only a few feet to spare either side of the rotors. No sooner are the blades clear of the top of the reservoir than the chopper's turbine engines roar and we are pushed into our seats as it thrusts upwards and forwards, southwest, just clearing the trees.

After no more than a couple of minutes I look over at Mike and, nudging him, eye-point down to the M20 just northwest of us. "There's Jeff and John."

"Bet they wish they had one of these," smirks Mike.

"Jeff would, but John loves any excuse to blatt around in his Audi."

I call Coops. "How's it going?"

"Not bad. Just finished speaking to Suzi, and she's got the lab boys ready for the test – quick and simple for them really."

"Excellent."

"Yeah, the thing I'm really worried about is the report Suzi got back from her water expert."

"Indeed, made my gut churn."

"She's on the phone to them now checking a couple of things out. Expect she'll call you shortly."

"I presume you're still trying to get a fix on the goons?"

"Yep, been getting the odd hit from the CCTV and road sensors, and I've been trawling the Traffic England database. Last fix is Lidl, London Road, Sevenoaks."

"Why Sevenoaks? And why the hell Lidl?"

"Not a clue, oh Great One, but I checked the Lidl systems and their number plate recognition has them parking up nearly an hour ago. And the van's still there!"

"Brilliant. Call Alex – he lives over that way."

"Will do."

I close the call and glance at Mike, who is now looking at me quizzically.

"Seven Oaks?" says Mike. "Don't tell me, oaks, seven of them!"

Despite the dire situation, I just can't resist. "No. In fact the name comes from the Saxon word 'Seouenaca', which was the name of a small local chapel in 800AD."

"You need to be on a freakin' quiz show!" replies Mike, shaking his head.

"Something Helen discovered, as Sevenoaks School was her first teacher placement. Apparently it's the oldest secular school in England: 1432!"

"Anyway, my learned limey, why there? Doubt it's the school?"

"Not a Scooby I'm afraid, Mike."

"What? Goddamn limey lingo again!"

"Not a Scooby Doo – clue!"

Mike again shakes his head as we sit silent for a few minutes, being whizzed through the air over the Kent countryside.

My phone buzzes and, as expected, it's Suzi. "Hiya."

"Hi Suzi. How did you get on with your expert guy?"

"Oh, my Landscape Limnologist you mean?"

"Blimey, another fancy title."

"True, but apt. Limnology is from the Greek *limne*, which is lake, and *logos* which is knowledge – cool huh?"

"What's the limnologist guy found?"

"Well, *Rebecca* reckons there's no water treatment works near Dunkirk, I didn't tell her precisely where, but she did mention there's a major underground stream in that area." She sighs. "But I've been speaking to Coops and she says the goons are now in Sevenoaks?"

"Yes, she told me the same, but not a clue why."

"Rebecca reckons these streams under Dunkirk feed deep in the chalk and go down to Sevenoaks and then on into an aquifer below London."

"Holy shit!" I lean forward and rest my forehead on my hands.

"Exactly!" Suzi sighs.

"Okay, you get back on to your limnologist and find out precisely where the aquifer comes out in London… and let me know soonest!"

FIFTY TWO

I sit back in my seat, gently shaking my head, and then turn to Mike. "I guess you got all that?"

"Cut me a break! You guys rattle things off so quick. But it didn't sound good?"

"Bottom line: the stream at the foot of our borehole runs into an aquifer in Sevenoaks, which in turn connects to an aquifer below London!"

"Jeez – clever bastards!" Mike says, wide-eyed.

We chat for a few minutes before, impatient, I phone Coops. "Hi. Found those guys on the CCTV yet?"

"No, but I've got footage showing them leaving the store on foot. I'm trying to trace them around Sevenoaks, but there's not much local authority or police CCTV, and so I'm trawling streams from shops and domestics."

"Let me know soon as you've any news."

"Will do. How'd it go with Suzi?"

"There's an underground stream from our borehole at D1 to an aquifer under central London, via Sevenoaks. Can you liaise with Suzi as she's still speaking to her limnologist–"

Coops interrupts, sniggering. "Is that her kitchen lino fitter?"

"Very droll." I give a mock sigh. "Apparently she's the leading expert, and we need to trace exactly which water treatment plant in London takes water from the aquifer."

"Okay, on it."

My phone buzzes in my ear and I look at the screen: Call Waiting – Helen.

I close the call to Coops and pick up Helen.

FIFTY THREE

I close my eyes while the line rings, and take a deep breath. "Hi darling, how's things?"

"Brilliant!" she replies sarcastically. "Where are *you*?"

"At the moment I'm–"

"That was bloody rhetorical!" She cuts me short. "Daisy's recital starts in an hour… eight-thirty, after the awards ceremony!"

"Ah," I reply, somewhat stunned.

"Is that it? 'Ah'… like you're late getting breakfast?"

"I'll be back as soon as I can, but right at the moment I'm trying to save–"

"You're *always* saving someone! Why don't you try saving your bloody marriage… your family. One bloody night she gets to do this. *Knob*!"

The line goes dead. I try calling back half a dozen times but her phone's "not contactable". Probably turned off.

"Shit," I mutter, furious with myself, and I bang the handset on my leg. Mike gives a supportive, nervous smile.

After staring at my phone for a minute, trying to work out what I can possibly do, I call Coops. "Hi, can you triangulate Helen's phone please, and drop a pin on my Apple map."

"Sure." I hear Coops tapping her keyboard. "All okay on the home front, Master?"

"Terrific," I say through a sigh.

"Bad huh?"

"Not good."

"Phone's live but off, and it's at the St Andrew's school, in the theatre. Do you want me to–"

"No, no, just confirming where she is." And I close the call.

Checking my iPhone's map, the best landing spot in Sevenoaks, near Lidl, is the Fire and Rescue Service (FRS) car park, just off London Road.

FIFTY FOUR

I call Suzi and get her to phone the Fire Chief at Sevenoaks FRS and clear Mike's chopper to land in their rear car park.

Five minutes later, at 7.35, we are flying over the Sevenoaks wildlife reserve, with the pilot advising he's readying to land in the FRS car park at the junction of Morewood Close and London Road. From there it's only a 300-yard dash to Lidl.

I'm still struggling to keep focused on this case as my mind keeps flashing back to Daisy's recital.

"Okay, Mike," I smile. "Ready for a quick sprint?"

"Damn right, starting to get stiff sitting here. Not sure what we can do with the goons having gone already?"

"Me neither, but my gut's telling me to check out the van."

"Oh… that hi-tech gut again!"

"It's been right over the years."

The Black Hawk zooms in over rooftops and is dropping so fast it feels like we're going to crash, but as usual the pilot maxes out the thrust at the last moment and puts her down. It feels like landing on a Tempur mattress.

****

Mike and I jump out and run like the clappers down the road towards Lidl, where we see a plainclothes local copper standing at the entrance to their car park.

"Morning officer," I shout as I run up to him, holding out my badge. "I trust no one's touched the van?"

"No sir," he says, pointing to a plain white van bounded by "crime scene" white-and-blue striped tape, "and the low loader's ready to tow the vehicle." He gestures to the adjacent ten-ton flat-back truck adorned with fluorescent yellow and blue squares, and Kent Police emblazoned across its cab doors.

Before I can answer he continues, "Also, I had a call from your colleague Suzi," he gulps, "who informed me in no uncertain terms not to touch *anything* until you arrive."

"Excellent," I smile, and pat him on the shoulder. "I wish everyone was this good at preserving a crime scene."

"Thank you sir." He grins.

"We'll take it from here. If you can just make sure Joe Public keeps your side of the tape."

As we approach the vehicle from behind, Mike goes down the left hand side, while I go down the right and jump into the driver's seat. I lean across and open the passenger door.

"Dammit," he says with a grin. "Still can't get used to you limeys driving on the wrong side of the road."

"Yeah, right. We were driving first, and anyway, you lot started off from this side of the pond – what did you do, forget which side of the road to drive your wagons?"

"Jeez, you crack me up!" he replies, oozing with sarcasm as he kicks old copies of The Sun, takeaway coffee cups and other rubbish on the floor, making way for his size twelves.

FIFTY FIVE

With Mike finally settled in the passenger seat, we start searching every nook and cranny of this Ford Transit. Fifteen minutes after moving from the cabin to the rear of the van, we finally scramble out, at which point Mike loses his footing. He ends up standing bent over with his palms on the tarmac and arse sticking out at me.

"Bloody hell," I splutter, laughing. "What you see when you ain't got your gun."

"Kiss my ass!" As he gets to his feet I notice he's eating, and he waves a crisp packet at me. "But I didn't drop my freakin' chips!"

"Crisps! Where did they come from?"

"On the dash, shame to waste 'em!"

My phone buzzes. "Hi Coops. What have you found, liddle lady?" I say with a snigger.

"That's an improvement from Mr Grumpy Pants earlier."

"Well, yes… just been having some fun huntin' bear!"

Mike shouts, "Don't listen to the moron, Coops."

"What do you mean?" Coops asks me, "hunting bear?"

"Oh, never mind, tell you later. So why the call?"

"Finally finished playing hide and seek with the goons; found a few frames of them breaking into, and driving off in, a Toyota Yaris – 65 plate, light metallic blue."

"Brilliant work Coops. Guess you're tracking?"

"Ah, now, that's the difficult bit. There was a power outage to the CCTV at the junction on to the M25; I don't know yet if they've gone east or west. But I will find out soon. Sorry."

"Never mind, Coops, keep on their tail." At which point I can't help giggle again at the image of Mike's arse in the air.

"Come on, Lucas, what's the joke?" she asks tetchily.

I hesitate a second. "Okay, just before you called, Mike tripped and fell getting out the rear of the van. He ended up bent over in front of me, and seeing his builder's cleavage, I said, 'It's amazing what you see when you ain't got ya gun!'" and we all start laughing.

After a few minutes, we finally calm down and Mike chirps, "Hey Lucas, can I speak to Coops for a minute? I got an idea."

I put my mobile on speaker, and pass it to Mike.

"Hi Coops, ignore Lucas's juvenile humour."

"No problem, Mike, how are you?"

"I'm well hun, you?"

"Yeah, I've got a sweet number here."

Mike smiles. "Anyhoo, just wonderin', you said earlier you got some CCTV from this car park?"

"Yes, front of the van with the goons inside, sat chatting for a good five minutes."

"How 'bout some lip reading?"

"Ah, I was just going to tell Lucas. I got our polyglot, Dave, to have a look at the footage, but the two guys were wearing caps and with the height of the camera he says there's nothing there, not even mirrors or another surface to get some reflection of their mouths."

"Shit," Mike mumbles through his munching.

"What you eating Mike? Hope you're not resorting to Lucas's diet of crisps and coffee?"

"Yeah. Only useful thing in the van was this unopened bag of chips on the dash. All I need–"

Coops interrupts, "Hang on, Mike, I have an idea! Lucas!"

Mike thrusts the phone at me and mops crisps from the edge of his mouth.

"What is it, Coops?" I ask.

"Those crisps Mike's eating were on the dashboard?"

"Yes," I say, looking at Mike and shrugging my shoulders.

"So would have been picked up by the CCTV?"

"I guess," I reply, frowning.

"Well, you know James who works on the new tech?"

"Oh, the lad with the gait analysis system."

"Well, he sent me some new software he's testing for remote audio monitoring; it could help us find out what the guys were talking about."

My phone starts beeping: Battery Warning 2%. "Coops, batteries dying. Call Mike's mobile."

"Will do."

I stand wondering what a crisp packet has to do with audio.

FIFTY SIX

After a minute or so, Mike's phone rings. "Hiya Coops, I'll pass you to Lucas." He hands his phone to me.

Before I have time to speak, Coops is already talking. "Okay. First go get a lighter socket charger or boost pack and get your mobile charged!"

"Will do." It's not enough I have Helen nagging me, but now I have Coops stating the bloomin' obvious.

"Please put Mike's phone on speaker," which I do immediately. "Mike, go get a bag of crisps, same brand and flavour as the ones you're eating, and then put them in the same place on the dashboard."

"Okay… dare I ask?" replies Mike.

"I can teach or I can do," she replies, a little snappily, and I can again hear her frantically tapping keys in the background. "Sorry. Please just get those crisps."

"No problem. I'll phone when back at the van," confirms Mike.

"Okay. Speak later guys." And Coops closes the call.

I pass the phone back to Mike and, as per instructions, we both scuttle off to Lidl. Within five minutes we're back in the van, Mike the passenger and me behind the wheel. Again, with Mike muttering about limeys driving on the wrong side.

I slot the in-car charger into the cigarette lighter and then into my mobile, whilst Mike dials Coops, putting his phone on speaker, and placing it on the dash next to the new bag of crisps.

"Okay Coops, we're back in the cab," I say, putting my recharging mobile into a cubbyhole in the centre console. "You're on speaker, and the crisps are on the dashboard."

"I'm going to send you a sound file which I want you to play with the phone's speaker pointing at the bag of crisps. Keep absolutely still and quiet until the track's finished, then come back to me."

"Okay," I confirm.

"Before you do, though, turn on the media player in the van and tell me if the last track played was Under Pressure by Queen?"

Now this really throws me; is she psychic? I glance at Mike, who again shrugs and puts his hands up in the air as if to surrender. I press the van radio's on button and the screen lights up with the words *Undr Press Quen*. "Coops, amazing, how did–"

"Now turn it off, and play the audio file I've just sent you."

The phone beeps and an audio file named TestCrisp.wav pops up on screen.

"Okay, I'll play it and then call you back, right?"

"Yes please." She sounds a little calmer, but still there is frenetic typing in the background.

I play the track through the phone's teeny speaker, which actually doesn't sound half bad, pointing it at the crisp packet. The track only lasts thirty seconds or so, and I redial Coops. "Okay? I presume you were listening?"

"Yep. Give me five mins and I'll call you back with their conversation."

But before I can ask any more, the line goes dead.

Sometimes Coops' focus makes her come over as rude, but it's just, as she puts it, a pink mist that appears with really exciting shiny things.

What the hell has this little minx come up with this time?

FIFTY SEVEN

We wait for Mike's phone to ring, which it finally does after only ten minutes.

"Hi Coops," he says expectantly. "Yes, yes, okay." Mike puts his phone on speaker and sits it on the dashboard. Looking at me quizzically, he puts one finger to his lips for me to stay silent.

Within a few seconds two voices start talking, as clear as a bell.

"Okay, Coops, who's this we're listening to?" I ask, perplexed.

"The goons in the van," she says matter-of-factly.

Mike and I look at each other in stunned silence.

Then I chirp up, "How the hell..."

"Simple really. This new software takes the video image of the crisp packet and its minuscule movements, created by the pulsing air coming from the spoken word, and converts them back into the spoken word."

"What the hell?" Mike says in total amazement. "I know there was a paper at MIT, but our guys are still trying to perfect it." He scratches his chin. "Run it by me again?"

"When you look at a working speaker, the diaphragm moves very rapidly back and forth, which makes the sound; the different frequency airwaves. Well, when those soundwaves hit the crisp packet, it moves in the same way – minutely. We convert that minuscule movement back into the original sound."

"So why the Freddie track? And why the sound file I played?

"The Queen track and sound file were purely to get a baseline of frequencies against crisp bag movement, and we wanted to remove the Under Pressure soundtrack from our re-recording."

"And how did you work out the very high frequencies?" Mike asked inquisitively. "The camera is standard CCTV so it's only sixty frames a second."

Obviously something his guys hadn't achieved.

"Now, Mike," I interject, smiling, "you can't expect Coops to give you all her secrets."

"Fair enough," he says grudgingly. "Real impressive, liddle lady." And he sits back in his seat looking a tad disappointed.

I look at him and shake my head. "What do you reckon,

Coops, let Mike know? They will owe us once again!"

"You sure, Lucas?" Coops teases.

"Yeah, go on, he can owe you dinner as well."

"That a deal, Mike?" Coops says with a chuckle.

"Certainly is, liddle lady, dinner *wherever* you want!"

"It's easy," she says, and we sense her grin. "We just interpolate a double-duplex analysis of the rolling shutter original image. This gives us frequencies twenty times higher than the fps rate of the camera."

Mike looks at me in stunned silence – like me, he's lost after "interpolate", and merely tries to memorise the words he's just heard. "Okay, well I won't pretend I understand, but seriously impressive, Coops," he says, heartfelt.

The goons tell us not only their names but also where they are going next.

FIFTY EIGHT

It should have been obvious really. Лев (Leo) and Николай (Nikolay) are going to Biggin Hill, and chartering a plane to Moscow. But we've also discovered they're using the company PrivateFly. My stomach churns when memories from my last case come flooding back to me at the mention of a Gulfstream G650.

At the same time as we listen to the recording, Suzi has our resident polyglot David earwig these Russians, and, from Leo kindly reading out their full names on their passports, he determined that Николайа Александревич and Лев Викторович are their patronymic names.

Therefore, if you take the евич and the ович off the end of the names respectively, and then their given names off the front, then what is left in the middle is their father's given name.

Hence Leo's father's given name is Виктор (Viktor) and Nikolay's father's Александр (Alexander). Along with their surnames, this will be a huge help to Coops in tracing them.

Turning on my mobile, I see it's sixty per cent charged. So Mike and I leave the van in the local plod's capable hands and rush back to our Black Hawk.

When we get there, a small crowd of interested Fire Station guys have gathered. Being the consummate professionals they are, they keep a safe distance, but can't resist shouting a couple of double entendres, comparing our chopper to their hoses. Mike and I smile, thank them for allowing us to drop in, and promise that if we had more time they could go for a spin.

Ducking under the rotors, we run over to the chopper's door and jump into our seats, as the navigator slams shut the sliding side door behind us.

(Ducking under the blades always makes me smile, as they are rotating six feet above our heads – but everyone ducks.)

Helmets and headsets on, Mike looks at me. "Biggin Hill?"

"Yes please, chauffeur." I smile at him.

Mike turns and looks out of the window. "Take us to Biggin Hill, please, pilot, and navigator, can you locate a firm there called PrivateFly? We need to pay them an impolite visit."

Back through my headphones, I hear the pilot and navigator confirm Mike's requests.

The turbine engines roar, the blades thwack the air and we are pushed into our seats again as some seemingly unearthly force thrusts the Black Hawk up and forwards across the nearby houses.

FIFTY NINE

At least the flight to Biggin Hill is straightforward. Then my phone bursts into life.

It's Helen. "Hi darling," I say, hoping she's in a better mood than earlier.

"Where are you?" And, without giving me time to respond: "Because in thirty minutes you break your daughter's heart – *again*!" she says coldly, making me gulp.

"I'm in a CIA chopper on my way to a bust. I can't just drop everything, and get back home in time for–"

"For bloody anything – you utter *bastard*!" The phone goes dead.

I slump in my seat like a beaten animal, and rest my forehead on my hands.

"What's up, pal?" says Mike, nudging me. "The wife?"

"Yes… my Daisy's recital this evening." I reply, with a posture like Eeyore.

"Look, get John and Jeff to meet me at Biggin Hill, I'll scramble another bird to there and you take this one down to see your girl – you really *can't* miss that, and we sure as hell can handle any developments over the next few hours."

"No, I couldn't possibly–"

He cuts me short. "I promise I won't shoot anyone or blow anything up until Jeff gets there. In fact, we'll land nearby and won't even move in until he turns up."

"Well, if you're sure."

He stares at me unblinking. "Pilot, I need you to drop me at Biggin Hill, near the main entrance. And then you're under the command of Lucas here. Just a short hop down to Eastbourne and back – he'll provide you with some grub."

"Roger that, I presume this is related to this mission?"

"You bet your stripes it is… it's family!"

"Roger that, sir."

I look Mike in the eye, and gripping his hands with both of mine, say, "Thank you."

He smiles. "Some things are sacrosanct, buddy!"

Not wanting to explain, I text Helen, *"I'll be there in 25 minutes – on my mum's life."* She won't question that!

SIXTY

I call Jeff, to update him on the Russian guys, their plan to charter a plane, and tell him and John to reroute to Biggin Hill. I also let him know my domestic plight and having to get to my daughter's recital before my marriage disappears down the toilet.

Being divorced once already, Jeff appreciates my predicament and happily agrees to the diversion of the Black Hawk. In any case, it's Mike's chopper.

"Thanks, Jeff. It may also be a good idea to get Alex to meet you over there – he has more firepower in the boot of his motor than John!"

"Sure will, Lucas. You just sort things out at home, and get back up to Thames House as soon as you can. I'm pretty sure this hasn't played out yet."

"Will do. Thanks."

I close the call and dial through to an old friend – Pat in the Sussex Police force; he'll be in Eastbourne, somewhere. We go back a few years, but he has known Matt twenty-plus, and they've come through a few close scrapes – so he allows me a lot of leeway through my association with Matt.

His phone rings out, so I leave a brief message, but before I've finished he's calling me back. "Hi Lucas. It's been a while mate. How's tricks?"

"Not bad." I pause on an in-breath. "To be honest, I'm in a bit of a fix and need an urgent favour."

"Typical, phone when you want something," he chuckles. "Go on, if I can I will."

"I need to land a Black Hawk in the playground of St Andrew's school in Eastbourne."

"Okay, I can probably get clearance. When?"

"Twenty minutes?"

"What the fuck! Don't tell me… you're in it?"

"Uh, yes."

"Lucky… bloody… sod!"

"Well, what do you think? Possible?"

"Shit. I'll try." Laughing, he adds, "This'll cost you, mate!"

"That's not a problem – it'll probably save my marriage."

"Enough said, mate. Call you in ten."

With everything set up, hopefully, I sit back in my seat as we approach the boundary of Biggin Hill airfield.

Our pilot radios the control tower and, with a few specific clearance phrases and using the sign BH1 for the Black Hawk, we are authorised to land wherever we wish; this particular landing will not be logged.

The pilot finalises details. "We need to land near, but out of earshot, of the hangar for the company PrivateFly."

"No problem BH1, they are at the south-east end of the airfield, and so I suggest you land adjacent the south-west car park."

"We're coming in from the south, Sevenoaks direction."

"No problem BH1, go to lat/long 51.320595 0.029543 and I'll have one of my men meet you there to give you the lie of the land. Then he'll come back to the main building, to await your colleagues."

"Roger that, Biggin Hill. Appreciate this at such short notice. I'll be dropping off one person, Mike. He has the full authority of the US government in this matter. Out."

"Oh, uh, right. I understand," replies the very nervous tower manager.

Minutes later we land, again as near silent as humanly possible. Certainly it would not cause suspicion; this is an airport, and only someone outside having a crafty fag would hear us.

We have put down next to a small white Ford Transit Connect, with yellow and blue fluorescent squares, similar to the police, but with "Airport Security" down its side panels. The somewhat portly security guard gets out of the driver's seat, puts on his cap, adjusts his unbuttonable collar, tie and undersized hi-vis, and strolls toward the Black Hawk.

I turn to Mike as he unbuckles, with an outstretched hand, and say, "Thanks. I owe you big time."

"Damn right," he replies with an ear-to-ear grin.

He then jumps out and strolls over to the security guard.

The pilot comes back on the radio. "Okay, Lucas, we're gonna make straight for the centre of East Bourne. Let me have lat/longs as soon as you can."

"Will do." I smile at his pronunciation of my hometown.

And with that we take off, gently this time, and head for the south coast.

Just need to hear back from Pat now, I think to myself.

SIXTY ONE

It is now just before eight fifteen and the Black Hawk is flat out at a thousand feet above the A22, and after checking my iPhone's satnav I radio the pilot. "Hi pilot."

"Yep."

"Our destination in Eastbourne is long/lat 50.75403 0.266207. It's the sports ground of St Andrew's school. Aim for the rounders diamond."

"Rounders diamond?"

"Think of it like your baseball diamond, just a quarter of the size."

"Roger that."

As we go over Little Horsted and the East Sussex National golf club, my mobile startles me and displays Pat's name flashing on the screen. "Hi, any luck?"

"All sorted, you'll be met there by one of our plain-jane BMW patrol cars running with the story you're backup for a police helicopter, your pilot needs his rest break, and the Eastbourne hospital helipad is not big enough for your Black Hawk."

"Bloody hell, well done matey, owe you!"

"Just get your pilot to mention the Official Secrets Act, give them a sit in the cockpit, and they'll be sweet."

"No problem. Thanks again Pat."

"Where are you?"

"Just came over East Sussex National."

"Cool. You'll be at St Andrew's in five mins. Oh, and their assistant head, Deborah, and the bursar, Stephen, are also aware – same story as the traffic cops." Pat chuckles. "They might need a sit in the cockpit as well."

"Will do." It's amazing how many people love helicopters.

"I gotta go, just had a shout for Eastbourne pier, something's kicking off… probably another one of Sheikh Abid Gulzar's gold lions has appeared. See ya."

"Bye, Pat, thanks again, and–" but he's gone.

I'm now the one grinning from ear to ear, safe in the knowledge I will make it to Daisy's evening. Just hope she and Helen understand that afterwards I have to go straight back to

Thames House.

****

Sure enough, a few minutes later we've flown over Arlington, Folkington, Jevington and the Eastbourne Downs golf club, and rapidly drop the 500 feet down past the Royal Eastbourne golf club, before arriving at the St Andrew's school playing fields.

The landing spot is made easier by the bright blue flashing lights behind the grille of the black BMW 5 series patrol car, in an otherwise dark sports field. As we approach, the searchlight below the Black Hawk lights up the rounders diamond.

Standing next to the car are two smiling coppers, a grinning chap in a smart dinner suit (probably the bursar), and a lady struggling to hold down a flowing bright red evening gown (presumably the assistant head).

The navigator slides open the Black Hawk's door and I jump out and beckon the two coppers. They run across, ducking the blades, and jump in. After a quick explanation that we will probably only be here for half an hour or so, and our case is covered by the Official Secrets Act, I leave them chatting to the navigator.

While the chopper's rotors slow down to a stop, I go over to meet the assistant head and bursar and apologise for my little misdirection, and explain this is the only way for me to see my daughter's recital at their fabulous school.

The assistant head thanks me for my candour and gives her apologies but has to rush off back to manage proceedings in her theatre. Smiling, she adds, "It would be fantastic if you could drop in again during our summer fête…"

"I will see what I can arrange."

With that we shake hands and then she picks her way, in heels, across the grass, leaving me to walk with the bursar.

Looking back over my shoulder, I see the pilot move over, and a grinning copper slide into his seat.

I explain quickly to the bursar that this is going to be a surprise for my wife and daughter, so his help in getting a good seat would be very much appreciated. Again, the promise of a sit in the Black Hawk's navigator seat seals the deal.

But I needn't have worried: he is a veteran of the Desert Storm conflict and is more than happy to oblige in any way he can, and will get me into a seat near his, at the front of the auditorium.

****

It's only taken a couple of minutes to be guided round the rear of the building and into their pitch-dark theatre, where he flicks on a tiny keyring torch and guides me to my seat. The bursar then wanders off to return to his seat, confirming he'll meet me back at the chopper at the end of the evening.

I have a grandstand view, at the right of the stage and two rows back, behind a dozen teachers who smile and eye-point for me to sit before the one nearest me turns and puts a finger to her lips and whispers, "Shush."

I surreptitiously text Helen, *'here, second row right side, see you after x'* and then turn my mobile to vibrate as the teacher next to me gives a gentle scowl, and another "Shush."

As commanded, I sit silently just as the curtain goes up.

SIXTY TWO

The recital lasts for just under thirty minutes, and Daisy is amazing.

Somehow, she seems to sense I am here, and, glancing around whilst receiving applause, she finally meets my eyes. She gives me an enormous beaming smile, which I return, as would any delighted parent.

I admit a tear rolled down my cheek; so very, very proud.

Times like these reaffirm that my life makes sense.

The theatre lighting slowly rises and illuminates a roomful of proud and, like me, enthusiastically applauding parents.

After a five-minute standing ovation, the noise level drops to a low chitchat hum of mums and dads as they congratulate their children and make their way to the school canteen for coffee and cake. I stand to one side of the exit aisle so teachers can get to the canteen first, as they will greet their proud students and their parents.

It's not long before Daisy drags Helen to find me, and whilst receiving a huge hug from Daisy, Helen hesitantly kisses me on the cheek, and whispers in my ear, "Thank you."

And I whisper back, "My absolute pleasure; she was amazing!"

"Indeed she was. You will be coming back to the house?"

I note she says house rather than home, which has been a trend since the end of my last case. But it's still early days in our reconciliation, and there are far greater hurdles to overcome.

"Sorry darling, I really have to get back to Thames House. In fact, the chopper is waiting for me on the playing field."

"No problem." She smiles. "Just have a few minutes with Daisy before you go, and give me a call in the morning."

Well, you could knock me down with a feather.

I turn to Daisy and, with another hug, "You were brilliant!" I say proudly, with an errant tear in my eye.

"Thank you *sooooo* much for coming Dad." She adds, looking at Helen, "And you too Mum." She grins cheekily.

We all hug and for now the world is put to rights.

I nudge Daisy. "So, come on, lead me to the coffee and cake, but then I must get back to London – really sorry."

"No problem Dad, I know you've got a lot on, just glad you're here now." And again she beams at me before administering yet another hug.

Daisy has a green tea, and I grab a coffee. She takes great delight in gently scolding me that it's not healthy.

This is bliss.

SIXTY THREE

We end up spending half an hour as a family before the bursar finds me to say there are a few people now gathering outside, and hence I really need to get the Black Hawk off the sports field.

"No problem," I say, shaking his hand firmly, "and many thanks for helping me out this evening."

"Any time. The navigator let me have a sit in his seat, and I must admit, I'm glad I don't have to deal with all that technology!"

"Yeah, me too!" I smile.

I turn to Helen, and, eyes meeting, we kiss gently. It hurts to see the look of pain she hides: although we agreed to give our marriage another go, my job still stretches her patience to breaking point. Talking helps, but I need to get better at it, and to a degree she needs to accept the dangers I face. The worst thing is those dangers affected our whole family a few days ago – and that is not acceptable.

Anyway, we both know now is not the time for any discussion; this is Daisy's evening.

Looking at Helen, I say, "I will call you tomorrow, as soon as I get a chance."

"No problem." And, with a forgiving smile, "Thanks again for this evening. It really does mean the world to Daisy."

I turn to my little girl, who is still grinning at me like the Cheshire cat. "Nice one, Daisy. I'll be home soon, just got to crack this case."

"Everything's cool, Dad. Love you *sooooo* much. Be safe." She craftily blows me a kiss: it's uncool to actually kiss your parents, but apparently another hug is in order. "And my friends will be green when they see you get into the helicopter," she chuckles. "Tops their Bentleys!"

I turn and give a final wave, as I leave through one of the fire exits with the bursar, and he and I jog the fifty yards to the edge of the sports field where the Black Hawk is waiting.

The police car is long gone, and, seeing me, the pilot fires up the engines.

Turning to the bursar and exchanging another hearty handshake, I ask, "Can I give you a lift anywhere?"

"Oh, if only that were possible, Mr Norton, but I must finish the evening here."

I jump aboard the chopper and strap myself in, which the navigator confirms to the pilot. And we're off.

Looking down, I can see a few dozen surprised faces as the engines gently roar and the blades thwack, again lifting us skywards, but as quietly as the pilot can manage. Then, a couple of hundred feet off the ground, we turn 180 degrees and power north towards London.

It'll take the assistant head and the bursar a little explaining, but the families are far more focused on the recital evening than the Black Hawk.

Except the men, of course – shiny thing.

SIXTY FOUR

We are soon flying back over the East Sussex National golf club, then Uckfield, then again track the A22 north back to central London.

I check my phone and it's just gone 21.40.

"Hi pilot, do we have an ETA for Thames House?"

"I've been directed to the US Embassy pad, where Mike will meet you, ETA thirty minutes."

"Oh, okay, no problem. Did he give a reason?"

"Sorry sir, he didn't."

I need to phone Alex and get him to meet me at their Embassy, presuming he's finished at Biggin Hill, then he can drop me back to Thames House.

After tapping on Alex's photo on my mobile it connects almost immediately, "Hi Alex, you still got an Audi?"

"Yeah, overnight – sweet."

"Can you pick me up from the US Embassy in Grosvenor Square?"

"No probs, you going back to Thames?"

"Yes. Need to get back to Suzi and try and find out what the hell these guys are up to; my gut is doing loops like the Red Bull air race!"

"I'll be there in twenty minutes, and park up on the south side."

"Thanks. I'm in one of their Black Hawks, and will be there in about twenty-five. I need to have a quick chat with Mike, but can do most of that on the phone now, so shouldn't leave you parked up for more than, say, ten or fifteen minutes."

"No probs."

We close the call and I return to looking at the myriad of streetlights circling little villages as we near the M25.

SIXTY FIVE

With still no news from Jeff, who I presume is still at Biggin Hill, I call him. His phone rings several times before he answers – it's probably on vibrate. "Hi, Lucas," he whispers.

"Hi," I instinctively whisper – needlessly making it harder for him to hear me. "What's happening?"

"Nothing, still waiting for these guys to turn up!"

"What about the plane?"

"That was the easy bit; it's grounded. But the charter company has no clue as to what's going on. But they are being very co-operative."

"Okay, can you–"

"Sorry Lucas, movement. Back to you in five."

The line is instantly dead.

Whilst I'm waiting I call Suzi, just to let her know I'm on my way into the office. This is a very rare occasion – I have to leave her a voicemail.

I no sooner finish recording a brief message than my mobile buzzes with an incoming call from Jeff. "Sorry about that, Lucas."

"No problem. Got them?"

"Yes. No resistance. Only giving lawyer's number and saying 'no comment want lawyer'." Sarcastically, Jeff adds, "Great!"

"Well done. I'll see you back at the office. How long does John think?"

"Twenty-five minutes with blues and two's."

"Bet he's loving today, a bit different to his usual chauffeuring."

"Indeed. See you back there. Oh, and Alex left a short time ago for the US Embassy, leaving some of his armament!"

"Ha! He doesn't travel light, does he?"

"You're telling me!"

The call closes, and I sit back into my seat, and enjoy the next twenty minutes whizzing through the clear night sky, looking at the stars above, and the town lights below.

SIXTY SIX

As promised, one of Mike's team meets me from their Embassy's rooftop helipad and escorts me straight to the lift, and straight down to Mike's office.

"Hiya. How's it goin' limey'?"

"Your taxi is returned in full working order, and my domestic calm returns, thanks in no small part to you!"

"Just glad I could help."

"Any developments, Mike?"

"Jeff's got it in the bag. I got picked up from Biggin Hill by another Black Hawk and shuttled back here. Got one of my boys to drop the swabs over to Suzi."

"Thanks for that."

"One strange thing, though: back home, our platform 61 in New York has been evacuated due to a major water leak!"

"Never rains but it pours!"

"What?"

"Just another limey saying," I reply, grinning to myself. "So, have you got to return home?"

"Yeah, out of Heathrow on the 9.30 flight tomorrow morning." He adds, in a concerned tone: "Have your guys got any more leads?"

"Nothing as yet, but I'm just going to call Suzi to let her know I'm on my way into the office, and if she has anything I'll let you know."

"Well I'm damn sure if anyone can sort this it'll be Suzi and Coops!"

"True."

"Okay bud. I'm going back to my hotel now, but one of my guys will take you down to the Embassy's rear carpark, then Alex can whizz you to your office."

"Thanks, Mike."

"No problem, see ya."

In a couple of minutes a young, close-cropped agent swings past Mike's office and escorts me down to the main lobby, through reception, and out to Alex in their rear car park.

I jump into the passenger seat, and the Audi's dashboard clock shows just past 22.25.

As I click in my seatbelt, I turn to Alex. "What's the story you being parked in here then?"

"Apparently," he replies grumpily, "I looked suspicious sitting out in the street, and so they came over to speak to me." Then he grins. "I gave them Mike's number, and shortly afterwards they ushered me in here and fed me coffee and doughnuts!"

"Mike is pushing the boat out!" I smile.

"I hear you've been on a jolly as well?" He grins again. "How did the recital go?"

"Brilliant, Daisy was absolutely brilliant. And Helen's thawed a bit as well."

We're monitored as we leave the Embassy's car park into Upper Grosvenor Street.

"Back to the office? Fancy a decent coffee?"

"You bet. Let's nip to Grosvenor Gardens, cabmen's shelter café on the way, I'll treat us all to bacon sarnies."

During the late nineteenth century, cabmen's shelters were slowly added around the busy streets of London. They were places of shelter, and hot drinks and food, for London's horse-drawn, open-top (for the cabby) carriages. Today there are only thirteen of these green garden-shed-like buildings around the city.

In five minutes we're pulling up outside the cabbies' café on Grosvenor Gardens, next to Victoria train station. I go inside and get half a dozen coffees and bacon butties – God help anyone who snaffles mine when we get back to the office.

Alex blasts us back the last couple of miles, as the one-way system goes – it's a mile on foot! But that's the fun of the one-way streets of London, and hats off to our cabbies who know them like the back of their hand.

It takes a black cab driver a minimum of two years to learn the "knowledge", and in most cases four! But then, given the number of streets, and the ever-changing one-way systems, I'm not sure I could ever keep up to date.

SIXTY SEVEN

As we pull up at the underground garage barrier, my mobile rings. It's Suzi. "Hi there," I say, "we're just pulling into the car park."

"Cool. I presume you have provisions?" she says expectantly.

"Of course, coffee and bacon sarnies!"

With a chuckle Suzi replies, "Predictable – cabbies' café."

The shiny stainless-steel hydraulic security posts slide into the road and we move across the paved approach to the main barrier. The security posts return to their sentinel positions behind us. Alex's credentials are checked and his iris scanned, and, with the systems happy, the three-foot-high floor ramp barrier slowly drops into the tarmac, allowing us entry into this secure cavern.

The guards nod grudgingly, with some following us, whilst others remain focused on the closing of the barriers. Two of the guards approach us cautiously, with machine guns at the ready. Anything out of the ordinary and we will be treated as hostiles.

Sounds harsh, but in the ever-increasing war on terror, we presume guilty until proven innocent; but then, our attention is extremely rarely drawn to the innocent. It's not unreasonable, and with terror attacks the risk is always life-threatening. In many cases, threatening hundreds of lives, and sometimes thousands.

Anyway, Alex parks up and we walk over to the secure lift where again we are given the once-over by the guards. As protocol demands, they will watch us on their monitors as we travel to our floor. Not until the lift is again empty and doors closed can they presume this entrance is secure.

SIXTY EIGHT

Suzi is in her office tidying her desk, and putting a few papers into her fabulous, dove-grey, Smythson Burlington leather document folio. I recall it was part of a gift set from her dad when she got the job here. When I looked up the price of this writing pad, £495, I shuddered, but the matching £995 handbag nearly made me faint – especially as he'd also bought them in the Clay and Dew colourways. I literally can't afford for her to meet Helen.

I knock on the frame of the open door. She looks up and smiles. "Hi, Lucas, Alex. I've booked the Situation Room."

"Excellent." I likewise smile, wondering how she always manages to look so cool, calm and collected.

"David has just gone down to reception to fetch Rebecca, the on-loan water expert."

"So just the five of us." I smile at Suzi.

"Indeed," she replies, eyes smiling at my laden tray. "So, who's getting the extra coffee and butty?"

"Would that be… Lucas?" jibes Alex.

Suzi shakes her head at me, knowing Helen has me on a diet – well, lifestyle change, as she calls it.

"And why not," I say with a grin. "I've not had a hot meal for forty-eight hours."

"Fair go," Suzi concedes.

"So, Suzi," I ask. "Any thoughts?"

"Yes, a few. But I'd rather wait until we're all in the Situation Room, as something Rebecca researched could have a major influence on our next steps."

"Blimey, sounds ominous," chirps Alex.

Suzi nods, grabs her mobile and iPad, and we all make our way up to the Situation Room.

SIXTY NINE

As we arrive, David and Rebecca are waiting outside in the corridor. Suzi looks at David, then Rebecca, and then me. "This is Rebecca, limnologist, and Rebecca, this is Lucas Norton, and his colleague Alex," she says, smiling. "And Alex, this is David, our linguist."

We all shake hands, with the usual cursory nods and smiles.

"Good morning, Mr Norton, Alex, David," Rebecca says a little nervously. We try to reduce the formality for our visitor. But unfortunately, these surroundings tend to put people on edge – especially at eleven in the evening.

Suzi goes into the room and I let David, Rebecca and Alex follow her before I enter and close the door behind me. We all take our seats and I nod to Suzi for her to take the lead, as after all it is her meeting and her intel.

"Okay." She pauses, passing around copies of a two-page hand-out. "This is a summary of where we are, and what has taken place thus far."

We all pick up the document, flick a peek at the four sides of A4, and wait for Suzi to take us through it in detail.

She glances at David, Alex and me but holds her gaze on Rebecca. "It goes without saying this information is strictly confidential and stays within this room until I deem it fit to release. Even then, it will be controlled by our PR team."

David, Alex, and me nod compliance, and Rebecca fervently so – I expect Suzi has already drilled it into her that she has signed the Official Secrets Act.

"Right," Suzi continues with a smile. "As you can see from the bullet points, we've been taken on a bit of a wild goose chase, and ended up not quite knowing our next steps."

"I thought you had–" Alex says quizzically.

"We do indeed have more info–" she interrupts Alex with a slight scowl, "–which has been further verified by Rebecca. But I won't steal her thunder."

She makes a small hand gesture, and smiles at Rebecca to speak.

Nervously Rebecca clears her throat, and flicks back and

forth across two pages, until she steadies at page three. "Hi. Firstly, thanks for letting me get involved on this, it is quite thrilling."

We all smile and nod. Bless her, it's nice when externals are with us – not the usual inter-departmental or agency agendas.

Suzi replies, "It's very good of you to give us your time, especially at such short notice."

Rebecca continues, "I've looked into this a bit further, and I think I know what the gang are up to…"

"Really?" I chip in, excited.

"Um… yes… I think so," Rebecca says nervously.

"I agree," says Suzi in support, as she looks around the table, her eyes saying 'don't interrupt'. "Please go on, Rebecca."

"Um… well, the simple explanation is, there are several massive underground aquifers around the UK, and in a few cities there are some quite high water tables."

"What, seawater?" Alex asks.

"Oh, no." Rebecca adjusts her spectacles, and allows herself a small smile. "These are all fresh water, resulting from rain over our lovely island."

"Ah, I see," says Alex, smiling at his pun.

"Um… anyway, in a couple of instances these masses of water–"

I interrupt, "Sorry, but 'masses'?"

"Ah… yes," Rebecca replies. "I'm talking here of billions of gallons of fresh water."

Suzi again looks impatiently around the table. "Let's all just allow Rebecca to finish her findings and then have questions at the end!"

We all nod in compliance, and Rebecca continues. "The work here is based on the principle it would be a contaminant – assuming that's what it is?" She looks at Suzi, who merely nods and smiles agreement to her assumption.

"Well," she frowns, "if introduced into the underground stream at Dunkirk, then it would travel to the small Sevenoaks aquifer, and then on to the massive aquifer below London." She then looks confused. "But it's a long shot that something would contaminate the stream at Dunkirk, as it is over eighty metres below ground. Anything entering the ground there would be filtered out by the eighty metres plus of downland chalk."

I look up from my notes. "So, Rebecca," I say, staring at her, "what if the contaminant was dropped into a nearby well?"

"Um… that would be extremely unlikely, as a well, typically fifteen metres deep, would merely go into the top of the water table and again be filtered by the chalk, and Dunkirk is right at the peak of the North Downs."

"So," Suzi summarises, "We would be looking at some direct access to the underground stream that feeds the first aquifer in Sevenoaks?"

"Absolutely right, Suzi. But, as I say, the stream is some eighty metres plus below ground."

Again I look up from my scribbling. "What sort of timescale for the movement of this contaminant, assuming it somehow goes directly into the stream?"

Rebecca removes her glasses, puts them on the table, and lets out a slow breath. "Oh, I don't know exactly, but it would take a couple of weeks to finally get into the London aquifer."

Alex pipes up: "You say these aquifer things are very deep below ground. So, the contaminant couldn't get into the domestic water supply?"

Rebecca now has a real look of concern. "Yes it could, and easily. You see London is fed from nine boreholes, and in total they extract some seventy million gallons of water each day."

We all now sit bolt upright, and wide-eyed.

Suzi frowns. "So, this is *all* the fresh water for Londoners?"

"Um… yes," Rebecca replies, "and many of the businesses in London as well."

"Seems a hell of a lot of water – no supplies taken from rivers?" Suzi pushes.

"None of any real consequence for central London. There used to be, but when the old boreholes went into mothballs, the water table below London slowly began to rise. Then, in the last fifty years, we've had to re-commission the boreholes. And to be honest, seventy million gallons a day just about keeps the water table in a status quo."

While the rest of us scribble notes, I see Suzi merely write one word, "flood", and glances at me, concerned.

She then looks around the table. "Any other questions for

Rebecca?"

We all shake our heads, smile and thank Rebecca.

I look at Suzi and then over at Rebecca. "No more questions, but thank you very much for your hard work, and of course, you will remember this is completely confidential and restricted to those in this room."

Rebecca stutters slightly. "Um… indeed, I certainly understand the sensitivity and confidentiality of this meeting, and there's no problem in Suzi contacting me further."

Suzi wraps up the meeting and, walking to the door, arranges for David to escort Rebecca to reception. The rest of us remain in the Situation Room.

She returns to the table and sits down, solemn-faced, as are we all, now we know the final game plan.

I start the conversation. "So: catch-22. These bastards are going to try to infect London with something, and if we stop it by turning off the boreholes, then we flood the City!"

Suzi grits her teeth and grimaces. "That's pretty much it!"

I look around the table. "What the bloody hell do we do now?"

SEVENTY

We've sat in the Situation Room for fifteen minutes discussing Rebecca's comments, before I state the obvious: "We must find out exactly what these zepto-bots are programmed to do; there must be a solution!"

Suzi clicks one of the fast-dial buttons on the conference call phone in the middle of the table. After one ring, Coops answers.

"Hi all, so what's new? Any diviner intervention?"

"Very droll," I reply. "Not much, other than we have ten days to find and neutralise the zepto-bots before whatever they are going to do happens in central London."

"Ah, I might have some news on that shortly – sorry, must stop calling you shortly."

"Have you been at the Mars bars, Coops?" chuckles Suzi.

"I guess… my soul needs it when I'm under this level of pressure!"

"So." I nudge them back on topic. "What have you found?"

Coops is quiet for a minute. "Well, it may be nothing, but I've managed to decrypt another one of Pete's project files, and it's something to do with fertility."

"What," I say in disbelief, "he wants kids?"

That causes a brief lightening of the mood, with sniggers all round.

"No," she continues through a laugh, "it's much scarier than a mini-me Pete. It's about choosing the sex of a child, and how that's affected by the chromosomes – XY of the father and XX of the mother."

"Straightforward, then, Coops… he's just doing a PJ for a friend?"

"I thought a private job at first, but somehow it's related," she sniggers, "with the zepto-bot project."

We sit silent for a minute but my gut's liking this.

"So – next steps, Coops?" I ask. "What can we do?"

"What I'm thinking is the zepto-bots can be used for both the memory gene project, and the sex selection project."

Suzi chips in: "But how on earth can sex selection be used as a weapon?"

"Not a clue," Coops replies in a downbeat tone. "But, looking at these files and the nomenclature, there is some linkage – but it's mostly just a hell of a lot of gobbledy-gook!"

"Okay then. As I see it," I say confidently, "we only have two options, find and neutralise these zepto-bots, or turn off London's borehole water supply and flood the financial district!"

"Coops." Alex apprehensively chips in. "I presume these zepto-bots have a finite battery life?"

We all look at Alex, embarrassed, and a little annoyed that none of us had remembered Coops had told Suzi this yesterday. "They last about ten days," repeated Coops.

"Can you send a copy of Pete's chromosome project paper through to me, please, Coops?" Suzi requests.

"Sure can, but it's a bit weighty."

"No worries, just email as a PDF and I'll speed-read it."

I chip in a final word. "The main point is: both the 'memory gene' and the 'sex gene' scenarios seem credible. Our job now is to determine which one has been initiated into the Dunkirk aquifer, so, should the worst happen and these things do get into the water supply, we know exactly what we're fighting!"

SEVENTY ONE

The best thing to come out of this evening's meeting is that we have a ten-day window to find a solution to one of two credible problems. At least their method of implementation is the same: zepto-bots in the public water supply.

Having left the Situation Room and said my farewells to the team, I go back to my office, pick up my coat, and make my way down to reception.

It's now very late and so I text Helen, *"Hi. On way home shortly, first train 04:00 arr EB 06:47 I'll buy breakfast. What drinks?"* I know she will have her phone on silent, but she'll check it when she wakes at six.

It'll be sausage muffin for me, Daisy and Molly, with a cheese and bacon croissant for Helen, but the drinks may vary. So, I'll be going home via McDonald's and Nero's in Eastbourne.

It's a bit of a murky night, with a misty rain falling that is gently blown into swirls at the road junctions. But as it's warm and so atmospheric, and I have a couple of hours to kill, I decide to walk to Waterloo rather than the much closer Victoria train station. Therefore, when exiting Thames House, I turn left, north-east, and start my walk along Millbank, over the roundabout for the Lambeth Bridge, and then down the steps into Victoria Tower Gardens.

Halfway along the gardens I pass the Burghers of Calais monument, which is in honour of the town of Calais, besieged for a year by the English in 1347. At the end of these lawns I return to the pavement and Abingdon Street, which passes Victoria Tower on the south corner of the House of Lords.

This tower is a magnificent stone building, built originally of magnesian limestone, but latterly replaced with Clipsham stone from Lincolnshire. I love the massive stone lions holding golden flags who guard the huge arched Sovereign's Entrance.

Directly opposite on the west side of Abingdon Street is the Jewel Tower, a beautiful but modest tower and part of the original 14th-century Palace of Westminster. It was built in 1365 to house Edward III's treasures, and was one of only two buildings to survive the fire of 1834. Behind the Jewel Tower is the Pyx Chamber, where the trials of newly minted coins have been held annually since 1282. These "trials" are judicial, presided over by a judge and a jury of assayers who certify the metallurgical content of the realm's coins.

Then next I see the fabulous Westminster Abbey.

All of these buildings stand on the old plateau of Thorney Island, with Storey's Gate, Great Smith Street, and Great College Street following the streams that once surrounded the security-conscious island.

It is on nights like this I try to imagine the coppers back then, "walking the beat" of the dim, firetorch-lit streets, with boats patrolling around the island. It must have been a cold, thankless, and lonely task.

I continue north past the Old Palace Yard, then the Palace of Westminster, and finally the statue of Oliver Cromwell, before turning right onto Westminster Bridge.

Here, as I round the corner to the bridge, its lampposts greet me. They are large, magnificent, three-lamp-head affairs, dating back to when the bridge was built, and there are seven on each pavement.

What sights they must have illuminated since it was opened in 1862. I imagine the clatter of horses' steel-shoe-clad hooves, and the clang of their carriages' steel-rimmed wheels.

Even now, at three in the morning, it is something to behold, as the city is at its quietest: no party animals, no commuting animals, just a few diehards meandering home.

At the other side of the bridge, and to the east, is a massive sandstone lion on a plinth outside County Hall. Further north is the London Aquarium and the London Eye, which is a magnificent night-time sight, and a favourite of my girls.

It's then left up York Road for five hundred yards, across the walkover bridge, and into the northwest entrance of the Waterloo station concourse. Now to find my train.

It's the first of the day, so it's nearly empty. I easily find a comfy corner seat away from the automatic doors. I snuggle into my coat for a two-and-a-half-hour snooze, broken only by the alarms I set on my watch to make sure I don't miss the two train changes.

SEVENTY TWO

Shortly after quarter to seven, at Eastbourne, an overly polite Polish woman holding a bin liner wakes me, as she clears the few remaining newspapers and food wrappers from seats.

"Mornin'," she grins in a gentle tone. "Please you get off." And, with a gentle nudge to my right knee with her black sack, she asks, "Party night?"

"Working, I'm afraid," I reply, yawning, and putting my iPad under my arm. "Better go and get breakfast for the family."

"Oh… nice, you adopt me for breakfast?"

"If only I could, my dear." After a little ferreting, I brandish a crumpled fiver from my pocket. "Here, grab yourself something later."

You would have thought I'd given her a thousand pounds, judging by the breadth of her grin. "Bless you! McDonald's when finish shift."

As I squeeze past, she very gently holds my hand in both of hers, and looks deep into my eyes for a few seconds, gently tilting her head left and right. Again she says, "Bless you," and knowingly smiles: "Something trouble you… don't worry… it be fine… no sterilised." She laughs as she turns away to get on with her clearing up.

I continue out through the carriage door, and then along the platform to the automatic barriers, which are permanently open at this time in the morning. As I pass through them, I glance behind me and can see the little busy bee wandering down to the next carriage.

Something's lost in translation – *"no sterilised"*.

Then my mind flashes back to my dad when I told him I was going to have the "snip". "Don't worry, son, it won't hurt, as long as you keep your thumbs out the way of the bricks."

This still brings a smile as I walk out of the station.

SEVENTY THREE

As I walk across the concourse, I check my phone and, sure enough, there is a text from Helen, and one from each of the girls. Helen confirms a latte, and the girls require milkshakes.

I reply to Helen, *'At station. Home 07:15 ish with breakfast.'*

Leaving the station by the south entrance, I walk the fifty yards along Terminus Road to the 24-hour McDonald's and buy three double sausage breakfast baps, and two milkshakes. Then it's across to Nero's for the bacon and cheese croissant and lattes for Helen and me. With my two bags of breakfast supplies, I go round the corner to the taxi rank to get a cab home.

At ten past seven, I walk through my front door to a rapturous welcome. "Hi, Dad," says Daisy as she hugs me and slips the McDonald's bag from under my arm, whilst Molly kisses my cheek. "Love you, Dad," she says, and relieves me of the recycled cardboard drinks holder containing the milkshakes and lattes.

Even Helen gives me a brief hug and a kiss on the cheek. "Thanks again for last night," she whispers. "This is thoughtful of you, too."

The dogs, Ellie and Grace, glance fleetingly at me, and then, nostrils flaring, turn tail and follow the food.

Still in the hallway, I open the under-stairs cupboard door, hang up my coat, and call over my shoulder, "I presume the table is laid?" But it falls on deaf ears, as everyone has left me for the dining room to scoff their breakfast. I do the same, because, if I'm not quick, my double sausage bap will be divided up as extra spoils by Daisy and Molly.

We sit around the table and chitchat between the munching of baps and slurping of milkshakes, and all is normal, whatever that is in our household. More to the point, it is calm and quite jovial, and a very welcome change to the pressure of the last 72 hours.

The forecast on my mobile shows sun for the whole day, and Helen suggests we drop the girls off rather than letting them catch the bus. Then we can go shopping and have lunch out.

I just grin at her and nod with delight. Perhaps things

between us are slowly returning to normal.

****

Helen's planned shopping trip goes well, netting her a pair of red suede open-toe shoes, two tops, a summer dress, a clutch bag – apparently necessary to match the shoes and dress – and two pairs of jeans for the weekends. In the process, I get strong-armed into buying some more socks and pants, cargo trousers, and a couple of t-shirts.

Then we are off to Zizzi's for an Italian lunch. We go the full seven rounds with a half-carafe of house white for Helen, small glass of house red for me – nominated driver – and starters, mains, puds, and of course lattes.

When the time comes to leave, we both feel like over-inflated spacehoppers and decide to head via Bolton Road and Devonshire Place, to the seafront promenade, where we can walk off at least some of these calories. In fact, Devonshire Place comes out right opposite the bandstand with its blue-green tiled dome shimmering in the bright sunlight.

We walk down to the lower prom, which runs at the edge of the beach, and have a leisurely stroll down to the Italian Gardens, which takes the best part of 40 minutes. There we pop in to the Holywell Tearoom for a cuppa.

We take our drinks over to our two hired deckchairs at the edge of the beach, and sit back, listening to the tide gently push-pull the pebbles across the beach. The ocean vista is breathtaking, as is its backdrop, with the pier stretching out to sea in the east, and Beachy Head cliffs to the west.

I feel totally relaxed, with my nostrils taking in the mix of salty sea air and the occasional waft of a strong English Breakfast tea.

This is one of the best days we've had in the past six months.

SEVENTY FOUR

We've been sitting here in our hired red, white, and blue striped canvas deckchairs for a while. But it's not until my mobile rings, and I see the time on its display, that I realise it's four o'clock. Apparently, I've been dozing for the best part of two hours.

Helen glances at the buzzing phone and then me. "Go on, answer it," she says with a begrudging smile. "If you don't, it'll bug you for hours."

This is a turn up for the books, and it's patently obvious I don't have to do much to keep things on an even keel. I just have to "do", as Daisy told me during a daughter/father moment the other evening.

I click the green button on my mobile. "Hi, sorry to interrupt," Suzi sighs. "I know you texted *'Don't disturb unless someone's dying and even then try Jeff first'*, but this really is bloody urgent."

"It's okay, Suzi, I'm on the beach with Helen, and she told me to answer your call."

Suzi answers sharply, "Blimey, that's a first!" Luckily, it goes unheard by Helen. "Oh, sorry, I shouldn't."

"No problem, Suzi, we know the demands of the job." I smile at Helen. "So, why the call?"

"Well, my diviner, as Coops calls her, says the calculations she made are out due to the massive rainfall a few days ago, and now she's saying we've barely more than a week's grace before the zepto-bots are in the London aquifer."

"Holy shit!" I shout. Helen gives me a stern look and an elderly couple sitting next to us raise their newspapers and shake them pointedly.

I mouth *sorry* to Helen, and the couple next door. "Okay Suzi, what do you need me to do?"

"I'm afraid we need you here. Goodness knows how we are going to avoid a catastrophe of one description or another."

"Okay, I'll be there first thing in the morning. In the meantime, you and Coops collate all the intel we have, and get Rebecca to produce her findings formally – calcs and everything!"

"Will do, Lucas. See you first thing."

I close the call, put my mobile back into my trouser pocket, and nervously look at Helen. "That okay?"

"It's fine," she says smiling. "Maybe we can rent a film this evening, and get a bottle of wine?"

"Sounds like a plan, but as you heard I have to get the first train to London in the morning."

"I said that's fine," she repeats softly, stroking my arm and closing her eyes momentarily. "This is a lovely day."

Again I close my eyes, and let my mind drift away to the mesmeric sound of the sea lapping the pebble beach.

SEVENTY FIVE

We had a fantastic day, followed by an equally fantastic evening, streaming James Bond: Spectre in HD from Netflix, with me quaffing a rather scrumptious Hardy's Malbec and Helen a bottle of Oyster Bay Sauvignon Blanc.

This morning, having woken at 4am and disturbed Helen, I bring up her requested cup of English Breakfast, two slices of Hovis brown wholemeal with Wilkin & Sons Tiptree orange marmalade, and a glass of freshly-squeezed orange juice from my hand press.

As I walk into the bedroom, she finishes puffing up her pillows, sits upright, and grins. "Thank you for breakfast, darling," she says as she takes the tray from me and puts it on her lap. "A real treat."

"No problem. Thank you for yesterday."

As I rummage through my tallboy, she smiles, munching a mouthful of toast. "Hope all goes well at the office today."

"It'll be fine, don't worry." Though I know she will.

I pick up my pants, socks, shirt, trousers and toddle off to my shower. By the time I finish my ablutions, Helen will be back asleep until her alarm at six.

When I get downstairs I'm again greeted by Ellie and Grace, and I let them out for their final pee before I leave the house to get the 5.08 Eastbourne train to Victoria. When they come back inside, their little faces are a picture of soulfulness as they think I should be doing their breakfast, but that will have to wait until nearer seven, when Helen gets down.

I'm not a morning person – these early starts are a pain – but as I trundle down past the Greensward with the car windows down, the chilly spring morning wakens the senses. Without streetlights, the whole estate is in darkness, with only one light on in a bedroom, a hundred yards away on the other side of the green. The four benches dotted around the Greensward, from bereaved estate families, are a ghostly reminder of mortality, particularly after Helen's shooting.

At the station, the barista at the mobile café recognises me, and interrupts his stall setup to make me a double-shot latte.

Then, as I go to platform one for my Victoria train, I spot the little Polish lady from yesterday morning as she scurries toward a similarly aged man in a Vauxhall Viva – the one I remember from the 70s, not the "city car" they've recently released under the same badge. She jumps in, they kiss briefly and then drive off; her shift must have just finished.

Looking down the platform, I see the doors are open on my train, and so I wander to the front carriage and grab a quiet corner seat. It only takes fifteen minutes to drink my latte, and ten of those are after the train has set off.

Now I can just sit back, relax and get ninety minutes of shut-eye until my arrival at Victoria station.

SEVENTY SIX

It seems like no time at all when the train comes to a stop at London Victoria station. I must admit I do feel refreshed, which I think is due more to yesterday on the beach than the hour-and-a-half doze I've just enjoyed. But my calmness is jolted as I get jostled off the train, and I realise I'm back in the land of impatient, hygiene-challenged commuters.

The twenty-minute walk from here to my office is at first a zigzag through very busy main roads, followed by side roads of immaculate Victorian buildings. I always find myself thinking how nice it would be to live in one of these old houses and only a ten-minute walk from the office.

But first it's down Vauxhall Bridge Road, which is your usual busy and boring London road, and then it's left just before the BP station into Hatherley Street. This, and the next part of the walk around Vincent Square playing field and along Vincent Street, is like another world, with the aforesaid large and immaculately restored Victorian houses; way above my pay grade.

Then it's across into Fynes Street, and at the next junction I nip into the Regency Café on the corner of Page Street to grab my daily second double-shot latte and a warm almond croissant. With sustenance in hand, I continue on down Page Street and then around the corner to the front entrance of Thames House.

It's only after I've gone through the turnstile and am waiting at the lobby for the lift that I get my first work call of the day; it's 7.15am.

"Hi Suzi, I'm in reception. Shall we meet in my office in say… twenty minutes?"

"Yes, no problem, you go finish your coffee and croissant," she replies with a smile in her voice.

I get the lift to my floor, wander along the corridor, across the empty corral team room and into my corner office. Sure enough, after fifteen minutes Suzi strolls through my door.

"I hear you had a great time at Daisy's recital. Apparently the taxi service was very efficient? And then a nice day off at the beach yesterday?" she says, grinning, as she sits opposite me at my small circular meeting table.

I look up from discarding my empty cardboard cup and pastry wrapper into my waste paper bin. "Indeed. The black cab was very efficient; avoided all the busy roads." I grin back at her. "Any developments during my day off?"

"Only that we need a solution within the next few days, so we can implement it before the one-week cut off."

"Yes… and a plan B, assuming we don't make it."

We both sit silent for a moment. "In summary, then," I say, somewhat downbeat, "we either find the antidote or we shut down London's' public fresh water supply boreholes and somehow supply the same daily volume in bottled water."

"That's about the size of it," she says, "along with some form of water table draining to stop the London City basements flooding."

But before I can say more, my mobile buzzes on the table. Coops' name pops on to its screen, along with a text, which I read to myself: *"Need to speak urgent."*

I tap out a reply straight away, *"Call on the Situation Room conference number. Here with Suzi."*

In seconds, the unit in the middle of the table springs into life; again Coops' name comes up on its small LCD screen.

Suzi presses the green "call open" button. "Hi Coops, only Lucas and me, and we're discussing what options we have over the next few days on these dammed zepto-bots."

"Brilliant!" Coops replies excitedly. "Just what I need to speak to you about."

"Good news?" I chip in.

"Sort of," Coops replies uneasily. "I think I've found a way to kill the zepto-bots."

"Bloody brilliant!" I say excitedly.

Suzi, though, looks concerned. "Is that *before* the zepto-bots are in the public water supply, Coops?"

"Probably not, as even attacking them while they're in the boreholes cannot guarantee all will be killed before they get into the general supply pipes."

"But what about the UV – are we absolutely sure it won't kill them?" asks Suzi.

"I'm now certain it won't, not these new ones," replies

Coops. "There are two models of zepto-bots and I believe the ones they're using now are unaffected by anything – other than a sort of ninja zepto-bot I'm creating."

"So, what do you predict as the kill rate of your ninja bots," I ask daringly.

After a moment's thought, Coops replies, "Forty eight point seven per cent. Mainly because it's not targeted, but rather just chucking a bucket-load of them into the water supply, and crossing our fingers."

"Shit." I gently rub my face. "We will have to find a better solution."

"There is more, but definitely bad news."

"Go on, Coops," I say, a little dejected.

"The purpose of these zepto-bots is definitely to do with human genes, but it's to alter the XY chromosomes."

"What?" I say, confused.

"Basically, they make the female X chromosomes into Y chromosomes. This means all future children will be male."

"No females?"

"Nope," confirms Coops.

We fall silent for a second.

Suzi's mobile rings, her first call of the day and almost an hour after mine, at 8.10. "Oh… yes… really… okay, um… Send him up and I'll meet him at the lift." With every answer, her face expresses greater and greater concern.

She stays silent a moment, eyes darting a few times from me to the conference unit in the middle of the table, before finally settling on me.

"You okay, Suzi?" I say, concerned.

"I've just had a call from reception. You will never guess who's just strolled in, and is making his way to our floor!"

"Johnny Depp?" I say sarcastically, as he would get this reaction. "How the hell would I know?"

She pauses, giving me a tight-lipped look of mild despair.

"Pete Skinner!" she says flatly.

"Bloody hell!" For a moment I'm in shock. "Okay, as you said, meet him at the lift and bring him straight here. Coops, you give Tony a shout, and stay on the line."

"Abso-bloody-lutely, fearless leader!" replies Coops, excited, and I can hear her typing frantically, no doubt an email in capitals telling Tony to get to here pronto.

SEVENTY SEVEN

It only takes Suzi ten minutes, and she's walking back into the Situation Room with Pete.

I stand, walk over to him, and look deep into his eyes.

Unspeaking, he stares straight back at me.

For a moment I search for the right thing to say, and then I just hug him, like a long-lost brother.

As we both lean back to look at one another again, I break the ice: "What the fuck do think you're doing? You scared the living daylights out of me! Out of all of us!"

With a lopsided grin he replies, "You? Scared? I thought you were just sitting on your fat arse waiting for me to return?"

Suzi looks at us both, nonplussed, as these are not the welcoming exchanges she had expected. Pete and I smile, and I hug him again, whispering into his ear, "Bastard… but bloody glad you're okay."

"Yeah, I know," he whispers back. "All those bloody forms you'd have to fill in."

I gesture to a seat between Suzi and me. "Come on, matey, sit your arse down and bring us up to speed."

She slides a notepad and pen in front of him. "While we are talking, just scribble anything that comes to mind… anything."

As we go to sit, a voice yells from the conference phone. "Pete, it's Coops. So pleased you're okay."

"Me too," seconds Tony.

And, leaning toward the speakerphone, Pete replies, "Trust you guys are looking after my 'doughnut'?"

"Well, our bit, certainly," replies Coops. "Your bit is still out of bounds, and has 24-hour armed guards wandering around."

"So, Pete…" I say, staring at him. "What's been going on?"

SEVENTY EIGHT

Pete leans forward and rests his chin on clenched, praying hands. "Simple answer: they have the latest zepto-bots, and those have been introduced into an underground freshwater stream in Kent."

I lean toward him with a comforting gesture, and look into his eyes. "We know," I say gently, "but what's their endgame?"

"I hoped you would know about Kent," he replies with a half-smile, "but I've overheard they're also going to target the aquifer below New York!"

"Bloody hell!" Suzi gasps.

"Christ," I blurt. "Suzi, you best get hold of Mike and bring him up to speed."

"On it." And Suzi walks out into the corridor to call Mike on her mobile.

"So." I turn back to Pete. "Where have you been, and did you manage to find out anything else?"

"Not much, I'm afraid," Pete says, dejected. "Spent most of my time blindfolded in the back of a van and with headphones playing Classic FM. They only needed me for access – they already knew a hell of a lot about the zepto-bots."

"But they had your codes as well, and you used your coercion code!"

He looks at me like he's been caught scrumping. "I had to; they have eyes on Katrina!" Then he starts welling up.

Few people know about Katrina, who was born to a beautiful, dark-haired and olive-skinned Italian lady from Lake Garda. The fact of Katrina's existence was even kept from Pete until, in her late teens, she decided to track him down. That was after he had been married to, and subsequently divorced from, an English woman from Minchinhampton, Gloucestershire.

He told me in confidence, in case anything should happen to him. Considering his job, he wanted it to remain secret at least until he retired; then he would try to mend fences with her mother.

"Come on, mate, let's get some coffee – have you eaten?"

"Coffee's fine, but I will need a few sugars!"

I lean toward the conference phone. "Coops, Tony, I'm going to grab a coffee with Pete, we'll touch base again later."

"No problem," says Coops. "Keep well, Pete."

"Likewise," echoes Tony.

I close the conference call and Pete and I get up and exit the Situation Room.

"Coffee?" I mouth, nudging Suzi as we pass her just outside in the corridor.

Muting her phone, she says, "No, I'm fine. You'll get a call from Mike in a second."

I turn to take us to the canteen, but Pete puts a hand in his pocket, and mouths at Suzi, "Is that Mike?"

"Yes, why?"

Pete drops something small into Suzi's hand. "You and he will need this," he says, crestfallen, as we all look at the micro thumb-drive in her palm. "It's their demands."

Suzi turns in her tracks. "Hang on a second, Mike, call you back." She immediately returns to the Situation Room and speed-dials Coops, as Pete and I take our seats next to her.

Before Coops answers, Suzi picks up the memory stick and pushes it into the conference's USB data hub.

"Who plugged that in?" Coops squawks. "Where's it from?"

I lean forward. "It's a memory stick from Pete which contains the demands of the gang. Treat it as hostile; don't let any viruses escape."

"Don't worry," she replies, "it's locked down better than Bruce Forsyth's wig cupboard!"

"I'll leave you and Suzi to have a look at this and advise, once you're happy to open it, Coops."

"No problem, Master, go get Pete a coffee!"

"We'll be in the canteen." Pete and I wander out of the Situation Room and along the corridor toward the café.

A few minutes later, we've just sat at a small square table in the canteen, when Mike's name comes up on my phone.

"What the bejesus is going on, Lucas?"

"Hi, Mike. I'm in the canteen de-briefing Pete, but the bottom line is, you need to cancel your BA flight, and get your private jet fuelled and your ass over to New York sharpish."

"What the heck?" shouts Mike.

"Zepto-bots are going to be put in New York's fresh water supply."

"Holy crap! What's your plan?"

"Let me finish with Pete, whilst you just get your plane, UK, and NY teams mobilised. And speak to your water authority in New York, as you're probably gonna need their help."

"Okay, buddy, but for Christ's sake call me back pronto with something more concrete, cos jeez I'm gonna get some serious flack!"

"Will do."

I close the call and look at Pete, who's again got his head in his hands. Speaking in a near whisper, he looks at me. "What the hell have I done, Lucas?"

"Nothing we wouldn't all do, and nothing we can't fix."

"God I hope so, Lucas; this has gone seriously tits-up!"

"Before we do anything else–" I squeeze his wrist hard, "–look at me mate, do they have Katrina or are they only eyes-on?"

"I'm pretty sure they are just watching her."

"Good. Let's get back to the Situation Room and you can give her details to Coops and Tony, and they'll send out a grab team to make her safe. Is there anyone else we need to pick up? Any more leverage they could have?"

"No one."

"You sure?"

"Yes," he says with a tear rolling down his cheek. "She's my world. Nothing and no one else even comes close."

"Okay, let's get back."

We go to the café, which has just opened for the day, and get some coffees, a couple of chocolate bars and a few rounds of cellophane-wrapped sandwiches, and make our way back up the corridor to the Situation Room.

SEVENTY NINE

Suzi gives Pete a supportive smile, whilst talking to Coops and Tony on a conference call. At a pause in the conversation, I interject, "Hi Coops, Tony. I'm back with Pete. We need to trace his daughter, Katrina." Suzi looks at me in astonishment, and I hear a little gasp from Coops. "I'll hand over to Pete."

Pete leans a little nearer the conference phone, as if not wanting anyone else to overhear. "Hi, Coops, Tony."

"Hi Pete. Don't worry, we'll soon have her safe with you at Thames," Coops replies.

"I'm fine. Just need to get Katrina to safety."

"Of course," Tony says comfortingly. "What can you tell us about Katrina and her whereabouts?"

"Well. She lives in Minchinhampton, and has a gift shop in Cirencester." This brings him near to tears, but, slowly lifting his head, he takes a breath, and gives them her mobile number.

"That's great," says Coops as she taps away on her keyboard. "What about a description?"

Pete sighs again. "She's 5'6", slim, has dark, shoulder-length, wavy hair, and she loves anything blue."

There's a second's silence, then Coops says, "Bet she's wearing something blue then?"

This makes Pete smile. "Oh yes, she's bound to be wearing something blue, and probably trainers."

"Ah, my kind of girl, practicality over fashion."

Pete gives a heartfelt chuckle. "Absolutely."

But almost immediately he's sullen again. "You will find Kat, won't you, Coops?"

"Already got her mobile triangulated, and Tony's just sent this to our local team to go pick her up – she's in Café Nero, Market Place, Cirencester."

Pete leans back in his seat, looks to the ceiling, closes his eyes and gives a sigh of relief as he blinks away a tear. "And call her Kat, then she'll know you've spoken to me."

"Okay, Pete, will do." Coops continues. "I presume it's alright with you if we take the line of you falling ill?"

"Whatever you think best, Coops," Pete replies

appreciatively. "Just get to her quickly… and get her here."

I gently pat Pete's forearm. "Don't worry, matey, Coops has it all in hand."

Then I lean forward to the conference phone. "Coops, what's the latest on the memory stick Pete gave us?"

"Um… bad news I'm afraid."

"Go on."

"Bottom line is, the zepto-bots introduced to the London aquifer are moving to plan, and those destined for New York are believed to be landing at JFK soon."

"So, definitely a second batch?" I turn to Pete for confirmation, and he nods.

"Yes," replies Coops sullenly.

I stare at Pete, who's again looking at the ceiling, as if for divine inspiration, and gently shake his wrist. "Are you aware of any more info on this?"

"Maybe," he answers, looking at me apologetically like a naughty child.

"What else do you know?" I say with a tinge of frustration.

"They mentioned something about New Croton and Kensico, which I think are reservoirs in the States."

I give an exasperated sigh, then turn again towards the conference phone. "I presume you got that, Coops?"

"Indeed, working on it now. They're two huge reservoirs bordering New York State and Connecticut. From there they feed aquifers which supply New York's fresh water. They're some 35 miles north of central New York. Loads more info popping up, but I need time to assimilate."

"Okay. Keep on it, Coops, you too, Tony, I want to know all the intel you can get on the water supply and associated communications, and what options we have to counter the UK threat. And I want a two-hourly update."

"No problem," Coops and Tony reply in near unison.

"Anything else on the thumb-drive, Coops?"

"Yes, Lucas." I can hear the unease in her voice. "There's a ransom demand addressed to our governments of £100m from us, and $150m from the US."

I sit back in my seat looking first at Pete, then Suzi, and finally the conference phone. "Okay, I guess that's nailed it; this ransom gives the entire case total credence."

Any threat must have credence before we can be certain our countermeasures will have an effect, and we use the term credence literally – credible threat and confidence in our analysis of the threat.

"Okay, Coops." I glance again at Pete. "You and Tony do your thing and let us know as soon as Kat's on her way here, and when you've got more on the goons in New York."

"No problem," replies Coops. "And I think we need to share with Mike soonest."

"Absolutely." I look at Suzi. "You apprise Mike, and we'll all speak again later." And I close the call.

Yawning, I look at Pete again. "I need you to debrief with Suzi and me for ten minutes, and then I need to get my arse over to Mike's office, so I can go and support him in New York."

Then turning to Suzi, "As usual, I need you to run the op this side of the pond, along with Coops and Tony."

"No problem," she replies.

Pete slides the notepad she gave him earlier back in front of her. All the time we've been talking, he's been scribbling – maps, diagrams and bullet points.

A heavily underlined comment catches my eye: *"Women under the age of 34 – UK 14M and US 70M".*

We stay in the Situation Room for just under ten minutes while Pete runs us through his notes, and then I leave for my office.

EIGHTY

Just as I get to my office door, my mobile rings. "Hi, Mike, I was just going to–"

"Yeah, yeah, what the heck is going on, Lucas? I have teams mobilised, Black Hawk ready and our G650 waiting at Heathrow!"

"We will need all of that, and some bloody luck as well."

"Come on, spill!"

"There's way too much to talk through on the phone." I gasp as I run up the corridor, having grabbed my coat. "Trust me, it's all in hand and you'll get a summary email from Suzi in five minutes. I'm on my way over to you. Oh, and we need to stop off en route, at Kemble."

"What? Where the hell is Kemble?"

"Just get you and me to Heathrow. See you in ten."

"Okay buddy. This better be good!"

"Good! It's the biggest disaster our countries have faced since 9/11! Look, I've got to go."

"Well, get your limey ass over here and brief me."

I close the call and redial Alex. "Get the car round the front now, I'm coming down. Need to get to the FBI yesterday."

"No problem, Lucas. I'll be at the front door in two minutes, I'm just–"

I close the call before he's finished talking.

At just before 9.45, with blues and two's, all four tyres of the Audi screech and we take off like a bat out of hell for the American Embassy in Upper Grosvenor Street.

EIGHTY ONE

Somehow, thanks to Alex's driving, it's only a smidge under five minutes until I find myself being marshalled through the US Embassy's high-security cordon, then through a rear entrance, and finally into a lift up to the FBI's office.

As I jog up the corridor, I damn-near bowl Mike over when he dives out of his office.

"Slow down, buddy," he says to me. "No need to panic. The cream of the FBI are on the case now."

I turn around and follow Mike back down the corridor towards the lift. "Oh, thank the Lord. I thought it was just your team of KMAs."

"Damn limey's gotta nerve! And how'd you know about Kiss My Ass for retirees?"

"It was when Matt was having a few beers with Dan and a couple of his pals – apparently a fab time had by all." I smile at the thought. "But the two things which stuck in my mind are your nicknames for retirees, and women agents (breast FED's) – totally non-PC, but funny all the same."

"I'd like to see you tell that one to Suzi!"

"I can be daft, but not that daft!"

Mike looks at me with his grizzly bear face. "What's the latest? Coops said two goons with a tin of zepto-bots have flown to JFK?"

"Indeed. Info from a memory stick Pete gave her!"

"So, what gives?"

"We need to get to JFK soonest."

My phone rings. "Hi Coops. News?"

"Yep. I see you're with Mike; well, your phones are next to one another. Let him know that the goons' plan for JFK includes Volga-Dnepr cargo. It may be their way off the airport, or a way home – I don't know!" She sounds out of breath. "I've got to fly and get these modified bots sorted. Bye."

"Thanks. I'll tell–" but she's gone.

I turn to Mike. "Coops says the goons' plan may include them going to a Volga-Dnepr hangar. A cargo hangar?"

Mike shakes his head, pulls out his phone and hits a speed

dial button. "Hi… yep, it's me… the goons' plan may include Volga-Dnepr… Port Authority, NYPD, and five FBI teams… okay, keep local airport security up to speed – and out of the way!"

He then turns to me. "You probably got the gist." I nod. "There's gonna be dozens of our guys covering the hangars and airport boundary."

"That's no small feat!"

"Ya tellin' me. The hangars alone total 1.7 million square feet!"

We get into the lift and head for the rooftop helipad. The rotors are already near liftoff speed as, heads bowed, we run across the pad and jump through the main door into our waiting Black Hawk. We strap in and the attending navigator checks we're buckled up before advising the pilot to "launch it".

As with my now regular experience of US pilots, we are thrust down into our seats as the kite's famous climb rate is tested, then we disappear into the night. In seconds we are whizzing over Hyde Park and the Serpentine, the Round Pond, and then Kensington Palace; taking the path as the crow flies, as they say.

"Okay, buddy," says Mike, looking at me as he speaks into the intercom, "We're set to pick up our G650 from Heathrow and then haul ass to JFK."

"Don't forget you need to make a tiny detour, to pick up some bits from Coops."

"No problem… Kemble?" He turns again to look at me. "Where precisely?"

"Kemble airbase, in forty minutes."

"Cool. What's the cargo?"

"Zepto-bots," I say calmly.

"What the heck? You wanna take more of these bastard things on *my* plane?"

"These ones are different as they will carry an antidote."

"Holy crap! Antidote – what the hell is going on!?"

"It really should not be a problem."

"You used the word *should*?" Mike shakes his head.

"You're right, it's just one of a couple of options, which aren't finalised, but should be by the time we get to JFK. I hope."

Mike shakes his head again. "Shit – now you're using the word *hope*!" He's just about to go off on one when my mobile rings. It's Suzi.

"Hi, Lucas. Don't forget Kemble!" she says, reasonably chirpy.

"I won't. How's it coming along?"

"Coops has a package of zepto-bots – well, a small baked bean can – and Pete's helped her program them!"

"Do we have enough of Coops' zepto-bots?"

"Well, not for the whole population of London," she says, downbeat.

"So you've a plan to target women only?"

"Ah. Slight snag there, as water supply is agnostic."

"So that's it then?" I say, frustrated.

"But these zepto-bots will reverse the chromosome change, and kill the goon's bots by introducing an antibiotic, so it is only the targeting issue to solve." She says trying to sound more positive.

"What exactly are these little bastards programmed to do?"

"They will change the female XX chromosome to YY. This will ensure all offspring are male XY. Any YY chromosome fertilisation results in a non-viable pregnancy."

"What? How?"

"Sorry, the explanation from Pete and Coops got very technical, very quickly. I've told them to précis it and then Coops will email you, or discuss when you meet up at Kemble."

"Okay, but get her to send the email pronto as I need to brief Mike."

"Will do."

I close the call and look out of the window to my left, to see the Twickenham stadium. It reminds me of our company visit there a few weeks ago and watching England giving Uruguay a drubbing – but it should be easy when you play against a team of builders, clerks and mechanics.

But quickly my thoughts return to the task in hand: how the hell can we target only women, and why the hell do we need antibiotics?

EIGHTY TWO

At just before 10.15am, we are starting our descent into Heathrow. Again I find myself daydreaming as I look out of my window and take in the sheer scale of the airport.

This fascination, which I've had from childhood, has stayed with me. Although now I'm not staring through a plate glass window on the passenger side, but rather blasting along the south side of the airport only a hundred feet off the deck.

At this distance, some 300 feet to my left, are the Volga-Dnepr 747-8 freighters. They're massive, and at £380 million each, they need to be kept busy.

The pilot brings me back to reality. "This is as close as I can get; they're pretty hot on sticking to the helipad markings."

"No problem, buddy, even we can walk the 150 feet from here," says Mike. We grab our overnight bags and jump out onto the tarmac, again instinctively ducking the rotors.

The silhouette of the black Gulfstream G650 stands out 50 yards away, with engines ticking over. Bright blue LED lights on the edge of the step treads lead up to its open door. There are two armed agents at the bottom of the stairway and one at the top, all looking anxious, as their precious cargo, Mike and I, jog across to the waiting craft.

As we enter the luxurious leather-clad plane, an immaculate, white-jacketed steward turns first to me, and then Mike. "Welcome aboard. Please take your seats and buckle up as we've been given permission for immediate take-off."

"No problem, buddy." replies Mike as he wanders off down the aisle. Looking back over his shoulder, he calls, "Any chance of a couple of decent lattes, steward?"

"As soon as we're in level flight, sir."

We sling our cases up into the overhead locker, take our seats and, following the gently pulsing instruction on the orange sign over the cockpit door, buckle up.

"Ya still like my flying taxi?" Mike gloats.

"I can only dream of such resources," I reply with more than a hint of jealousy.

"No wobbles about our previous adventure with the G650?"

"Nooo," I reply with a slight tremble in my voice.

My mind flashes back to that *adventure*, our 'Misdirection' case, where we were travelling around in a G650, the updated model recently reapproved after engine failures with several planes. Then to top that, as part of the case, Mike authorised two to be shot down. And that experience has left me with an unreasonable fear of the G650.

Already I'm already feeling nauseous, which never happens on other planes.

In minutes we are taxiing, and then, in a seemingly fluid movement, we're accelerating down the runway. The rumbling wheel noise stops as we become airborne and a gentle humpback bridge feeling ripples across my stomach.

The plane turns as it accelerates skyward, and we start our 3,470-mile journey to JFK.

Mike turns to me. "Not long and we'll be home in New York."

"Can't wait. If we can wrap this case up quickly, perhaps you can treat me to another legendary New York steak?"

"Sure thing, buddy."

After a few minutes, the plane levels, the seatbelt lamp goes off, and the steward makes his way to us. "Would you like anything with the lattes, maybe some bear claws?"

"Oh yes, please." I grin back at the steward. "I presume they have raisins as well as almonds?"

"Definitely." He smiles, gently nodding.

"Quite the aficionado of the American staple – after doughnuts, of course?" Mike grins.

"Indeed. Any pastry with almonds to be honest."

Mike turns his attention back to the steward. "A couple of large Amarettos as well, please."

"Not a problem. With ice?"

"No way, it'll water it down," Mike replies, and I chuckle, having had the same thought.

The steward disappears into the rear galley and Mike and I get our iPhones and iPads out of our man-bags.

"So?" Mike nudges me. "Got that email I need to read?"

"Bouncing it to you now."

For the next few minutes, Mike furrows his brow as he reads

the information from Coops. The steward returns with our hot and cold drinks, and *massive* bear claws, which are put on the shelves either side of us.

Mike turns to me, stabbing a forefinger at his iPad to a perplexing paragraph of Coops' report. "This bit about the antibiotic is great!" he says, and he leans a little closer. "Will this really work? Antibiotics kill the zepto-bots' organic power supply?"

"If Coops says so, it will, and she's got Pete as backup; the inventor of this technology."

"This shit is inspired!"

"But there's still the problem of targeting one gender," I remind him.

"Well, it is for you guys… they're already in your water supply."

"Thanks," I reply with mock resentment.

"Come on, I'm only joshing."

"Yes. And if we don't catch these goons in New York, you're going to have the same problem."

At that thought Mike's face drops, as, with no word from his office back home, this is becoming a distinct possibility.

EIGHTY THREE

It's just gone 11am when the peace is broken by the pilot coming on the radio: "Approaching Kemble. Cleared for landing in four minutes."

My phone vibrates and, looking at its screen, a little envelope icon tells me I have email. Sure enough, there's one from Coops, and I open it.

Hi Lucas. These are brief notes on the plan so far, should the zepto-bots get into the NY drinking water system. Obviously the same plan for the UK, but in both cases we need a method for targeting only one gender with our reprogrammed zepto-bots. The options for NY are similar to the UK with the goons probably introducing the zepto-bots on the outskirts of NY. Talking to our water expert Rebecca, this is most likely the Jerome or Hillview reservoirs. I'll be at Kemble before 11am as it's taken a little longer than hoped to test the microscopic little sods.

The attachment to the email is a single page of A4 but summarises Pete's research paper, which is over ten thousand words. To be fair, I don't need to understand all the technicalities, but it does help to get a handle on the basics, just in case something goes pear-shaped – as it often does.

I turn to Mike and speak over the intercom. "Just forwarding you an email from Coops."

"Okay." After a few moments he turns to me, waving his mobile. "Holy crap, so this is why you want me to liaise with our water guys. And what the bloody hell is she going on about 'targeting a gender'?"

"Long explanation, and I suggest we wait until we're on the leg to JFK. Zepto-bots must target females."

In a rare, almost calm moment, Mike replies, "Okay, buddy. If Coops and Suzi are on the case, I'm happy to wait a little while longer."

It never ceases to amaze me how Suzi and Coops seem to put people at their ease.

EIGHTY FOUR

The pilot flies the G650 low over the 29 Regiment Royal Logistic Corps/Joint Air Mounting Centre (RLC/JAMC) at South Cerney, swooping low over Kemble railway station, before finally dropping fast into RAF Kemble.

We still refer to it as RAF Kemble despite it being privately purchased from the MOD in 2001 and changing name in 2009 when it became the Cotswold Airport. It is the spiritual home of the UK's Red Arrows, though it has been the repair shop for Thunderbolts and many other planes over the years. First coming into service with the RAF in 1938, it still has a runway long enough to accommodate a Boeing 747.

It's not the nearest meeting point to GCHQ, but Coops lives just around the corner. In fact, she parks her 48-year-old Beagle Pup 150 here, having known the airfield's owner since she was at nursery. I've been up with her in the Pup, and her flying skills near match her wizardry on the computer.

It's the only time I've seen her truly relax, and she has a magical smile when piloting. It's to do with the memory of her late dad flying one, and her Pup's birthday being the same as his, June 1967. She always says to me when mentioning her lovely little plane, painted in her dad's favourite petrol blue and silver, that she only wished he were here to be passenger. But unfortunately cancer took him a few years ago.

The G650 landing, though near perfect, jolts me from my reminiscing. Looking out of my port window, I can see Coops' Fiat 500.

Whilst the plane is still slowly moving, the steward drops the passenger door down, and she excitedly runs up the steps, along the aisle and plonks herself opposite Mike and me. "Hi, Lucas. Hi, Mike."

"How are you, Coops?"

She just grins at me, and then leaps forward, giving me another of her bear hugs.

Mike smiles. "I wish my team gave me a hug now and then!"

Coops lets go of me, and turns to Mike with a cheeky grin. "I'll ask Dan to give you a hug!"

We all laugh at the thought of that happening.

"So." I nudge Coops. "What have you got for us?"

"Well. Pete says this is the most practical method of transport, looks ordinary, and will be humorous when you open the tin."

I take the Heinz tin from her and show it to Mike. He looks completely nonplussed.

"These are the zepto-bots, Mike – carrying the antibiotic."

Mike looks at the tin's label, and suddenly gets Pete's joke. "Ah, you can spill the beans!"

Again we all have a chuckle, which is not bad going, given the situation.

I frown as I look at Coops. "Any more thoughts on resolving the zepto-bots in the UK?"

"No, not yet," she sighs. "How the hell can we target one gender in the entire population of London? That's 770,000 females under 34!"

"Guys, you gotta tell me what's going on here. And why 'under 34'?" Mike jumps in.

Coops looks at him impassively. "The bulk of adults bearing children are younger than 34." She pauses a second. "Lucas can explain the details over the Atlantic. It won't take too long, but you need the whole story."

"But you're the one with the inside track–"

She just leans over, gives him a hug and kisses him on the cheek, which stops him in his tracks.

Then she starts to make her way down the aisle. At the top of the exit she turns to us, smiles, gives a brief queen-like wave and then disappears down the steps.

The steward closes the door behind her, and the captain announces our immediate departure.

EIGHTY FIVE

The pilot taxis the G650 the last few hundred feet to the runway, opens the taps, and we rocket off on the next leg of our journey to New York.

We make our way to the stateroom at the rear of the plane. It was only some six months ago I was in Mike's "Air Taxi", as he refers to it, but even since then it's had a tech upgrade: the walls and ceiling are entirely covered by 8k super-high-resolution monitors, curved to match the fuselage. But the highly polished wood trim and leather seating remain, as do the concealed armament cupboards and extra wide armrests, which hold the Glocks, and a discreet under-seat drawer for the Heckler & Koch MP7s.

We've no sooner got our iPads and iPhones on the table than the steward knocks. Two lattes, and yet another two pastries; obviously our tiredness and lack of sustenance is showing. He checks if anything else is required and, with nothing more to do, advises he will be at the front of the plane, grabbing a few minutes' sleep; apparently we're not the only ones pulling double shifts!

As soon as the stateroom door is closed, Mike looks at me expectantly: "So, come on then, give me the down-low?"

"The short answer is that in the UK, the goons' zepto-bots have been introduced into an underground stream, which then feeds the major aquifer which supplies the drinking water of the City of London."

"And what exactly are these little bastards programmed to do?"

"They will somehow infect the population of London."

"Infect? With what?"

"Well, not so much infect… they are programmed to change the female XX chromosome to YY. This will ensure all offspring are male XY. Any YY chromosome fertilisation results in a non-viable pregnancy."

"Holy shit!" Mike blurts, sitting back in his seat with his palms on the table.

"Holy shit indeed."

"How the hell are we gonna stop these little critters getting into domestic water?"

"Well, in the case of London we can't, not without risking the City flooding."

"What?" says Mike indignantly.

"The fresh water supply for London is taken from the aquifer through boreholes. They were unused for several decades until it was realised the water table was rising and threatening the basements of buildings, particularly in the financial areas." I pause for a moment, rubbing my brow. "Therefore, if we turn off the boreholes, we again risk flooding the capital as well as causing a massive logistical problem of providing bottled fresh water."

"Hell, this is some kinda nightmare catch-22."

"Indeed. Following some modelling by Coops and Pete, and our water expert, we've decided the only option is to allow these zepto-bots into the water supply, and find some way of targeting the YY chromosome-affected females, to correct their chromosome to XX."

During my pause, Mike has caught up. "Ah. Male has XY but only affected females will have YY?"

"Exactly. We only have a limited supply of old zepto-bots that we can reprogram to make this change, and they will change all Y to X, hence we need to target only females. We don't want to change male XY to XX. Somehow we've got to find a way, and Coops, Suzi and Pete will get no sleep until a solution is found!"

"So the antibiotics aren't the solution?"

"No, they're purely there to kill the zepto-bots' organic process in their electrical power unit, which is derived from an organic complex carbon battery. This will happen after the chromosome changes are made."

"This sounds like science fiction!" says Mike, perplexed.

"As Arthur C Clarke said, 'Any sufficiently advanced technology is indistinguishable from magic.'"

We both sit back in our seats, and finish our coffee and pastries, while Mike fidgets with the Heinz tin he's taken from the middle of the table. "Who would have thought… It's like war of the worlds, but with electronic bugs trying to kill off mankind?"

"Pretty much – certainly for London if Coops and the team don't find a solution."

Shaking his head, Mike picks up his phone and calls Dan to bring him up to speed and reinforce the urgency of catching these goons at JFK.

We leave the stateroom and make our way back down the aisle to our seats for some shut-eye. Coops or Suzi will get hold of me soon as they have anything.

EIGHTY SIX

I've been asleep for about an hour when my phone vibrates in my breast pocket, but I'm so knackered it barely wakes me. Bleary-eyed, I look round and see Mike is still asleep, and the steward is pottering about in the forward galley.

I get up and quietly move down the gangway to the stateroom. Halfway there I click the green button and whisper, "Hi, Coops. Wait a second." Once in the room, and after closing the door quietly behind me, I ask Coops to continue.

"Just woken up have we, Mr Sleepy Head?"

"How did you guess?" I say, yawning a smile.

"Well, good news, my fearless leader."

"Excellent. You've found a way to target affected females?"

"Uh, no."

"So what *is* the news?"

"The goons are going to target the Hillview reservoir!"

"Blimey, Coops, how do you know?"

"I managed to hack into their plane's voice recording software, located the flight attendant call button above our goons' seats and set their mic to permanently on." She gives a small snort. "Without activating the lamp." She pauses a second. "It's taken a while, but I've picked up a few words in Russian about Hillview reservoir."

"Brilliant. I presume you've not told Mike, as he's still slumbering in his chair."

"Thought I'd let you have the pleasure."

"How's the team?"

"Suzi, Tony, and Pete are grabbing some zeds. I said I'd call you, and then I'll turn in for an hour as well."

"Don't blame you. Maybe fresh minds will give some fresh ideas?"

"Hope so, because at the moment we've all drawn a blank."

"How's Jeff doing, Coops?"

"We're letting him deal with the politics; the Home Secretary is being an arse, as is the Mayor of London!"

"Can't blame them. This is the biggest crisis they've had for the City since the threat of flooding before they built the

Thames Barrier."

"Indeed, and that was back in '82, before I was born!"

"You're just a puppy." We chuckle. "It was quite a feat of engineering at the time, spanning 520 yards, protecting fifty square miles of central London, and costing a mere £500 million pounds!"

"Dread to think of the cost of this little escapade if we cock it up!"

"Billions, I should think, Coops; or possibly the whole UK economy if we flood London's financial districts."

"Okay, I'm off for some kip," she says, yawning, which sets me off again.

"I'll grab some coffee and bring Mike up to speed. Speak later."

I close the call, and put my phone down next to the iPad, aligning them squarely on the table. Yawning again, I wander out of the room. Walking down the gangway, I pass the gently snoring Mike and, when I get to the steward, I request yet more coffee and something hot.

"No problem, Mr Norton. I've bacon bagels?"

"Superb! I'll wake Mike and we'll have the drinks and food in the stateroom."

"No problem," says the steward cheerily, and with no sign of fatigue. Mind you, he's in his mid-twenties and probably needs a fraction of the sleep we old guys do.

I go and sit back in my seat, as there's little to do until I update Mike.

EIGHTY SEVEN

Mike really is like a big ol' bear in many ways, not just stature, as at the moment he's snoring like Baloo. It seems a shame to wake him but, judging by his twitching nose, he's already smelt the bacon bagels.

I get up, and, standing next to the gently snoring bear, I nudge him and whisper, "Bacon bagels and latte."

It grumbles, shifts in its seat, opens one weary eye, and half-consciously sniffs and gently licks its lips. "Do I smell bacon?"

"Indeed you do, and a latte."

"Fantastic, just what the doctor ordered."

"The steward's bringing it to the meeting room. See you there in ten minutes?"

"No problem. But first I need the head."

I leave Mike stretching as I walk off up the aisle to the stateroom, and when I look back, there he is rubbing his back against a wall cupboard. I smile to myself: Baloo!

As I'm checking my emails, the door opens and Mike comes in and sits opposite, closely followed by the steward with a tray. After placing the plate of four bulging bacon bagels and two large lattes on the table, the steward slides the now empty tray under his arm and looks at Mike. "Anything else, sir?"

"No thanks, buddy," says Baloo, licking his lips. "This looks A-okay."

Smiling, the steward leaves and Mike sinks his teeth into one of the bagels. I'm a little slow off the mark as I take one of the paper napkins and put it on my lap, along with a paper tea plate onto which I place one of the bagels and cut it into quarters.

Mike grins at me. With his mouth full, he begins, "Very ladylike, you–" but he's suddenly interrupted by a piece of tomato-sauce-covered bacon as it drops out of his bagel, bounces onto his tie, and then onto his white shirt, before landing in the centre of his lap.

It all seems to happen in slow motion, and during the bacon bit's journey his face moves from surprise to shock/horror, and then anger. He chucks the bagel back onto the large oval plate in the middle of the table, and looks up at me as he's trying to remove the blood-red stains from his clothing. "Don't say a word… not one goddamn word."

"Sorry, I was only going to offer you a napkin," I reply, with a laugh gurgling in my throat. Mike scowls for a few seconds, and then likewise starts to laugh.

When he's finished cleaning himself up, he looks at me, as I slowly consume my last quarter of bagel. "So, any news from your gals?"

"Nothing as yet, but Coops is monitoring everything, and will no doubt call me when I start my second bagel."

"She's good… but not that good."

Just as I'm picking up another segment, my mobile rings. "Bloody hell, it's Coops!" I shout, putting my mobile on speaker. But in my hurry to swallow my mouthful of bagel, I start to cough.

Mike's so surprised he splutters some coffee down his tie before starting to choke, causing him to spit a lump of masticated bagel onto the table. He too then starts choking.

"Lucas? Lucas?" shouts a concerned Coops. "Are you two okay?"

"Don't worry, it's just Mike inhaling a bagel."

He looks up at me as he grabs a napkin to dab his watery eyes. "Jesus, guys, you trying to choke me to death?"

"I only rang to give you an update," she says, sounding hurt.

"It wasn't you, Coops, it was me," I say, grinning at Mike. "I had only just commented on your expert tracking skills, and I said you'd probably call before I could eat my bagel – and, almost immediately, you rang."

Mike, having finished his convulsions, says, smiling, "That's right, hun, just you surprising me with your skills again."

We laugh for a minute, and then Coops continues, "So, want my news?"

But before I can answer, Mike's phone starts to jig across the table. "Hi, Dan. What's up, bud?"

I pick up my mobile. "Hang on a second, Coops," I say, "Mike's got a call from Dan."

Then we get a few a-has until Mike, explaining Coops is on another line, closes the call. He puts his phone back on the table. "Dan's had an update from the local Bears and Barneys on the case, with every route from JFK to Hillview reservoir eyes-on. Just in case they give us the slip from the hangar."

"Mike," teases Coops, "that sounds like an attempt at cockney slang?"

"Wow, something you guys *don't* know?" smirks Mike.

"I guess the Bears are cops." I get this from watching Smokey and the Bandit many times in my youth. "But Barneys?"

"Well, the slang Barneys comes from TV – Barney Fife on The Andy Griffith Show of the 60s – it was great: won five Emmys!"

"Blimey, Mike, good memory!" I grin.

And Coops chips in, "I wasn't even a twinkle!"

"Yup." He shrugs off the cheeky comments. "Don Knotts played an inept cop brilliantly; born in 1924 and passed in 2006."

There's a brief silence whilst Mike reminisces.

"So – want some news?" Coops gets us back on topic.

"Yes please." I answer.

"Well, I got hold of the steward on their plane, and got him to serve them iced fruitcake, and, after *accidentally* dropping some on the floor, smear a little marzipan on their shoes." I sit back in my chair, part-covering my mouth with my hand, trying unsuccessfully to stifle a laugh.

"Nice, huh?" chuckles Coops.

"What's so damn funny?" says Mike, looking at me.

"Have you not heard of this trick?" I ask, surprised.

"No," replies Mike grumpily.

"Go on, Coops, you tell him, it's your idea."

"Well, you know the old-style sniffers and wipes customs use for plastic explosives and so on?" she says.

"Yeah," replies Mike with a confused frown.

"Almond marzipan sets them off in the same way as C4!"

Mike grins like a kid, and slaps the table with his palm. "Jesus, Coops, fantastic!"

"One I got from my old Master," she says with a chuckle.

"Less of the old, thank you madam," I say with mock indignation.

"So, customs should definitely pick 'em up," chirps Mike, impressed. "Nice one, liddle lady."

"Your John Wayne is getting quite good," Coops teases.

We close the call, thanking Coops for her foresight, and quickly scoff our coffee and bagels while they're still warm, this time without spillage. It won't be long before the goons land at JFK, as they are only an hour or so ahead of us. If they manage to get out of the airport then we really do have a problem. I just hope the Bears and Barneys are on their A game.

But it won't hurt to "have a backup plan", as Jeff would say, "and keep refreshing it until you finish the game".

Always sounded like overkill to me when I first worked with him, but I soon learnt.

EIGHTY EIGHT

Mike fast-dials Dan and puts his phone on speaker.

"Hi Mike," Dan says cheerily. "Have you been updated by Coops?"

"Yep," replies Mike with a gentle chuckle. "She's on the money with this marzipan trick."

"Very nearly." Dan's tone sounds a little downbeat. "The goons got pulled in customs, but somehow, after being there for an hour, they got out fifteen minutes ago."

"Hell! What's wrong with the customs guys!" shouts Mike, banging a fist on the table.

"Dunno, they just said several people got picked up by the sniffer. They thought there must be a technical problem with it. Then they got a phone call from the Senior Partner at a law firm called Whyte & Chase, and they let our perps go!"

"Bullshit," says Mike, and we share a knowing glance. "I bet they sussed the steward and themselves marzipanned a few other guys!"

"What's our ETA, Mike?"

"Dunno, I guess an hour… I'll check with the pilot." Then he scowls. "Dan, where the hell are these goons now?"

"We're tracking them on CCTV, and the Bears and Barneys have put out a BOLO (Be On the Look Out). We've got all our teams on alert, and the FBI are monitoring comms traffic and CCTV."

"Okay, sounds like you've got the bases covered," replies Mike confidently. "Make damn sure you liaise with Coops and Suzi as they seem to be ahead of the curve!"

I can't resist a smile as Mike again acknowledges the skill of my two ladies.

The call is closed and Mike goes off to speak to the pilot, and no doubt give him the hurry-up.

I take this opportunity to phone home.

EIGHTY NINE

It's nearing 9am in the morning in New York and 2pm at home; the US being five hours behind the UK.

The home phone rings half a dozen times before it's answered. "Hi," says a laid-back Daisy.

"Hello sweetheart, how are you?"

"Dad! I'm fine, how are you, how's America?"

"Not quite there." I look at my watch. "A few hours yet. How's Mum doing, and your sister?"

"Molly's her usual high-maintenance self, and even more stressy than usual... Just because I broke the screen on her iPhone, it wasn't my fault!" she says indignantly. I guess it's just the way of sisters, or brothers for that matter, though I was effectively an only sibling, as my sister is fourteen years older than me, and so more like a second mum.

"How about Mum?"

"Don't know," Daisy replies in a tetchy tone.

"Can you put her on?"

"No."

"Why not?"

"She's not here. Went out last night with one of her WI friends. Not seen her this morning."

"Maybe she's just popped outside?"

"No. I'm not stupid, I've checked everywhere."

I get an overwhelming sense of Daisy's false anger, which can only mean one thing.

"Don't worry, I'll phone Mum's mobile."

"Okay."

"Sorry, I've got to go, as I need to have a quick word with Mum. I'll speak to you later, have a great day."

"You too."

"Miss you, Daisy... love you lots."

"Love you lots too, Dad, come home soon."

Daisy closes the call immediately. Something is not right. I'll call Coops and get her to check the house monitoring systems, and have a word with Tim.

NINETY

As Mike has not yet returned from his visit to the pilot, I quickly call Coops: "Hi, got to be quick. Need you to check the house monitoring system and Helen's mobile. Just spoken to Daisy and Helen's not been around since last evening; apparently went out to a WI meeting and not around this morning."

"No problem, Lucas, but I expect she's just popped out early for some milk, or something equally innocuous."

"I'd like to think so too, but–" I stop suddenly as Mike walks into the room, startling me, "–it's just a gut feeling."

"Okay. I'll get back to you in five minutes."

After staring at my mobile for a few seconds, I look up at Mike, who is already in mid-sentence.

"… and so should land at about 3am local time."

He looks at me, concerned. "What's up, buddy? Look like ya seen a ghost!"

"Eh, nothing really."

"Come on, buddy, it's me you're talking to."

"Well, it's Helen. She went out last night, and apparently wasn't around when I phoned just now."

"Ah. They do that occasionally."

"What do you mean?"

"Behave like inconsiderate assholes," he says, grinning at me, knowing full well we do the same on an almost weekly basis.

"Point taken." I sit back in my seat, trying to relax and refocus on the case. "Any news on the goons?"

"We've tracked them out of JFK and they're in an old truck northbound on the I-678 Van Wyck Expressway. The last CCTV sighting is at Meadow Lake, so it looks like they'll be at Hillview reservoir in about an hour, just after we land at JFK!"

NINETY ONE

As I'm mulling through the timings of us landing at JFK and Mike's Black Hawk air-cab to Hillview reservoir, Coops calls.

"Hi Coops, any news on Helen?"

"Sure is. She's home cooking breakfast, apparently."

"What? But Daisy didn't know where she was?"

"I've spoken to them, on the auspices of losing Helen's mobile signal, and they say it's a misunderstanding." There's a long pause before Coops stutters an answer. "It's not for me to speculate, but…" She pauses.

"Come on, Coops, I know you know something!"

"Helen's mobile has been on a bit of a jaunt, basically… to Brighton."

"Route and timings?" I demand angrily.

"Don't shoot the messenger – and there are probably a dozen good reasons." But her tone believes that is more of a hope than a certainty.

"Come on, I don't have time for this. The goons are nearing the reservoir."

"Okay, okay. Eastbourne Grand Hotel until eleven, then Brighton at midnight and then home for 7.30."

This hits me like a ton of bricks.

What the hell is she up to? And why is Daisy covering for her?

"Thanks, Coops."

"No problem. But don't jump to conclusions."

"Got to go, Coops. Let me know if you get any intel on the goons."

"Will do. Let me know if–"

But I've closed the call, cutting her short.

My mind is in a whirl. I want to ask Coops for more detail, but that will just distract me even more. But my gut tells me something is not right. There's going to be more heartfelt conversations when I get home.

NINETY TWO

We've been flying and discussing options for the last forty minutes when the G650 starts its fast, final approach into JFK.

"Blimey, sharp descent," I say, stomach churning.

"Don't want to waste a minute getting to the Black Hawk," replies Mike sternly.

"Any more news on the goons?"

"They're on the last leg to Hillview, but not had eyes-on yet, maybe in the next fifteen minutes."

As I'm bent double, having located the sick bag under my seat, my mobile lights up again with Coops' name. "Hi… Coops…" I say through a sharp intake of breath.

"Sounds like you're not enjoying the rapid descent?"

"Braille yawn any minute!"

"Lucas! Really!" she says like she's tasted lumpy milk in her coffee.

"Or pebble-dash… when it's… stuck to… the ceiling."

"Gross. Stop now!"

"Okay. What have you got?"

"Well, I've been tracking the NY CCTV and it looks like the goons were on track and westbound on the I-95 Cross Bronx Expressway."

"Okay," followed by a puke-preventing gulp.

"And then northbound on the Bronx river parkway."

"Okay?" This time a small (ish) burp.

"But then their trail's gone cold – they turned off eastbound onto East Fordham Road and then north again onto Southern Boulevard."

"Again, okay… I've not a clue where these roads lead… what's wrong?" Gulp.

"It's the wrong route for Hillview reservoir, but the right one for Jerome Park Reservoir!"

"Oh, bugger." I poke Mike in the ribs to get his attention and then put my mobile on speaker. "Say again; you're on speakerphone so Mike can hear."

"I think the goons are going to Jerome Park Reservoir."

"Holy shit! Thanks Coops, I'll verify with my guys as they still have them going to Hillview – dammit!"

I tell Coops we'll phone back once we've landed as Mike needs to call his team and I need to focus on keeping my stomach contents at bay.

In minutes the "buckaroo" descent finally stops and we're trundling along smooth tarmac as we taxi to the waiting Black Hawk. Luckily, my dignity remains intact.

Mike has received confirmation the goons are somewhere in the Bronx, and their van has recently been spotted travelling west on Bedford Park Boulevard. That road terminates on Goulden Avenue – metres from Jerome Park Reservoir.

Shit! Were we looking at the wrong reservoir?

We exit the G650, run across the tarmac and jump into the Black Hawk, which, as we tighten our belts, powers up its engines for take-off.

NINETY THREE

We're flying low and fast across New York in the Black Hawk, ETA at Hillview reservoir five minutes, when I see Mike's mobile light up.

He looks at me. "It's Dan, I'll put him through our headphones." He clicks his intercom Bluetooth button, connecting his mobile to our headsets.

"Hi Dan, how's things?"

"We've just had a police patrol spot the goons' van."

"Where?" Mike demands.

"It's parked down the side alley of 2854 Webb Avenue. It's a tiny old close-boarded house between two massive apartment buildings. Reminds me of the small house in the movie Up."

"Where's that road? I can't picture it?" asks Mike.

"Right next to Jerome Park Reservoir!"

"Holy shit, get everyone over there now!"

Mike barks at the pilot. "Change of destination. Jerome Park Reservoir ASAP!"

"Roger that, sir," the pilot replies impassively. "New ETA four minutes," he advises.

My guts are wrenched as the Black Hawk veers sharply left, and with my head now pressed against the window I can see Bronx Park and New York Botanical Garden as we continue flat out towards Jerome Park Reservoir.

Mike's dulcet tones now bellow over FBI and police radio channels, who are rushing to Webb Ave to meet up with the local cops at the scene. "NYPD 50th, this is Mike, FBI. Block off the street and empty buildings either side of the target house." Then after verifying on his map, he adds: "We are coming in fast in a Black Hawk and will land at the far north end of Webb Avenue immediately outside Our Lady of Angels parish church." Sure enough, after a couple of minutes we are landing on the street in Webb Avenue, only a few hundred yards from the house where the van's parked.

With the helicopter a foot from the ground, Mike leaps out and runs over to Dan, who's there with the 50th Precinct Police Lieutenant, Senior Officer in Charge (SOC). "Okay guys, what's the state of play?"

Dan looks first at the lieutenant, who nods to confirm that the FBI are running the show, and then at Mike. "Adjacent buildings vacated, van and house secure, waiting our instruction to enter."

"Go for it!" Mike bellows with a growl.

The SOC instructs his team to enter with maximum "shock and awe". There is complete silence on their approach – and then a massive amount of noise as the SWAT team enter, barking that they are police and everyone must lay down their weapons. They visit each room and declare it "clear!"

After a few minutes, the whole building and the van are declared clear – no one is present.

Mike, Dan and I stand at the rear of the van. The doors are wide open: it's empty.

Well, virtually empty. The only items we can see are an empty box from a child's remote-control drone, and what looks like its charger plugged into the van's cigarette lighter socket.

Mike picks up the box. "What the hell is this about?"

"Dunno," shrugs Dan. "Maybe it's the van owner's. This vehicle was stolen from outside JFK."

"Could be," shrugs Mike, and hands the box to Dan. He reads from a side panel: "Thirty-minute flight time, colour camera streams to a mobile phone." Smiling, he adds, "I could do with one of these."

As he turns the box over, a roll of black electrician's insulation tape drops out and rolls across the concrete. It travels only a couple of metres and hits the shoe of an elderly gentleman, who now stands on the sidewalk at the end of the driveway, staring up at the house.

"Hey," shouts Dan at the old boy. "What the hell are you doing? Please, go and stand behind the police tape."

The guy, looking a little dishevelled, slowly lowers his head to look at Dan. Cupping his left ear, he shouts back, "Sorry, son, a bit deaf…"

Dan walks over with the copter box under his arm, picks up the roll of tape and then speaks again, much louder and slower: *"You can't stay here, it's a crime scene!"* He gestures down the street. *"You need to go stand behind the tape!"*

The elderly man winces. "No need to shout. I live here, son. What's going on?"

"It's – a – crime – scene," Dan slowly enunciates.

The old boy shrugs, and looks down at the box under Dan's arm. "What ya got there, son?"

Dan is now starting to get a little tetchy, but nonetheless he tries to placate the old-timer. "Just a box from a toy helicopter."

Poking the image of the quadcopter with his walking stick, the old boy grins and shouts excitedly at Dan. "They had one of these!"

Both Mike and I spin on our heels and walk over to the two of them, with Mike demanding, "*Who* had one of these?"

"The boys who came out the back of that there van."

"What did they do with it?" barks Mike.

"Just threw it in the air."

"What?" Mike says, confused and angered. "Did it fly?"

"Yup," says the old boy. "Straight up in the air." He excitedly points north up the road. "Then up the street and clear over the trees."

Dan, Mike and I look at each other in disbelief. Mike shouts on his radio, "Black Hawk captain, get your kite up and see what you can spot over the reservoir – you're looking for a quadcopter – but don't go near."

"Roger that."

Immediately we hear a roar from the chopper as it thrusts vertically into the sky. Its rear rotor glints in the sunlight as, hovering, it swings left to right.

Almost immediately the pilot replies, "Nothing over this reservoir but our radar shows something, probably the copter, hovering 50 feet above the centre of Hillview reservoir about three and a half miles away."

"Shit!" shouts Mike. "Get back down here and take us to Hillview reservoir. And everyone else listening, haul ass over there now!" He gestures for Dan and me to go with him.

Whilst we're running, Mike's back on the radio. "And someone track down the goons – they can't be far away."

NINETY FOUR

Minutes later, we're at Hillview reservoir, and we drop down on the northeast side car park. A few cars from Yonkers Police Dept 2nd Precinct are back here already, as they had only just left for Jerome Park, and are again unpacking their electronic monitoring gear.

Mike, Dan and I are standing on the grass verge of the reservoir, looking south. The body of water is split perfectly in two along its length by a walkway, and we can clearly see a glinting quadcopter in the middle of this eastern half. It's hovering some fifty feet from the water's surface, and 500 feet from the east bank, where we are standing.

"How the hell are we going to get the damn thing?" says Dan, hands on hips.

"Dunno," replies Mike with a growl. "But we must."

"With the best will in the world, I'm not sure it's possible," I say, frustrated.

My mobile rings. It's Coops, and she immediately starts talking. "I see from the CCTV images you're at Hillview. But I can't see what you're looking at."

"It's a bloody quadcopter in the middle of the reservoir!" I reply frustrated.

"Just hovering?" she says, quizzically.

"Yes. What are you thinking?"

"First, I need to know its battery life, and second, a close-up. Your phone won't be steady enough."

"Okay, leave it with me, Mike's guys have got some pretty techy kit here."

"Cool," says Coops.

I turn to Mike. "Can your guys get a close-up for Coops?"

"No problem." He turns to Dan, who is still transfixed by the copter. "Get the guys to sort out a close-up of that thing and get it put through to my cell."

"Will do, Mike." And Dan runs over to the techies, who have just finished unpacking their kit.

Smiling at me, Mike continues, "I presume Coops can get it off my cell?"

"Did you hear that Coops?" I ask.

With a smile in her voice, "Yep, already connected."

I shout to Dan as he's running. "What's the quad's flight time?"

"Thirty mins-ish." He looks at his watch, and then back at Mike and me. "About fifteen left, I guess."

Mike gets back on his radio. "Listen up, everyone. This is a terrorist attack. No-fly zone two miles. Cell and WiFi antennae off within two miles, this radio channel only, and keep it open. Only speak if it's *urgent.* We have fifteen minutes to retrieve this toy copter, then it's game over."

One lone voice dares to raise a question.

"What do you mean, game over?"

"If I hear your voice or anyone else's asking stupid questions, they will be picking up cat shit at the zoo. Radio silence for God's sake!"

We stand here, useless, staring out to the middle of the reservoir at this buzzing, fifty-buck piece of electronics, which is holding New York City to ransom.

A voice comes over the radio. "Mike, Tech Support. Our AV feed's coming to your iPhone."

"Thanks," replies Mike, simultaneously checking his phone. Peering over his shoulder, I see a crystal-clear picture pop up, showing the quad as if it was near enough to grab – if only!

My mobile rings. Coops again. "Mike's got a feed to his mobile," I say excitedly.

"Yes, got it," replies an equally excited Coops.

"How the…? Never mind."

I nudge Mike and mouth that Coops can see his AV feed already. "I might have guessed." He shakes his head and smiles.

"Coops, I'm next to Mike and putting you on speaker, what are your thoughts?"

"Basic quad. IPhone taped on with black electrical tape. Probably pre-programmed for that lat/long and hover," she gulps, "until its battery fails."

"Agreed," I reply.

After a moment's pause, Mike says, "You *can* hack it, right, Coops?"

"My first thought, but I'm guessing you've already activated the cell tower and WiFi shutdown?"

"Yep," he replies with a grimace. "All locked down."

Again we're silent for a minute.

"You okay, Coops?" I ask.

"Not really. There's something else taped to the quad copter, and I'm pretty sure it's a small Easter egg!"

"What the…!" exclaims Mike. "They're taking the piss!"

"I bet that's how they got the zepto-bots through customs – probably used an emptied chocolate egg injected with the bots, and then recovered it in a Cadbury's Creme Egg foil wrapper. Neat!"

Mike asks, frustrated, "Coops, can you do this?"

"I'll have a blooming good try," she says.

"Anything you need, tell me now."

"Okay. First get the nearest cell antenna back online, and get your techies to send out a code spike to set all phone Bluetooths on. They'll have to do the opposite once I've finished. And I need them to get Dan's cell gaffered to their copter and then get it hovering equidistant between the goons' quad and your phone."

Mike runs the fifty yards over to the techies who are chatting with Dan. I follow, talking to Coops, having turned the speakerphone off.

"So, what are you up to?"

"No time, Lucas. I'll call you soon as I'm done. Just make sure Mike does exactly what I asked: this is our *one* chance."

The line goes dead, and I simply watch Mike bellow orders to the techies.

NINETY FIVE

Several minutes pass before Mike finally gets confirmation that the local cell antenna is online, and then another few before the techies have got their quadcopter into position. But it's another minute or two before the FBI confirm the Bluetooth code has been sent to the local antenna. Almost immediately, our phone screens blink as their Bluetooth is turned on.

Seconds later, Coops rings my mobile. "Okay, all fine here. Just get Mike to keep his phone in his hand, and not make or take any calls."

I do as I'm instructed and then stand here with my mobile to my ear, watching Mike at the very edge of the reservoir – holding his phone at arm's length. One of the techies stands next to us with an iPad showing the two Bluetooth data streams: one from the goons' quad and one from the FBI's quad.

My phone's silent and I start to sweat. "Coops, everything okay?" I ask nervously.

"Nearly. No need to panic unless the red and green LEDs under the quad start flashing; thirty seconds of battery remain."

I immediately stare at the image on the iPad and focus on the quad's LEDs, currently a steady glow of green and red.

The techie looks at his watch and taps Mike's arm. "We got two minutes, max! Then it's a slam dunk."

We all stand here, staring at the image, willing the goons' quad to start moving towards us.

Coops mumbles an expletive, then, "Okay, I think I'm there!"

As she speaks, the goons' quad starts to jig around, as if giving a little celebratory dance.

"One problem, no camera on the goons' quad," says Coops. "I've no clue which way I'm facing!"

The techie shouts, "The red LEDs on the *rear* of the quad are facing us!"

"Okay, I'm not going to waste its battery turning around." After a short pause, "I'll reverse it over to you guys!" she exclaims.

Very, very slowly, the image on the screen gets bigger until the quad is only some fifty yards away.

Then, suddenly, it bounces around and the green and red LEDs on its underside start to flash.

NINETY SIX

The quad copter takes another forty heart-stopping seconds to get to us, and the last few after its rotors have stopped are at the edge of the car park, where, after narrowly missing Mike's head, it crashes into the gravel twenty feet behind us.

"Coops – you little bloody marvel, you!" shouts Mike, grabbing my mobile from me. "You sheer bloody marvel!"

"Guess you owe me dinner as well as Lucas then?"

"Too damn right, liddle lady." And he grins like a man possessed, passes my mobile back to me, and starts running around, high-fiving everyone within reach.

"Brilliant work, Coops. Best log yourself out of the FBI's secure mobile system now, though?"

"Already gone – they won't find a trace – but they'd let me off *this* time anyway; else I'll set Mike on them!"

We have a chuckle, and I watch Mike back-slapping a couple of techies, making them wince, and high-fiving Dan before he gets on the radio and stands everyone down. I hear him shout at the techie to get the Bluetooth command "thingy" sent out to the antenna to turn *off* all local Bluetooths: that'll be another glitch attributed to the service providers on tomorrow's local radio.

At least this side of the pond is sorted. Now I need to find a solution for the UK problem.

NINETY SEVEN

I figure Coops could do with a little peace, and in any case I need to speak to Suzi to find out the latest situation on the UK zepto-bots. So I take Mike up on his offer to stand dinner for Dan and me; as he says, it's the very least the city can do.

Mike confiscates one of the FBI GM trucks and instructs Dan to get in the back and me to ride shotgun.

As usual, they both have a chuckle as I go around the left side of the vehicle, and Mike teases, "C'mon, limey, you must have got the hang of this by now – you guys drive on the wrong side, remember?"

"As I repeatedly explain, most of your ancestors came from Ireland, and they drive on the right side of the vehicle. It beats me how you can forget by just crossing the Atlantic!"

"Yeah, yeah… our way is better–"

"Or was it the French and Spanish influencing you, driving on the wrong side?"

That always makes Mike bite, with his proud Irish ancestry. "Goddamn argumentative limey. Let's just go and fill your face with some decent American steak!"

I grin at him. "Now with that I *can* agree – your steaks are heaven!"

Mike shouts a few words out of the driver's window to the techies clearing up their gear, and thanks the local Barneys, before he boots the throttle and showers them with gravel.

"Next stop your hotel, Lucas, then I'll pick you up at seven for the restaurant."

"Fantastic." I sit back in my seat and grin. "Thanks Mike."

We steam off down Central Park Avenue, which I never realised stretched this far out of central New York.

NINETY EIGHT

Having refreshed myself at my hotel, the Ritz-Carlton, with a quick shower, shave and a clean shirt, I sit in my room's large corner chair. With a panoramic view of Central Park, I dial Suzi to get the SP on the case back home, and, as usual, she answers within a couple of rings, "Hi, Lucas. I was going to give you a call in the morning. How're things over there? I hear Coops came up trumps again?"

I suddenly realise it's midnight at home. "Sorry, Suzi, I forgot the time difference. She literally saved the day!" I reply, with heartfelt admiration for Coops. "What's the state of play with you?"

"The Home Secretary can't make the decision to stop the water supply, so it's down to you. Unless of course it's a success, then it'll be his idea!"

"No change there then, Suzi. Politicians!"

"Anyway, we really only have one viable option: let the zepto-bots get into the water supply and then kill them, and reverse their chromosome change."

"Agreed." I pause. "We know we can kill them. But what about the chromosome reversal?"

"The team here have looked at every angle, but they've not found a way to target only women. And it's also obvious now, given the timescales, that the goons had no intention of taking the ransom."

We remain quiet, deep in thought, until Suzi breaks the silence. "So… what are you doing tonight?"

"Mike's splashing out on some top nosh, but I expect I'll stick to my steak."

Suzi laughed. "So predictable!"

"Yes – easily pleased."

"Well, you get off to your slap-up dinner, and make sure you get your money's worth. I'll carry on researching here with the team first thing."

"Call if you need anything, particularly if Mike can help – they owe us – big time!" I close the call and drop my mobile into the inside pocket of my loaned blazer; apparently it's a jacket and tie affair this evening.

There's a knock at the door and Dan announces himself. "You ready, Lucas?"

"One second."

I grab my black clip-on loaned tie and check myself in the full-length mirror; I brush up quite well for an old-timer, as Alex once said. Satisfied, I make my way over and open the door.

Dan's standing in the corridor, pulling at his collar. Like me, he looks awkward in his borrowed jacket and tie. "Mike's getting the drinks in; he's already negotiated a window seat." Which causes Dan and me to smile, as we imagine the brief, non-negotiable discussion that took place with the waiter.

We head down to the Star Lounge dining room on the second floor, and, after having our names checked at the entrance, go into the wood-panelled restaurant. We are ushered over to a window table that would comfortably seat six, but has just three settings, one of which is taken up by Mike and his huge grin. "What do you think of the view, Lucas? Pretty spectacular, huh?"

"Breathtaking," I reply as I stare out across Central Park.

In the near distance is an expanse of water, reminiscent of the Serpentine in London. "What's the lake, Mike?"

"Jacqueline Kennedy Onassis Reservoir. Nice touch, huh?"

"Very apt!" I reply with a smile. "No quad copters, I presume?" And we chuckle.

The maître d' gestures for us to sit, and introduces our table waiter, who efficiently places an elegant brown leather-bound menu in front of each of us and a wine menu in front of Mike.

We have a general chat about wine, but Mike is a gentleman and acquiesces to my liking of a good Malbec – two bottles, he suggests, to start with.

NINETY NINE

What an evening, as far as I remember. But it's now seven in the morning, and some idiot playing music at a deafeningly loud level wakes me. I finally realise it's my phone's alarm, amplified and distorted by my hangover.

"Bloody hell!" I mutter as I roll over to the bedside cabinet and turn my mobile face down, which immediately stops that mind-bending noise.

As I gently move back across the bed, aiming to be more central, I roll on to an arm – and it's not mine!

My heart stops. I gingerly turn over, mortified at the thought of what could have happened last night.

"What the bloody hell!" I shout.

"Jesus, what the feck!" shouts a startled Dan, as he withdraws an arm, which appears to strayed under a pillow and into my zone. We stare at each other in total disbelief, which is quickly followed by embarrassment and a quick check there are pillows and quilt between us.

I have a vague recollection of Dan collapsing in a drunken stupor, and Mike and me carrying him to my room, but after that it's all a bit of a blur.

Then I recall having neckache and, having taken the spare pillows from the wardrobe and placed them between Dan and me, clambering onto the bed from the armchair.

After a few minutes, as we both seem to remember the same events, we start laughing. That immediately brings back the head pain, and we both wince.

I get first dibs on the bathroom, and after we're both dressed we head down to breakfast sure in the knowledge that Mike will be there, ready to royally take the piss.

ONE HUNDRED

We have a couple of large lattes, and extra strong Nurofen Plus, which certainly helps Dan's and my headaches.

But one voice still penetrates, as somehow Baloo's metabolism appears unfettered by his intake of copious amounts of alcohol.

The waitress, Emma-Jo, is a delight, and loves my British accent, which, as per the last time I was in NY, pisses off Mike and Dan.

"So where in England are you from?" asks the petite, brunette twenty-something.

"You won't know it, but it's Eastbourne, a small town in Sussex, on the south coast."

"I know it! I got an aunty who moved there, after her partner died, to be near one of her old university friends."

"Blimey… small world." I sit back in surprise. "Does she like it there?"

"Oh yeah," she says with a smile. "She says it's quaint, and loves afternoon tea at the Black Cat Tearoom in Meads, or, on special occasions, the Grand Hotel."

As I'm looking at her, the morning sun catches her earrings, which act like a dispersive prism and split the sunlight into the seven glittering colours of the spectrum. With my currently over-sensitive eyes, this makes me blink madly, and she looks at me, concerned. "Are you okay?"

"Sorry, the sun on your earrings dazzled me," I reply. "They're very nice."

"Oh, these," she says dismissively, gently rolling one of the drop earrings between thumb and forefinger. "These are from the two-dollar stand at Wal-Mart." And then, with a slightly sad frown: "Everyone gets their earrings from Wal-Mart. Unless you're one of the bottled-water brigade; then you can afford the real thing!"

I just sit, staring at her… well, at her earrings.

"You sure you're okay?" she says anxiously.

I don't answer immediately, just switch my stare to the bottle of spring water in front of me. "Eh, sorry, yes, I'm fine thank you. I think you may have solved my conundrum."

Mike and Dan look at me as if I've lost the plot, but Emma-Jo merely smiles. "Little ol' me – fantastic," she exclaims. Then she leans in to me and whispers in my ear, "What's a conundrum?"

"It's like a puzzle, and if I'm right we'll make you an honorary detective."

She grins at each of us. "Bon appétit!" She has a slight skip in her step as she goes back to her station, and I hear her quietly mutter, "Honorary detective Emma-Jo".

Smiling to myself, my headache waning, I tuck into my massive plate of eggs benedict with extra crispy Canadian bacon.

"What have you dreamed up this time, limey?" asks Mike.

Between mouthfuls, I reply, "Not totally sure. I need to finish up here and get on the phone to Suzi and Coops."

As I go to pass Mike's napkin to him, he drops a fork-full of scrambled eggs down his shirt front. "Jeez, not again!"

I burst out laughing. "Do you think it would be worthwhile Dan and me chipping in to get you a pelican bib?"

"Very funny, guys." Then he joins in the joke.

ONE HUNDRED ONE

Breakfast finished, and wiping my mouth on my unstained napkin, I pull up Suzi's number on my mobile, and stab the green button. Within seconds, she answers. "Hi Lucas. How are things? On your way home?"

"Just about to leave the hotel for the airport, but I need you to liaise with Coops and maybe Pete's daughter – I think she was in the jewellery trade for some years."

"Jewellery?" she exclaims. "A present for moi?"

I spend the next five minutes roughly outlining my idea.

"So, what do you think, Suzi?"

"I'd prefer a nice platinum and diamond necklace – something simple and classic, perhaps?"

"Really, Suzi, come on, what do you think?"

"It will take a *lot* of organising, especially at this short notice – but it's possible!"

"If anyone can do it, you and Coops can," I declare with absolute confidence.

"But what if we can't?"

"We have to. What other option do we have?"

"Well, Coops and Pete reckon the zepto-bots might be deactivated with infrasound, as it was something he was working on."

"But what about the magnitude and duration of the sound burst?"

"Pete reckons it's possible."

"And they would need to cover the whole of central London with the sound burst?"

"That's the real stumbling block, and the main reason Pete thinks it won't be fully effective."

"Okay. Keep going with the infrasound, but also look at this new angle."

ONE HUNDRED TWO

I say my farewell to Mike, who has a mid-morning meeting with a very appreciative mayor. He has left Dan to chauffeur me to the airport. At least it will be a comfortable flight, as, to show his appreciation, the mayor insisted Mike lend me his G650 to get back to Heathrow. Apparently there will be a couple of US London Embassy employees joining me on the plane.

The passage through customs is uneventful, since we don't go through the usual rigmarole but rather we drive straight through to the waiting G650.

It's only 9.15am, but Dan looks knackered, and several times between yawns he tells me he's dead beat. All his yawning doesn't help me and, as I turn at the top of the plane's steps to wave him goodbye, I put my hand over my mouth to stifle yet another yawn.

On board, the steward formally introduces me to my two Embassy companions, then sees me to my seat and fetches me a coffee and a bear claw – my reputation precedes me. I finish the pastry and half the coffee, click my mobile to silent, and snuggle into the sumptuous beige leather seat.

My last thoughts are of crushing tiredness…

ONE HUNDRED THREE

What the hell does she want now? *Stop poking me, Daisy, can't you see I'm trying to sleep?*

I stop myself in mid-sentence as I suddenly wake, and stare into the amused face of the steward who is nudging my arm.

"Mr Norton, are you okay? We land in thirty minutes, would you like a drink?"

"Bloody hell… I've been asleep for eight hours?"

"Yes, like a baby, not even the turbulence woke you."

"Well, I must have needed it." I drag my mobile out of my pocket and take a couple of stabs at the on button: no calls, texts or emails. No news is good news – I hope.

I send a pre-planned text to Alex to pick me up at Heathrow. He'll be there already, but it'll get him off his backside in the police unit café and out to go warm the car up.

"So, Mr Norton… latte? Maybe I can make you some eggs?"

"Yes please. A couple of scrambled eggs would be fantastic."

I get up and nod at my travelling companions and make my way to the facilities at the rear of the plane. A quick flannel face wash is just what I need to freshen me up. It still surprises me how they fit all this stuff into such a relatively small plane. I spend the next ten minutes imagining I'm a film producer returning from Hollywood – we can all dream.

I'm back in my seat after only ten minutes, as, sure enough, my breakfast arrives.

"I did you four eggs as they're the last and won't keep."

The plateful of beautiful orange atop fresh wholemeal looks most inviting. "Just what the doctor ordered – thank you."

"Blast from the past," says the steward.

"What?" I reply, confused – still not fully awake.

"What the *doctor ordered!*"

"Oh, I've said it for years. Got it from my father I think."

"Yeah? Well, he got it from an American at some point. It comes from the prohibition years: 1920s."

With a mouthful of eggs, I ask, "How so?"

"Something to do with the 18th amendment and doctors prescribing alcohol; a loophole around prohibition. There was a huge fight about it in Congress. Prohibition eventually ended in December 1933, but the phrase stuck."

"Well, you learn something new every day." And I smile at him, thinking it's one for my next quiz night.

Twenty minutes later, the seatbelt sign lights up and we are readied for our descent into Heathrow.

ONE HUNDRED FOUR

Alex meets me at the arrival gate next to the Customs area, and, with one of his armed police pals, ushers me through to the Audi. "Posh trip back then?" he asks, grinning, as he looks past me to the G650 being replenished for its return flight.

"Not too shabby." I smile, and recall what some believe is the origin of "posh" – Port Out Starboard Home – from the days when the upper classes would sail from England to India, specifying their preferred cabins on the shady side of the ship: port side out and starboard side home.

"We'll be back at the office in twenty minutes; 22:35," advises Alex. "Apparently Suzi and Pete have an update."

"What?"

"Won't tell me, they say it has to wait until you're there – sounds like a hefty decision in the offing?"

"Oh well, at least she'll have some decent coffee at the ready. I had some on the plane, but barely half my morning quota."

Alex smiles back at me, shaking his head. "Too much bloody coffee."

In just under twenty-five minutes we're back at Thames House and I'm walking into the Situation Room.

"Hi all."

"Welcome back, Lucas," says Suzi with a hug. "We've made some good progress here."

"Indeed. Glad you're back safe and sound," says Pete with a sturdy handshake. "We hear all went well in the States?"

"Yes, they're well chuffed – thanks to Coops!" And, with a smile: "So, what do you have for me?"

"First thing…" Suzi looks at Pete. "Would you like to do the update?"

"Oh no, Suzi," he replies. "It's your gig – you run with it."

"Bottom line: infrasound is out," she continues. "It just won't get the effect within the aquifer, and it would mean having systems at each of the nine boreholes."

"So?" I ask with a drooping smile.

"There's still no contact from the goons, so the ransom is definitely a red herring. I've been in touch with the FBI and their analysts came to the same conclusion for the unsuccessful New

York attack."

"You're right: Mike said there was the first demand, but then nothing." I pause. "Okay, so have you managed to firm up any alternatives?"

"Well, your idea seems to be the only viable option. I've spoken to Pete's daughter Kat and she in turn has been in touch with some of her old contacts."

"Any progress?"

"One of them is the co-owner of the company which supplies the vast majority of shops across the UK with fashion jewellery – phenomenal coverage."

"Wow. So we have a delivery method and coverage, but how do we get the take-up? This *can't* be left to chance."

"The owner has agreed to meet Kat and Coops tomorrow, and once she's signed the Official Secrets Act, we can brief her on the full plan."

"Which is?"

"Coops suggests we spray all their earring stock with our zepto-bots. We can get it done under the auspices of a pest control fumigation for imported products."

"Excellent! Sounds doable, but are the ninja-bots up to the task?"

Suzi looks and nods at Pete to cue him.

"It's simple, really," he says, smiling. He's in his element. "The bots we introduce will be self-powered for seven days, but will have their organic recharging system removed. This way the antibiotics will kill the goons' bots but not ours. And then our bots can administer the antiserum, turning the female YY chromosomes to XX."

I can't help grinning. "This still sounds like sci-fi to me, but if you guys say it'll work, let's get to it."

Suzi looks at me. "The only thing we haven't worked out is a way to ensure the take-up of these earrings en masse rather than just normal weekend shopping."

"I'm sure we'll think of something. Let's at least get the jewellery firm on board, and get all this kit in play."

ONE HUNDRED FIVE

I go with Suzi to meet the owners of the fashion jewellery giant Jewels Unlimited, based outside Brighton.

As far as their Board are concerned, we are from Her Majesty's Government Customs Office, following up on suspected imports which may be contaminated and require fumigation.

The owners have already met us at Thames House and signed the Official Secrets Act; they have an absolute commitment to the project following our visit to see the Home Secretary. This included them joining him for lunch in the Members' restaurant at the House of Commons. A rare treat, but well deserved, considering the assistance they are providing.

Anyway, we arrive promptly at their offices, and, wasting little time, our team start inspecting their main warehouse. It's not long before we establish that all of their warehouses require isolation and fumigation. This causes some consternation with their warehouse manager Steve, until an email from the Ops director allows him and his teams two days' extra leave, with overtime to catch up with getting the stock out to stores.

With military efficiency, our vehicles arrive ten minutes later. It takes only 24 hours to "fumigate" the earring stock. This is in part due to Pete's ingenuity in programming the zepto-bots to attach themselves only to the plating on the earring posts, after they've created minuscule holes to enter the clear plastic packaging. Once they touch the skin of the pierced ears of their hosts, they will detach themselves and get to work in their bloodstreams.

Our team's work complete, we sign off the "expenses" incurred by the firm, which the Home Office will be covering, and leave the owners to placate their teams and get ready for the picking and packing of these freshly-fumigated lines for their clients.

The next part of the equation needs a solution. How can we make sure women *everywhere* in London go and buy these earrings – preferably within three days of them reaching the stores?

ONE HUNDRED SIX

It's Thursday morning and, as they say, the stage is set.

Every last pair of earrings has been sent to stores, with treble stocks in London – much to the bemusement of the staff.

But it's now or never, as the goons' zepto-bots are already starting to pop out in London's fresh water supply.

The Home Office clerk, and, on several occasions the Home Secretary himself, have phoned me to check the status of events.

The media has not had a sniff of the issue, and we pray it stays that way. Any information in the public domain would cause pandemonium, and scupper the chances of Coops' ninja-bots' success.

We have a direct data feed from Jewels Unlimited's head office so we can track the sales, which thus far have been a little disappointing, but normal for midweek. Apparently, it should pick up today, but it's Friday and Saturday alone which bring in sixty per cent of their weekly turnover. So that's when we need to push uptake of these earrings.

Somehow, we need to get people into the shops and buying earrings – *this* weekend.

We're sitting in the Situation Room, hoping for the best, when I get a call from James, our techie.

"Hi, James, how are you? Thanks for the video-to-audio software on the crisp packet; it worked a treat!"

"Thank you, Mr Norton. I'm well, how are you?"

"Not too bad, but in the middle of a case at the moment. Is it a quick one?"

"Oh, sorry… it can wait… well, it can't really… but it can, if you know what I mean."

I smile to myself, understanding his dilemma. "Go on, James, what can I do for you?"

"Actually, it's what I can do for you!"

"Even better."

"You mentioned about me keeping an eye out for a new iMac Mini for one of your daughters."

"Yes, Daisy – it would make her year. A great help for her packaging design course."

"Well, PC World mucked up their website pricing and offered

the iMac with a 16Mb upgrade for the price of just the memory – I bought four before they corrected the error. I only need one for a friend, so your Daisy can have one, and I'll put the other two on eBay."

"Are you sure?"

"Of course – it'll be £149 – is that okay?"

"More than okay, it's bloody brilliant. Thank you, James."

"No problem, Mr Norton."

After a moment's pause, I ask, "How on earth do you hear about these things? Or was it just lucky timing?"

"I'm on a site called Moneysavingexpert.com and their chat forums list dozens of errors like this. They're mainly markdowns that have been incorrectly keyed into the retailers' head office systems. Last year I got my mum a Swarovski necklace for a tenth of its price just because some numpty keyed in £9.99 instead of £99.99."

I sit in stunned silence.

"Mr Norton? You still there? Hello?"

"Sorry, James, just going to put you on speakerphone so you can repeat the last bit about your mum's jewellery – Suzi will find it fascinating."

"Oh, um, alright," James replies nervously.

"Okay James, you're on."

"Hi, Suzi," says James warily.

"So, James. What's this about your mum's jewellery?"

"Erm. Well I was just telling Mr Norton I got my mum a silver Swarovski necklace for £9.99 instead of £99.99 just because some twit keyed the price in wrong at the shop's head office, which is what comes up on the till."

Suzi, Pete, Jeff and I exchange looks of amazement, which slowly turn into massive grins.

"Hi… are you there? What have I said?" James asks, this time even more nervous than before.

"Don't worry, we're here," I reply. "You've just solved a problem that's been bugging us for the past couple of days."

ONE HUNDRED SEVEN

I immediately dial the Home Secretary and outline my proposal. He agrees – reluctantly, as this will cost an additional half a million pounds, but could guarantee the success of our plan. With his agreement in an email, I phone one of the owners of Jewels Unlimited to outline my plan.

She agrees to the proposal and promises to personally ensure her team resend all earring retail prices to their dozen or so clients. And she will call me when it's set up.

A little over six minutes later, my phone rings. "Hi, Carly. All okay?"

"Indeed it is, Lucas. My team have sent the necessary re-pricing files. These price changes will be activated by our clients' central systems overnight and will be live in the stores tomorrow morning; earrings will be scanning at 80% off their stickered price. We've also sent emails to our store staff, advising that they are to ensure the earrings remain on sale over the weekend."

"Fantastic. Thank you, Carly, could be a good weekend for you!"

"For both of us hopefully, and I presume your team will handle any media aspects?"

"Yes, already on it. Releasing later this evening with full coverage by the morning, and then we'll give it a few nudges during the day."

We say our goodbyes, and I get onto Coops to make sure she has everything ready.

"Hi Coops. All set your end?"

"Yes, oh great one. I have blogs and adverts ready to drop onto Facebook, Twitter, Moneysavingexpert, and a few other bargain tracking sites and Twits." She laughs after the last one.

"Well done. Nothing left to do now but cross our fingers."

ONE HUNDRED EIGHT

I 'm back home on a lovely Sunday morning, sitting at the dining table with a fresh French-press of coffee and some honey toast. I'm smiling as I read an email on my iPhone. It informs me that the reaction of the bargain-hunting public has been incredible on Friday and Saturday, with earrings sold out in all stores.

This is the equivalent of two pairs of earrings for every female in London.

It's going to cost the Home Office a few million quid, but from our laboratory's preliminary test results, the effect of the goons' bots has been reversed, with a hit rate of nearly 96%.

Without doubt the women of London are safe, and, should they have a child, the chances of it being a boy or a girl remain about fifty-fifty, as normal.

It's been three days since my family and I received the all clear from our sniper attack two weeks ago, and the teams, and the eye-in-the-sky, have returned to their normal over-watch duties in London.

We still don't know who was behind the attacks – the sniper, the zepto-bots – but despite the fact that the only call leads to Rome, we still believe it's the Russian, rather than Italian, Mafia.

Helen is currently herding Grace, Ellie and Molly for our usual Sunday walk down to Belle Tout, as Daisy won't be joining us today. She is in her room with a permanent ear-to-ear grin, setting up her new iMac Mini.

Helen told me she lent her phone to Daisy the night it went walkabout to Brighton. Helen's spoken to her and she's promised it won't happen again, with a plea of, "Please don't tell Dad." So, I will keep my word and ignore it – for now.

I just want my family to be happy and safe.

The End

AUTHOR BIOGRAPHY

Martin Link earned a BA in Technology from the Open University in support of his nineteen-year career with the Post Office. He studied analogue and digital electronics, as well as materials science.

He has been involved in security matters at very high levels, including building security, cash centres, and with large blue-chip companies. He has always been fascinated with the premise of something being "impenetrable".

Link brings this expertise to bear both in this sequel Credence, and his debut novel Misdirection, which are part of a series of international crime thrillers which follow MI5 agent Lucas Norton as he chases down high-tech criminals while dealing with life's everyday problems at home. Link sees his protagonist as a modern-day Bond, except he is someone with whom the reader can identify as a regular person.

Martinlinkbooks   @linkbooks   www.martinlink.co.uk

71499098R00138

Made in the USA
Columbia, SC
29 May 2017